It's a Kink Thing

ON KINK'S EDGE

M.C. ROTH

On Kink's Edge
ISBN # 978-1-80250-564-1
©Copyright M.C. Roth 2023
Cover Art by Kelly Martin ©Copyright September 2023
Interior text design by Claire Siemaszkiewicz
Pride Publishing

ON KINK'S EDGE

Dedication

For Q

Chapter One

Keady
Three months ago

"*Yes, Sir. No, Sir. Thank you, Sir.*" Keady rolled his eyes as he strolled to the bar, slipping through the middle of a scene that looked like it was about to get intense. The Dom shot him a glare at the interruption, the sub hardly noticing from his position on the floor.

That glare was like a taste of the thrill he'd been seeking for months. Too bad he wasn't welcome.

The Dom had no right to be pissed at him. That was what happened when you set up a scene in the middle of the bar area. There was an open play area in the club for a reason.

But at least that Dom was looking at him with something other than mild contemplation—not that Malone, Keady's own Dom, didn't *look*. He was just too sweet, too careful and too fucking gentle. It drove Keady insane. Instead of 'Yes, Sir,' 'Go fuck yourself,

Sir' had been on the tip of his tongue before he'd excused himself and headed for drinks. Malone had only smiled and nodded obliviously, sending him another patient look.

He didn't get it — or Keady — and it was infuriating. There were so many couples at Unkinked — a club for kinky bastards like him — and they all seemed so much happier than he was. They all appeared to know exactly what they wanted, when he was still tripping over limits like some newbie.

If lust had a smell, it was Unkinked, with music pounding off the bodies that were all searching for the same goal. Sweat and sex mixed with the latest cocktail, coating his tongue and skin. Some members came to get drunk, and others wanted to submit, but the outcome was the same. They all left satisfied. *Except me.*

Leaning against the bar top, Keady bit his lip before looking over his shoulder. Malone was looking his way, speaking with another Daddy Dom like him. Keady had thought that maybe he was little, but now he wasn't so sure. He loved to color, could play video and board games for hours and the thought of wearing a diaper was positively thrilling.

But it didn't push him the way he wanted to be pushed, and after a few months of being his 'Daddy's boy', he'd reverted to 'Sir'. He'd hoped that Malone would punish him for it, but he never had, taking it all in stride and grabbing him another coloring book from the store to doodle in.

"What can I get you?" Clint sidled up to him from the other side of the bar, and Keady sent him a smile filled with relief. If there was any person he'd spill his guts to, it was Clint. Owner of the BDSM bar Unkinked and former nurse, Clint had patched him up enough times that he knew almost everything about Keady – *except for the part that matters.*

"Anything…please. I'll double the tip if you spike it with something fun." Keady lowered his head into his palm, scrubbing the sweat from his skin. "And for Christ's sake, turn up the air conditioning. It's packed in here tonight."

Clint only chuckled, slipping him a ginger ale and a smile. "Don't want to get you in trouble."

Keady grasped the fizzy drink, struggling down a swallow while wishing for something so much harder. He must've been insane to sign a contract that prohibited alcohol. Then again, he'd been pretty fucking desperate at the time. He'd pissed off more than a few Doms before he'd finally settled for Malone.

"But could you?" asked Keady, his voice surprisingly desperate. Usually, he was better at hiding it, but tonight was getting under his skin in the worst way. The packed bar, sweet smiles and the sound of pain from other subs weren't helping, either.

Clint paused, narrowing his eyes and giving him another once-over. The dishcloth in his hand was well-loved and worn, the color all but faded away. "How long until your contract is up?"

Clint knew as well as he did that Keady would never break a contract. He was serious about kink, and he'd been in the lifestyle since he'd graduated high school – before high school had ended, really, if he counted the few choice boyfriends he'd put through the wringer.

"Three months." *Fuck,* that sounded so long. Ninety days of 'Sir' at the end of every sentence and unfulfilled orgasms… Ninety more days without subspace and probably more, if he were honest with himself… He hadn't been that deep in…years.

"That's not so bad." Clint scratched his chin where three days' worth of growth was. On most guys, unshaven and worn clothes would look sloppy, but on Clint, it was endearing. He was hard not to love when he spread his heart around to everyone. "We'll be in the new place by then, and who knows? Maybe you'll find your dream Dom."

The rumors that Clint was leaving the bar behind and building a house of kink instead had been circulating for months. It was nice to finally hear the gossip confirmed. It was also a little terrifying.

Unkinked had become a home to so many kinksters like himself, and the thought that they might be uprooted put him on edge. It wasn't so much the bar, the open play area and the themed rooms, but everything else. *The people.*

Keady snorted, taking another sip of the sweet bubbles. It reminded him of the days he'd spent sick on his mother's couch, flat ginger ale his companion when nothing else worked. Once they'd figured out that he was allergic to meat, the stale soda had become a thing of his past.

"You know I won't." He swirled his glass, tapping his foot as the song switched to something low and throaty. Hopefully, the new place had better music with speakers that could blast his eardrums out.

"I thought we talked about this," said Clint, swiping at a bit of moisture from the bar top with the cloth. Another man stepped up to order, but Clint ignored the guy. "Your dream Dom and your nightmare are pretty close to the same thing in your fantasies, but this is your life. I need you to be safe, okay? I don't want to go down that road again."

It was the road that had left Keady with a few scars on his back and a stern talking-to from Clint. He'd been terrified that his membership to Unkinked would be rescinded, but Clint had taken a different path. Six months of voluntary domestic servitude was something of Keady's worst nightmares, but he'd done it—cleaning the rooms at Unkinked and helping Clint with set-up and take-down on the nights he could.

It had driven them even closer to one another, and Keady had met Maddy along the way, a person whom he could call his bestie. Too bad Clint wasn't his type. *And off-limits.*

"Yep." Keady stared at his glass, his stomach rolling. "That's why I'm here." Sticking to Unkinked meant that his heart didn't pitter-patter during a scene, but he didn't end up injured or dead, either.

"Someone will come up," said Clint, tilting his head to gesture down the bar. Keady followed his gaze, gritting his teeth when he saw who Clint was trying to point out. "I imagine Cutler will be looking for a new sub again. His last one only made it twenty-four hours."

Keady shuddered, eyeing up the man in question. If serial killers had a look, it was Cutler's. Even his *name* sounded dangerous. He was tall and lean, his face twisted in a perpetual frown and a scar over his lips that had to be from some kind of fight to the death. The thick-rimmed glasses completed his look like some sort of Clark Kent disguise.

Keady wasn't sure if it was a coincidence that Cutler had just shown up one day without a sub or a backstory. Maybe he'd changed his name to run from the police, his hands still stained from a fresh murder. It didn't explain why Clint vouched for him, though.

Subs rarely lasted more than one scene with him since he'd arrived, and word was that he'd been kicked out of other kink communities. *But why?* He couldn't have disrespected someone's safeword or he would have had his ass handed to him by the Dungeon Master.

The peek Keady had caught of one of his scenes had been intense, but Malone had dragged him away before he'd witnessed much more than a heavy flogging and screams.

"He looks like a goddamned serial killer," whispered Keady, quickly averting his eyes when Cutler looked his way. A flush settled over him and his belly went tight. He could *feel* Cutler's eyes on him, raking through his skin to the vulnerability underneath.

Do I like it? He couldn't answer.

"Huh. I thought you would have been into that," said Clint, shrugging before he turned to grab the newcomer his drink. "Think on that one."

Bastard. Pursing his lips, Keady looked back to his Dom, frowning at what he found. Malone was still waiting patiently, his perpetual smile driving his nerves past what he could stand.

The worst part was that Malone had become a friend, which was the last thing he wanted in a relationship. A 'friend' couldn't give him what he needed. No, that took someone very special.

He glanced at Cutler, ice traveling down his spine when he caught his glare. That look was a thousand promises and threats all rolled into one, with a side dish of terror. Swallowing, he grabbed his drink, rushing back to his table. He felt Cutler's eyes on him with every step.

Chapter Two

Keady
Present

Keady pulled up to the new site for Unkinked, his jaw momentarily dropping as he tried to take in every bit. It was like nothing he'd ever seen, sprawling in the forest like some kind of modern castle. A few branches clawed at the edge of the building, the gray brick shooting through the piece of nature as if it had always been there.

Other than the upturned dirt and fresh gravel, it didn't look new. The forest looked like it had barely been disturbed and the house had just shown up one day, scooting into place without damaging more than a few blades of grass.

It smelled clean, with the small stream just down the lane and the crispness of trees dragging away the dirt of the busy streets. It was insane that this place had been only a short drive out of the city.

The gravel rectangle, which would probably be a future parking lot, had enough room for a dozen cars or so, and every spot was packed. The lane was the second option, already lined with vehicles with a few spots remaining. Keady circled back and pulled off to a grassy patch on the side so he didn't block anyone in, doing his best not to slip too far into the ditch.

On open house nights, the streets at the old bar would be crammed down the block, kinksters from every part of the city making their way there. The dozen parking spots didn't seem like much, but Keady wondered if there were a few people who wouldn't be making the move along with the rest of the crew.

Some had treated the place as more of a bar with a lovely view, while others seemed to get their kicks from watching a demonstration they would never want to take part in. Many of the members didn't have access to the rooms unless they'd been mentored by one of the more senior members, and even then, there was a hell of a lot of paperwork to fill out.

This place felt different—pure. He couldn't blame anyone for turning their nose up at the trek out of town, and he wasn't looking forward to it in the winter. A club was one thing, but a house? That was something serious where *couples* could come to play.

Kink and people were a strange mix. Some stayed for life, while others just visited. Clint was a lifer and seemed content about where things had rolled to for him. Keady wanted to call himself a lifer, too, but he certainly wasn't content.

"You made it," Malone called to him, and Keady shot him a smile, locking his car with a *beep* before sliding his keys into his pocket. It had been nearly a month since Malone had called it quits on being his

Daddy, only a few short weeks shy of their contract. It was the best thing that he'd ever done for Keady.

The second their contract had disappeared, their friendship had bloomed. It was worth every bit of disappointment and frustration to have a friend like Malone at his back.

Like most Daddies, Malone loved handing out advice, which was fucking infuriating sometimes. But it was something Keady needed from a friend to keep himself from slipping into dangerous territory.

There had been too many nights where he'd strolled down an empty street in the middle of the night, *hoping* something kinky would happen. It took Malone for him to realize that there was no trust in true danger.

"Hey, big guy, you look good." Keady grinned, throwing his arms around Malone's shoulders and giving him a quick hug. Malone looked the part of Daddy between his body hair and burly build, the silver streaks in his hair only adding to his attractiveness.

It was probably why their dynamic had devolved into friendship instead of blowing up in their faces. Malone wore his sweetness on his sleeves and offered hugs freely to anyone in need. If he hadn't been so big, he would have been positively cute. To strangers, he could be intimidating, a natural sternness creeping into his features.

"Did you find yourself a new boy? Maddy was saying that he saw you with a newbie."

Clint had hired Maddy as a bartender, and he had single-handedly encouraged most of the changes that had happened at Unkinked. He was as extreme of a masochist as Keady had ever met, with nerves like fucking steel and the scars to match. He also had an attitude a mile long once you got past the bleak politeness of his mask.

Malone flushed, breaking into a smile that made Keady's heart break. He looked away, unable to hold his gaze any longer than necessary. Malone had tried so hard to make it work between them, but that smile had vanished for almost an entire year. He'd seen so many fake ones that Keady hadn't realized how much his Dom had been hurting, too.

"That brat is a gossip," said Malone, peering at the house. "It's a good thing Derreck knows how to handle him."

That's an understatement. Keady had been introduced to Maddy in the same way he had been to many others. About a year before, he'd appeared at the bar, fitting in as if he'd always been there. His Dom Derreck had probably helped with that. Derreck was as intense as he was mysterious. He was also the only person in the world who Maddy wasn't a brat for.

"Look at this place, though." Keady let out a soft whistle. The more he looked at it, the more he discovered. The roof was curved on one spot, sweeping outward toward the forest so it almost melded with the boughs of the trees. And the sunlight hit everything just right, shimmering in spots and cool and calm in others.

"How have you been holding up, Keady? You look tired."

He jolted, biting the inside of his cheek as he looked at his feet. *Isn't that the truth?* He barely slept at night, preferring to log his hours between one and five. Once the sun was up, there wasn't much hope of resting, either, his mind racing just as much as the traffic and noise outside.

His last full night of sleep had been so long ago that he couldn't remember quite what it had felt like.

"I've been looking for a new place. I thought maybe it was time for a change." Keady shrugged, kicking at the gravel and scuffing the toe of his running shoes. His toes were nearly sweltering in the things with the summer sun pouring down at them. He should have opted for sandals, but once he'd heard about the new place being in the bush, his first thought had been poison ivy.

Most of the natural flora looked harmless enough, and it wasn't like he needed steel toes to go on a tour of Unkinked. He snorted. With some of the Doms out there, maybe he did.

"Wow." Malone squeezed his shoulder before letting his hand drop. "Never thought I'd hear you say something like that. You love your place."

He'd actually refused to give his place up when Malone had asked him to move in with him. When he'd been looking for a house originally, he'd watched the real estate market for three years, waiting for that exact condo to come up for sale. It had been easy to make an offer on his first walkthrough when he'd looked out of the floor-to-ceiling windows.

But the fact that he loved it may have been part of the problem. He'd gotten too comfortable with his life, and when he'd woken up on his thirty-ninth birthday, he'd realized he was *bored*.

"I'm just starting to look now. Nothing yet." It wasn't exactly true. He'd found four places in his budget, but they were all out of town. He worked from home, but his commute to the city would move from five minutes to an hour. The thought of it left a wrenching ache in his gut.

But something had to change.

"Well, good luck. I know a few guys in real estate if you want any names. I'm sure they'd be happy to help." Malone gave him that smile that he was all too familiar with. As a lawyer, Malone knew so many in the city and recognized who were the crooks.

Keady let the silence hang, glancing to the doors that hopefully led to paradise. *This is the first step.* New club, new him. He loved Malone in his own special way, but his friend couldn't be right about everything.

"Looks like the twins are here," Malone continued awkwardly, scratching at his short beard that was threaded with a few strands of gray. "I don't expect them to show off their boy any time soon."

That got Keady's attention. He turned to the beast of a car, raising one eyebrow as he eyed up the model and make. *I'm in the wrong business.* He was going to be extra careful about kicking any stones that way.

He had no desire to piss off two mobster twins whose middle names were 'badass'. Keady wasn't sure if he agreed with Clint's reasoning on letting Nikita back into the fold after he'd been banned from the bar, either. The new place apparently meant new rules for *everyone,* even if someone had a criminal past.

"So, tell me about your boy. Is he cute?" prodded Keady, looping his arm through Malone's as they headed for the door. It was easy to slip into his usual persona with Malone, putting a smile on his face as he let out a giggle.

The massive entrance door was all wood, only it had been streaked with paint in a way that looked like it should hang in a museum. There were a few artists in the community, one of them being his friend Nav, who was a new face to the club as well. His Dom Trick was another story.

He'd been close with Trick's fiancé Theo when he'd met Nav, and he still didn't forgive Trick for the way he had treated him. Trick adored Nav, though, and that was what mattered. Maybe he was a tad jealous of their dynamic, too. Consensual non-consent was positively drool-worthy.

The last he'd heard, Theo was looking to come back to the community after a stint of trying to get out of the lifestyle. Once someone went *that* kinky, it was rare they went vanilla.

"He's cute." Malone's gaze instantly went distant, a smile on his lips. He looked happy. *Good.* "I've never met such a sweetheart in all my life, and he does so well. He's just as happy to color with his crayons as he is holding Daddy's cock in his mouth."

Ugh. Struggling not to laugh outright, Keady skipped up the steps, leaving Malone behind. Some things were teeth-rottingly fluffy when it came to his ex-Dom. "When do I get to meet him?"

"He'll be here tonight. He had to finish up his classes before he could make it out." Malone grabbed the doorknob, fishing out his key card before he tapped it open.

"College boy?" That seemed a little young, even for someone like Malone, whose kink was age-gap. Keady had failed him at that, too.

"College professor," said Malone, holding the door open and motioning Keady through. "What about you? Any sadists catch your eye?"

No. Keady huffed, sagging his shoulders. The problem was that a lot of Doms caught his eye, but that didn't mean he was going to approach them. Some subs kneeled while they waited for a Dom to take notice, which was honestly a tripping hazard in Keady's opinion. Others took the straight and direct route and had an actual conversation before talking limits.

Keady usually didn't make it past the first word. It was a wonder that he'd ever managed the courage to speak to Malone, and he was one of the most inviting and relaxed guys around.

"I said hi to a few." He ducked his head as the air conditioning washed over them. It wasn't exactly a lie. He had said '*hi*' before he'd tucked tail and scurried away.

"And?"

Shrugging, Keady paused to gawk at the entranceway, which led into a hall where a stage, almost like a theater, had been set up. He still couldn't believe he'd missed the open house, but the idea of that many people in one place had given him hives.

Demos were going to be *awesome* with that kind of setup, with lots of floor space and seating. But where were the kinky shit and his favorite rooms? He had a few on his list that he wanted to check out. He hoped Clint hadn't changed things too much.

Change is good. He gritted his teeth.

"Keady." Malone's voice dropped into something stern, and Keady had to fight not to lash out. Any proper sub should have whimpered to that tone, but since when had he been a proper sub? Sometimes he wondered if he was just in it for the thrill, and that's where he'd gone wrong. If he hadn't figured it out yet, he probably wouldn't.

"I don't know, Malone." He lowered his voice as it echoed in the hall. There was only one other person in the hallway, bent over his phone as he sat in one of the chairs. He gave Malone a nod and Keady a wave that made him want to hide.

"I'm starting to think that maybe I should try a different community. I love this one, but maybe a change of scenery will get me what I need."

But change was *terrifying*. And quirks aside, the community that Clint and his late husband had started was amazing. It was welcoming and steady, with lots of play partners to choose from — if he managed the gall to talk to one, that was.

"What about a helping hand instead?" Malone led him down a hall to where Keady spotted the familiar engraved doors. He let out a sigh of relief. The rooms were his favorite part of Unkinked.

Grabbing the knob on the nearest open door, he pushed his way inside with a smile.

Ah, *Wet*. It was probably the one at the top of his list. There wasn't much that couldn't go down in a room like it. With the shower running and the spray hoses, *anything* could be washed away. Things weren't fun unless there was a bit of a mess involved. His cheeks must have colored because Malone gave him a knowing look.

Sometimes it sucked when your friends knew you so well. Malone had hardly ventured into the room before Keady had *convinced* him to try a few things. It had been early on in their contract when there had still been a chance for them. "I don't need your help. I know what I want. I just can't seem to find it."

"Correction," said Malone, grasping his shoulder and giving it a squeeze. "You know what you want, but you aren't *brave* enough to find it. You're many wonderful things, Keady, but brave isn't one of them. I'm a friend who wants to help, so let me help."

Keady grumbled, kicking the tile with his running shoe. *Fucking Daddy Doms.* It squeaked against the tile, leaving a small scuff of dirt on the otherwise pristine surface — a familiar white covered the floors and walls, with drains spotted throughout. It looked similar to what he remembered with a few improvements, like an extra fan.

Maddy had told him that he'd expected a room full of toilets his first time inside. He hadn't stopped laughing for a long time. Sometimes Maddy was too innocent for his own good.

"Cutler."

Keady locked up, peering over his shoulder as Malone said the name. His heart started to pound, and he took in a gasping breath as he searched for the named man. He'd done a great job at avoiding being close enough to Cutler to speak with him.

No one was there, the hall empty except for themselves. He shot Malone a narrow-eyed look.

"Uh-huh. I think I know what you want, even if you're in denial." Patting his shoulder, Malone moved to the next room, letting out a whistle of appreciation. *Impact* somehow had more implements than it had in the last setting, restraints and floggers of every kind lining the walls. There were canes, too, along with paddles and whips that made Keady's mouth water.

It had been way too long since he'd had a proper beating. Malone had been the furthest thing from a sadist.

"He's a serial killer...or at least a killer," said Keady, keeping his voice low and looking over his shoulder again just to make sure Cutler hadn't appeared. He seemed like the kind of guy who would walk into a conversation like that. "The last sub he scened with left the community the next day. Like how is that even okay?"

"Clint trusts him, so that's worth a lot to me," said Malone. "And don't listen to rumors too much. That sub who left didn't go by choice. His membership was revoked."

That was a lot to take in. Keady knew of a few Doms who had been banned, but it wasn't as common for a sub. He must've done something very wrong.

"I would hate for you to go looking in another community only to find a guy who will harm you. In almost a year, you didn't show an ounce of self-preservation, and that was with your limits. Besides, you can't tell me that the name Cutler doesn't make you hard."

It's my limits that are the problem. Malone did have a point, though. Keady wasn't exactly great at safewording when he needed to. He hated the words, actually. They were like missed opportunities. How far could he have gone if only he hadn't called 'red'?

Shivering, Keady adjusted himself, sending Malone a glare. "Stop saying his name."

"Cutler, Cutler."

Keady shuddered, slapping Malone on the shoulder. "Fucking stop it. He could appear at any time and hear you. That guy is seriously scary."

"Which is exactly what you want." Malone gave him a steady look. "Besides, don't judge him by his looks alone." Malone fingered the handle on one flogger, testing its weight before placing it back on the wall. "You've seen a five-foot-nothing sub take a six-foot beast of a man to their knees. You know better."

"Sorry." Keady looked away from the floggers that practically called to him. He doubted he would get to feel them anytime soon. "I've talked to a few of the subs that he's scened with and they all tapped out before they could really get into the scene. He's got some kind of weird following, like if someone can survive him without safewording, they get some imaginary badge or something."

He'd stumbled upon it during a conversation with a fellow sub. People were lining up to scene with Cutler, the mysterious guy who took intensity to a whole new level. No one had achieved the imaginary badge yet.

"Maybe they weren't a good fit." Malone shrugged before turning from the room. "Or he could be a bad Dom. Did he respect their safewords?"

Keady nodded, swallowing thickly as he trailed behind. "Yeah, and he warned them that they would safeword before the scene was over, too. Who does that?" he asked incredulously. "If he knew he was going to push them so far, then why even agree to the scene?"

And how did Clint allow that? Keady had grown close to Clint over the years, and he knew how much the man cherished the rules. He didn't put up with any shit in his club and safety was his top priority. Although lately he had seemed a bit lax.

"Maybe he's looking for the right match, just like you are," said Malone, pausing in the hall. The next door was shut tight. "Cutler might be looking for someone he can push and not risk breaking—someone strong and quiet, who doesn't think he can scream." Malone skipped the closed door and went for the next open one. Keady grimaced at the engraving. He'd hoped that *Feel* wouldn't make the cut. Feathers and sensation play were not his thing.

"And I know for a fact that subs think he's a bit of a joke. That challenge says enough. If anyone gets through him, they get five-hundred points. That's not what this lifestyle is supposed to be about." Malone trailed off before squaring his shoulders. "He'll be here tonight, Keady, and I'll be sending him your way."

"What?" Keady took a step back, his tongue sticking to the roof of his mouth. "Tonight? That's too soon. I need to get ready — to prepare. I can't just *talk* to him."

Three years probably wouldn't be enough time to prepare. No matter how many times he went over a conversation in his mind, it never went the way he planned. If only he were brave.

"Then don't." Malone sent him a knowing look that Keady absolutely hated. "Or do. It's your choice. But you've been a kinkster since you turned eighteen, Keady. It's time to pull your head out of your bum and go after something you really want."

Fucking Daddy Doms. How could anyone stand them?

Chapter Three

Cutler

Three minutes in and he already missed the bar. There was great lighting, rocking music and enough implements to make him salivate...but no bar. The floor was too clean, the air lacking that edge that always came along with sex, sweat and fear.

At least with a glass in his hand, he'd had something to hold onto to keep himself busy while he scoped out every person in the room. He'd liked the illusion that it offered — the barrier and the mask when he lifted his hand to cover his lips, glaring at anyone who didn't have the manners to look away.

The routine had been hold, sip and swallow as a random starstruck sub had eyed him from across the bar. Another sip as he'd dismissed them without words. He'd fallen for that look too many times. But no one interrupted him when he had a mouthful of whiskey. No one *dared*.

He could probably drag his own reusable water bottle from home, but he doubted it would have the same effect. There was something about buying booze that added sweetness to it.

The new Unkinked was one hell of a place, though. The rooms were bigger, and the stage was epic. The design of the whole thing was modern yet rustic, like two designers had fought every step of the way, both refusing to compromise. It was a good look.

A few people milled about, some getting ready to scene while others just chatted. They all looked fucking thirsty.

Cursing his empty hand, he headed to the open play area, which stretched the entire length of one wing of the house. It was a big upgrade from a room that used to house about fifty people, and even that number had been a bit of a stretch. Now it was the type of place that was made for orgies. All they needed were a pile of gym mats in the corner and *presto*.

The play area was also where *he* was supposed to be. *Keady*. The little sub who wasn't so *little*, at least, not according to Malone. Big dreams were dangerous, especially in kink.

Cutler remembered exactly what Keady looked like, with his dark hair, bright eyes and a speckling of gray that made him a touch more interesting. It wasn't often he found a sub of Keady's age who was searching for a play partner. By the time gray hairs sprouted, most of the good ones were usually taken, unless they had just stumbled into the lifestyle.

Keady hadn't been of much interest when Cutler had caught sight of him at the bar before, but he was attractive, at least. Cutler had always had a soft spot for older men. Age typically went hand in hand with experience, which was underrated as far as he was concerned.

The last thing he wanted was another newbie virgin who thought their first time should be a fantasy of rough sex and chains. That never went over well.

But every time he'd seen Keady with Malone, there always seemed to be something strained between them — something missing. Keady was the one who seemed to hold the power, but maybe that was because Malone was the less experienced of the two. Not by much, though. A year? Two max.

Cutler wanted his sub powerless, so there was no question as to who was in control. He wanted them to forget their own fucking name as they gave in to him. Brats never survived more than a few moments in his presence, and anyone high and mighty was quickly stripped of everything they thought to be true.

But maybe that was why he was often without a play partner. Forget contracts... He could hardly have someone finish a scene with him. He usually ended up calling it or his sub safeworded just like he'd told them they would. He'd been so close to fucking up enough times that he'd lost count. Maybe he'd even gone too far a time or two.

Rumors followed him like the plague. It was always the same thing when he started over in a fresh community. First came the welcoming smiles and the line of subs hoping to make an impression. Sometimes, he gathered a little following — like groupies trying to get a hit. But everything changed when people started calling red. Then, he was the bad guy.

As if I didn't warn them from the beginning.

It was hard for him to tell when someone was putting on a brave face and when someone was actually enjoying themselves. A moan was a moan, and some guys were great actors...until they weren't.

Everyone was a masochist until he flogged them until they bled. Everyone wanted to be degraded until he made it clear that they were nothing more than a useless cum hole.

He'd gotten great at aftercare as a side effect. No sub had ever dropped on him, and he always made sure that they understood their value before he released them back into the wild. But that didn't mean they weren't too scared to try again — too *traumatized*.

His repeated no-goes had gotten him ostracized from his last community. They didn't kick him out so much as they talked about him, thinking that he couldn't hear their whispers. Whispers could kill a man, and despite what they thought, he was *just* a man.

He'd stopped at Clint's door when he'd reached his limit, giving Clint a little taste before he'd eased his way into Unkinked.

That had been a scene that he would never forget. Too bad Clint wasn't looking for more than a one-time thing because *damn...* Clint had called it an audition at the time, putting himself on the line before he was willing to put any of his patrons at risk. From what Cutler had gathered during his short time in the community, Clint hadn't scened in years.

Clearing his throat as he entered the play area, Cutler crossed his arms, leaning against the wall just inside the entrance. It *was* bigger in every way, with enough restraints and displays that it must've cost a fortune. Some of it had been taken from the old bar, while others shone with fresh polish. Couches and loungers dotted the space, along with stacked chairs on the side for if a scene drew a larger audience. Whoever had planned it had put a lot of effort in.

One sub was leaning over a metal exam table, their ass spanked red and their Dom lubing up a toy and getting ready to slide it home. It was a pretty picture, even if it wasn't exactly his cup of tea. The stainless steel didn't turn him on in the least.

Another man was being flogged on a cross, his back and thighs blazing red while his ass was still pale. All that flesh was a missed opportunity, unless their Dom had other plans.

He spotted Keady on one of the loungers by a raised platform, his eyes bright and long lashes fluttering as he stared at a wicked scene. He was sitting at the edge of his seat, leaning forward as he bit his lip, completely entranced by the couple before him. *Maybe there's hope after all.*

Knife play was dangerous and could put someone into the hospital or worse, but that didn't mean it wasn't one of Cutler's guilty pleasures. Apparently, Keady's as well. The Dom in the scene was one of the many who Cutler didn't recognize, but he seemed confident and experienced. The sub was blissed out, barely crying out anymore as tears streaked down his cheeks.

The Dom would call it soon, if he knew what was best for them both.

Keady followed the blade carefully with his gaze, shifting at the sound of metal against flesh. There was hardly any blood at this point, the sub too sensitive to take much more. That didn't stop the sub from whimpering on the next stroke, his breath coming fast as his eyes rolled back.

Interesting. Cutler adjusted himself as he watched Keady's reactions, looking for clues. *Maybe not so boring, after all.* Keady gripped his hand into a fist, rocking on the couch slightly as his mouth dropped open and a look crossed his face that was both envy and desire. He was probably hard, but Cutler couldn't be sure with the way he was bent over, leaning ever closer to the couple.

"He's very shy, but I think your kinks line up pretty well," Malone had told him earlier, instantly piquing Cutler's interest. Only, he didn't want them shy. He needed someone who knew exactly what they wanted—or things could get…dangerous.

At the moment, Keady certainly didn't appear shy. If anything, he had an exhibitionist streak buried beneath a few layers.

Cutler could help with that. He was very good at peeling back layers.

Stalking across the distance, Cutler paused just beyond the platform, watching Keady's every move. His throat bobbed, sweat dripping down his neck despite the air conditioning. There was a reusable water bottle in his hand and Keady took a long chug, his eyes never straying from the couple.

Maybe the reusable bottle idea wasn't so bad, although Cutler wouldn't be caught dead with a purple one. It would clash with his, uh, personality.

"Like what you see?" Cutler asked softly, not wanting to disturb the scene as he got closer. He doubted the couple would hear him over the steady moans, but he wanted to be conscientious.

Keady nodded without looking away, unconsciously adjusting himself. He was hard, tenting the leather pants that were almost painted on. Did he know who he was answering or was it just automatic?

The lack of eye contact was an instant strike against him. Malone had let his brat get away with far too much in their time together, and it was almost like a beacon to Cutler.

"Have you ever tried something like that?" Cutler moved closer, standing his ground as Keady blinked and finally looked his way. In a moment, Keady went from calm to flustered, a flush breaking over his cheeks as he clenched his jaw tight. He widened his eyes, sitting ramrod straight on the lounger.

Shy was a fucking understatement. Was he even worth the effort? Keady couldn't even hold his gaze, staring at the floor before leaning away. He shuffled his feet, looking like he was about to run for it. The whole ensemble screamed of inexperience.

It was like seeing two very different people sharing the same skin, and it was almost enthralling. *Almost.*

Cutler didn't exactly have anything or anyone better to do tonight.

"N-no," said Keady, his soft voice barely audible above the moans. "I've never had a Dom willing to do knife play with me like that." He bit his lip before he seemed to find some resolve. "Have you?"

We're making progress already. Cutler nodded, glancing at the scene quickly before he looked back to Keady. Goosebumps broke over his skin, making him want to shiver. A sudden energy rushed through his limbs as he locked onto a hopefully willing target.

"Yes. Some of my most powerful scenes have involved a knife." He took a seat next to Keady, resting his hands on his knees. People always seemed to find him intimidating, and with a new play partner, he reveled in it. Fear was one of the best things to add to a scene to make it headier. With Keady, it took barely any effort at all.

Cutler tried not to smile much due to his partial facial paralysis, and he was tall and strong enough to make anyone look twice. But that wasn't everything. He'd been told by a few people that they sensed something in him that made their cocks go hard as they shivered with terror.

He took it as a compliment. Unfortunately, most of the people that had told him that had been very wrong about how far they wanted him to take them. It was interesting how many people didn't know their own limits. Luckily, Cutler was an expert at finding and breaking them.

"Oh." Keady flushed deeper, toeing the ground with his dirty running shoe. It had probably been white when he'd set out that morning, but it was coated in dust now. *Filthy, just like his reputation.* Malone hadn't spared him any details in that department. His shy boy was a dirty little slut.

"Did you want to try?"

Cutler left the offer hanging, turning back to the scene. It was rare for him to do the approaching in the first place, leaving it up to the subs to seek him out if that was what they thought they wanted. But Malone had assured him that if he were to wait on Keady, he'd be waiting for eternity.

An eternity that he didn't have. Between his work and sleep, he only had so much time to submerge himself in the lifestyle. Every moment without a play partner was a wasted one.

The sub in the scene had been reduced to quiet whimpers and the Dom had taken a step back as they prepared to wrap up, dragging the blade one more time over a particularly sensitive area before they cleaned it with a cloth. *Beautiful.*

"Yes."

If he hadn't been waiting for it, Cutler wouldn't have caught it. He grimaced, looking toward the door as he wondered if he should cut his losses early and head home. "Speak up when I ask you a question."

If he missed something during discussions, then he'd miss it in play, too. Clint was a nice guy, but ignoring a safeword, either intentionally or not, would mean a one-way ticket out of Unkinked.

"Yes, Sir," Keady parroted back, sitting up a bit straighter.

Cutler's frown deepened. "And don't call me 'Sir'. You certainly don't deserve that yet." He'd had enough of subs thinking that if they tacked 'Sir' onto the end of every sentence that it equated respect. They had to *earn* that privilege. "Address me by my first name. I'm sure you know what it is."

Keady nodded, his swallow audible. *Good.*

His mother had given him a fantastic name that put the fear of a blade into those who he'd just met. It was fitting, really. And better than 'Francis', which had been her backup choice.

"What are your limits?" He'd already asked Malone about injuries and Keady's background, but he needed to check in before he proceeded. Keady was a complete stranger and someone whom he absolutely didn't trust.

Keady inhaled sharply, looking to the side. His cheeks were no longer flushed but had gone pale as he fiddled with his thumbs.

Come on. It's a basic question.

"Well?" Cutler softened his glare. Maybe he was just too intimidating? The question couldn't have been a surprise. It started most conversations outside of his work.

"I don't have any limits."

Well, now I'm awake. Giving him a once-over, Cutler bit back the quip on his tongue. The idea of that was fucking ludicrous. He could see it coming from a newbie, maybe. Sometimes people tested the waters of kink, declaring they were up for anything, but pretty soon they ran.

"Malone said you were a seasoned sub, not an idiot newbie. Tell me your limits or we're done before we can get started." Cutler had his scowl back in place, and he aimed it straight at Keady. Malone had seemed like a nice guy, and they'd had a few conversations. Cutler hadn't thought he'd waste his time, though. And something like 'no limits' was definitely worth mentioning.

Keady finally turned to look at him, meeting his gaze full on. He straightened his back, clenching his jaw tight as he ground his teeth. "I don't have any limits. I know exactly what you're going to say about it, too. I usually make up a few for Doms, just so they'll play with me, but I've had enough. I know it's not *safe* or ideal, but it's true."

So, he does have a spine. Cutler wanted to dig in and pull out more of this glimpse of Keady, but he wasn't sure if it was worth the risk. Keady was probably just like all the rest.

"Fair enough," Cutler drawled, stripping Keady of his confidence with a single look. "If you want Derreck to start digging you an early grave now, that's up to you. I could start with a knife on your skin, but where would I go from there? I could choke you out and gag that pretty mouth of yours. You'd be safewording in minutes...if I *let* you."

Now was about the time that most subs hit the road. Cutler would *never* ignore a safeword, but he would certainly push — push until it no longer mattered. He needed someone to know what they were getting into, even if that meant setting them up for failure.

Keady's bravado instantly dropped away as he locked onto his scuffed shoes. Worrying his lip, he glanced at Cutler out of the corner of his eye. There was no fear in his gaze, just the same nervousness from before and something that appeared a lot like regret. "I don't know."

Fuck. Keady was already getting under his skin, and it had only been a few minutes. But if that's how he wanted to play, then Cutler was calling it. He wasn't going to lose his new community so soon because of one sub who didn't have their shit together.

Rising to his feet, he gave the scene one last look. The Dom had released the restraints, cradling his limp sub to him. The sub was blissed and deep in subspace. It was perfect. "Figure your limits out, Keady, then give me a call."

Simultaneously looking furious and dejected, Keady let out a huff. "Or I can find a Dom who can give me what I want."

What a little spitfire. *That*, Malone had mentioned. Once Keady got over himself, he was a brat through and through. He'd even refused to call Malone 'Daddy', despite their dynamic.

But Cutler refused to be drawn into this fucking nightmare waiting to happen.

Fuck. "I dare you, Keady." There was no way he would do it. Men like Keady were all talk and no play. "And when you're done being fucked over, and you're ready to be fucked out, call me. I'll leave my number with Clint. Try not to get killed before you can use it."

Cutler should have been running, but Christ, he was curious. If Keady ever did call him, it was fucking on. He'd always wanted to break a brat.

Chapter Four

Keady

When Keady had been eleven years old, he'd taken a boat out onto the lake by himself after dark. The old aluminum twelve-footer had been light and easily tossed by the wind, especially when the engine had stalled as soon as he'd pulled away from the dock. But for some reason, his younger self had thought it had been a great idea. He'd ended up in the shallows on the far side of the lake and it had taken him hours to drag the boat all the way back to the dock.

He'd thought that had been the peak of the humiliation he'd face in his life, but this moment took the cake. It was the pinnacle of bad ideas, and just as lethal as a kid on a runaway boat after dark. He gritted his teeth, refusing to break down before he was alone.

He fucking *hurt* — and not in a good way.

The Dom he'd messaged, who Keady was starting to doubt was even a Dom at all, had left him high, dry and bleeding. Maybe it would have been a bit better if he'd at least gotten off on it, but no. It was hard to get off to something like that disaster of a scene.

You know what? I'm not calling it a scene. That's just an insult to kink.

He stared at his couch from his spot in the kitchen, trying to keep on the linoleum so he didn't stain the carpet. There were a few spots that he'd need the steam cleaner for, but Windex would take care of the rest. *I hope.*

He was almost numb, the distant grumbles of frustration and belittling jibes slipping off him with ease. The Dom was handsome, with long, dark hair and strong hands, but that was as far as the attraction went.

He was also a big, annoying asshole who had the knife skills of a toddler. Keady was never trusting the internet again.

"I'm taking off." The Dom grabbed his jacket without another backward glance before heading out of the door and slamming it behind him. It left the condo gratefully silent, although the smell of cigarettes and aftershave still lingered.

Clutching his arm, Keady winced, his eyes stinging as he glared at the wounds he'd just managed to reopen. They weren't long, but they were *deep*, which made sense, since the guy had used something so sharp. *Fucking idiot.*

Keady had only been trying to recreate the scene he'd caught at Unkinked and the moments with Cutler that haunted him. It had been an impossible task with a man who had cut into him like he was a prime rib steak. Hopefully, the knife had been clean.

Oh fuck. What if it wasn't? The bleeding would probably stop soon, but there was still a chance he would battle infection or worse.

They had both been idiots, but Keady was the only one who had been left bleeding.

That's what happens when you try to catch someone's attention outside of your own community. He glared at his wall, wiping the tears from his cheeks before they could fall any farther. So much for 'change is good'. Change was an asshole.

The cheap box store art on his walls looked tastefully back at him, offering zero relief from the chill of his kitchen. His home had always been his haven and safe space, but in a few minutes, he'd ruined it completely.

A few slices in, and he'd already known it was going to be a shitshow. And after the guy had ignored his call of 'yellow', he'd instantly called 'red'. For a moment, pure terror had engulfed him, but the guy had eventually backed off. The 'what ifs' were endless.

It had been the first time that Keady had been grateful for his safewords. Any other time he would have just shrugged them off, enduring more and more to reach that level of subspace that had eluded him for way too long.

But he'd been on edge since the beginning, when the strange Dom had knocked on his door and stepped past him like he'd owned the place – even before that, when Cutler had ripped his world out from under him when he'd told him to hit the road.

One of the most dangerous Doms in the club, and terrifying as all fuck, and even he wouldn't play with Keady. It probably wasn't just the limits thing, either. Keady was too old for most Dom's tastes, especially since he still had no idea what he wanted and was too shy to communicate it in the first place.

Hands shaking, he grabbed for his phone, dialing the contact at the top of the list. 'Clint' landed just above

'Daddy', since he'd left Malone's name in his contacts as it was, just so he could glare at it and wonder what the hell he'd been thinking. That, and he loved teasing Malone, who took it all in stride. *Of course.*

If he didn't bleed out on his kitchen floor, Clint was going to kill him. It was probably best just to get it over with.

"Hello?" Clint's voice was threaded with sleep and Keady winced as he glanced at his clock. It was after two in the morning, and well after Unkinked would have shut down for the night.

Other than special nights, Clint had moved the hours up to a crisp one a.m. The only ones active would be the couples who had decided to stay in one of the guest rooms. And those were only open to long-time members who were trustworthy. Definitely *not* Keady.

"Hey, Clint, it's Keady. You got a minute?" He bit his lip, reaching for another strip of gauze from the pile he'd set on the kitchen table. He'd been lucky that he still had them in his old first-aid kit. The thought had crossed his mind to throw them out a few times to clear up space, but his rational side had thankfully won out.

The old white strip of gauze had bled through, leaving a mushy and soaked piece of cotton behind. Tossing it with the others in the trash, he wrapped the fresh one around his arm a few times. It must've been a cheap brand because it was soaked in moments, vermilion gathering to drip down to his fingertips. A warm drop hit his toe, and he hissed in frustration.

"Shoot, baby. What's going on?" He must've still been half asleep. Clint didn't call anyone 'baby', least of all his friends.

This whole situation was going to suck, especially with how pissed Clint was going to be. He knew basic first aid, as in Band-Aids and peroxide, but he needed some nursing expertise, and Clint was the only nurse he knew. Hopefully, he didn't have to go through a punishment again.

On second thought, he should have just called Maddy. If there was anyone experienced with knife wounds, it would be him. His Dom Derreck was intimidating as hell, though.

"I think I need stitches," said Keady, turning his arm over and patting at the escaping mess with a Kleenex. "Can you walk me through how to do them?" He peeked under the edge of the gauze next, wincing at the stickiness. He should have called 'red' at the first cut, not the fifth.

"That's one way to wake me the fuck up." Clint definitely sounded awake and more than a little bit pissed. "You finally found your dangerous Dom, I presume. You are such a fucking idiot, Keady. Did you not listen to anything I said? How badly are you hurt?" Something rustled in the background, and Clint let out a low sigh.

"Eh." Keady tilted his head and shrugged as he tried to stay calm. Yep, he was in for it. "I'm not going to die or anything, but I was hoping to stop the bleeding. This gauze isn't doing shit. I have a sewing kit for buttons, and the needle is still in the package. That should do, right?"

"Fuck." Clint let out a groan. "Just when I think I've finally got you guys trained. You are in so much trouble right now." There was a pause. "Give me a few minutes, and I'll get dressed — or, you know what? Can you make it here? I don't think I'm in any state to stitch you up, but there are still a few folks that live close by that could help you out. I don't want you to drive if you think you're going to pass out, though."

Was he safe to drive? He didn't want to bother Clint any more than he had to or land in his bad books any worse. He should have called Malone. He would have known what to do, but he was probably busy with his boy.

"I think I should be able to drive." He'd have to steam clean his car and maybe throw out his jacket, but they were both due anyway. "I'll just find a towel or something, then I'll head your way."

"A towel?" Now Clint sounded concerned, his voice going deep. "Fuck that. If you think you need a towel, then you are way worse off than you're letting on. I'll send someone your way. Just hang tight."

"Fine." He glanced down at the trail that had made its way to his wrist again. He wiped it away with a handful of tissues. He was in double — no — triple trouble. Safety had always been Clint's primary concern, and he took that shit seriously.

Maybe he'd move up his relocation just to avoid it. The city lights blinked in through his window, sending that thought right back out of the door. Every time he looked, they got prettier, the cars on the highway like streaks of fireflies in the night. *Fuck change.*

Biting his lip, Keady hung up the phone before ripping the useless gauze off his arm. After trekking to the bathroom and grabbing a towel, he padded at the wounds, wincing as the scratchy fibers terrorized his oversensitive flesh. Of course, all he had were white and beige towels, so they were going to be screwed, too.

He shivered, his knees going weak as he flicked on the light. He sat heavily on the toilet with the lid closed, letting his head fall into his hands. Everything was cold against his naked flesh, settling into his gut along with months and years worth of frustration and regret.

His hands were damp and sticky against his cheeks, the tacky blood diluting in the tears that had started to flow. He hadn't realized when he'd started to cry, but it was nearly silent—no wrenching sobs from deep within him. It was almost surprising how little he cared about them.

He'd fucked up...huge. Somewhere in the last few months, he'd turned reckless and desperate. It didn't suit him in the least. He'd always been so careful, vetting his play partners and talking to previous subs while trying to avoid talking to any Doms directly. Subs were easier, and they usually gossiped, until eventually, the Dom would head his way, searching for the fresh bit of bait he'd laid.

He'd never tell Malone, but their eleven months together had ruined him. With every sweet act and moment of understanding, Keady had only gotten angrier and more desperate.

He just wanted to feel the way he used to. When he'd discovered kink, it had been the lightning of his life and his single source of comfort in his lonely days. Friends, lovers and community had all become a part of him.

The adrenaline rush, the way every hair on his body prickled and his cock went so hard his entire body throbbed had become his crack. He wanted to come so hard that he blacked out and floated in subspace for hours. It had happened before, until suddenly, it hadn't anymore.

His preferences had changed along with his numerous partners, and things like simple floggings and degradation had lost their edge. He wanted *more*.

But every time he tried, it was just another failure — a meek attempt at normalcy. Tonight had been a last resort, and he'd fucked that up, too. All the yearning had led him to a place that was best left alone.

Maybe I should give up? He shook his head. Kink was such a huge part of his life, and he couldn't just leave it behind. Vanilla sex was just that for him — tasty, but ultimately boring and unsatisfying as hell. He needed the caramel drizzle and the half-pound of chocolate along with a side of strawberries and Skor bits.

Or just a Dom who wanted to take him flying without trying to kill him.

He didn't have any friends outside of the community, either. He didn't speak to his family, or rather, they didn't speak to him, and he worked from home. Maddy, Nav, Clint, Malone and a few select others were his best friends and the only ones he really cared about. *And to think, I disappointed them all on the same night.*

He startled at a knock on the front door, looking to the puddle that had formed on the top of his knee and had dripped all the way down his leg as he'd waited. Red circled each of his toes as it bloomed on the tile, the sticky film already drying.

That's not too much blood? Is it? It was hard to know when he could hardly see straight with how hard he was shaking. He kept his condo at a crisp and a few degrees below normal room temperature, but that was usually with clothes on and not bleeding. The cold of the tiles was like a rain that fell just on the cusp of winter.

"It's open," he called, his voice echoing in the quiet bathroom. Hopefully, they could hear him, because his knees were wobbling too much for him to stand. It was probably a good thing that he hadn't driven. He would have ended up in the ditch when he zoned out for the first time.

He heard the sound of the front door clicking open before closing again, then the shuffling of someone removing their shoes. There was a moment of silence before they must've caught the light from the bathroom. Their steps moved closer, each a thud against carpet, then linoleum.

His place wasn't small, but it was excruciatingly open-concept. From the front door, you could see almost everything, including the bedroom. It made everything easier to clean and it was a great excuse not to hang photos. The spots on the walls that existed were filled with cheap art, leaving no space for any sort of mementos.

He glanced up as the footsteps paused at the bathroom door, and his heart nearly stopped. Cutler was standing at the entrance, his broad shoulders threatening to take up the entire doorway. He probably could have tossed Keady over his shoulder with one hand or carried him for an hour without breaking a sweat.

Cutler's gaze was steady, his pupils constricting in the bright light of the bathroom. He didn't look the least bit tired, despite the hour, his face slightly flushed from the summer air that refused to release its humidity.

It was just another point in his favor on the serial-killer list. Murderers had to be great at staying up late. Everyone knew that was the best time to bury a body. *Am I the only one who has put the pieces together?*

His heart pounded, his teeth chattering as Cutler took a step into his bathroom. It was a small space to begin with, but with the two of them, it was unbearable.

Keady let out a gasp, biting his lip at the whimper that threatened to escape when the sting of his arm rushed back at full force. The wounds that had dulled to a slow throb, sprung to life, pain slithering beneath his skin all the way to his fingertips.

It hurts.

It was bad enough to partake in a terrible scene, but this was too much. The last thing he wanted was for this suspicious man and Dom to see him at his worst. He was bound to rescind his offer of a scene...not that Keady was sure if he was going to accept it or not.

He'd never admit that he'd only set up the date with the knife-happy Dom to prove a point. He was taking that fact to his grave. What was he worth if he backed out of a simple dare?

"Clint didn't tell you I was coming." It wasn't a question. Cutler's voice sliced straight through him. He sounded pissed and wide awake, his eyes narrowing when he caught sight of Keady's wounds.

Keady shook his head, unable to answer with his teeth chattering. He was so vulnerable and open right now, ready for the next predator to snatch him up. The old him from a few hours before would have been thrilled at the idea, but not now.

He needed Clint or Malone, not someone who made every sub safeword halfway through a scene.

"Is it okay if I take a look at you? I can leave if you prefer."

Keady took a second glance. Was that worry he detected? It was hard to tell when Cutler's face was cut in stone like it always was, as if expressions were the enemy. His face wasn't a terrible one, though.

Maybe his brain was acting funny from blood loss or maybe he just hadn't noticed before, but Cutler was *hot.*

It was a dreadful time to make note of it, especially when Cutler was in his space, making the small bathroom that much more claustrophobic.

But that leather jacket, which was ridiculous for how hot it was outside and the tight shirt underneath displayed everything that Keady had failed to notice before. The guy was cut, his jeans clinging to his legs to show off the assets, especially his ass, which Keady could see in the mirror above his sink. The whole package was like a fucking dream.

Cutler's usual glasses were missing, his face looking ten years younger without them. It was hard to pinpoint his age exactly, but he didn't have a single gray hair and his body was lean and strong.

Across his lips was the only imperfection in the form of a scar. It was more prominent against his flushed skin, white and stark in the shiny way that spoke of a serious injury. It could have been surgical — or maybe the result of one of his victims fighting back.

Definitely a serial killer.

"Come on in," Keady managed to say, his voice shaking as he startled himself with the invitation. *This is no time to be polite!* Cutler took a step, his blue eyes blazing over Keady's body.

Fuck, I'm naked. He'd forgotten somehow, but his skin flushed with the reminder. How many times had he been naked before strangers at the club? But none of that seemed to matter now. "Where are your glasses?"

It was an absurd thing for someone to forget, and it got Cutler to stop *looking* at him, even if it was just for a moment. Contacts didn't even register as an option at the moment.

Cutler grimaced, kneeling at Keady's side with a creak of leather. He smelled like polish, cologne and something else dangerous, banishing the last of the cigarette smoke that lingered from the stranger. Something in his gut unwound, and Keady took his first real breath in minutes, his toes curling.

"I can't wear glasses with my helmet. They'd just squish my nose. Here... Let me look at you," said Cutler, barely sparing the rest of Keady a glance as he locked his gaze onto the wounds.

Is he a vampire? He seemed to be fascinated by the vermilion streaks, his eyes narrow and focused.

Keady raised his injured arm, shuddering as Cutler carefully touched the dry portions of the soaked towel that had stained through. The movement zinged up his arm as Cutler pulled the edge back, revealing the mess underneath. His fingers were long and his grip firm as he held Keady steady. That grip could probably kill a man with how precise it held him.

Most people would probably feel queasy if they looked at something like Keady's arm in its battered state. Maybe not many in the lifestyle, but there were still those who fainted at the sight of blood. Cutler seemed to be as much of an exception as Keady was, leaning closer as if to inspect the area while dragging in a breath through his nose. The tang of it must've been strong, because Keady could *taste* it.

For the first time that night, Keady's adrenaline spiked and a long-awaited thrum washed over him. It caught him so off guard that he had to struggle to keep breathing, his eyelids drooping as he trembled for an entirely different reason.

Cutler furrowed his forehead, the corner of his lip twitching as he traced the lines with his gaze. The scrutiny just sent Keady higher, the focus dragging over his skin and cutting so much deeper than the blade. It wasn't the look of someone who was just there for kicks and didn't give a shit about him.

After snapping on a pair of white gloves from his pocket, Cutler touched the wounds for the first time.

"Fuck," said Keady quietly, clutching the toilet seat with his other hand. He bit back a groan as the pain became something else entirely, with so much potential that hope filled him to the brim.

It wormed its way deeper as Cutler examined each spot with sure, confident fingers, humming under his breath a few times as he paused on what he found. His breathing never changed, his face as calm as if he were taking a sip of coffee in the morning and not staining white with red.

He had everything that the other Dom hadn't—the confidence, calm and, of course, a nice ass. *God,* he was better in every conceivable way.

"I've seen worse." Cutler touched the deepest cut, putting a bit of pressure on it so it gaped wide for a moment, fresh blood welling up and dripping like tears. It was so deep that Keady wondered if he would see veins, bones and other things that he wasn't meant to see. His vision wavered.

Fuck. Keady crossed his legs as blood rushed to every part of his body, including between his legs. He leaned forward to try to cover the evidence of what the pain was doing to him, hoping that he'd pass out any second to spare himself the humiliation.

He wasn't sure if Cutler was ignoring his reaction or if he really didn't care, but he didn't seem to notice a thing.

"You need stitches, but hopefully not that many. You'll have scars, but I'll make sure they'll heal small, as long as you don't pick at them." Cutler was all business as he reached into his pocket, plucking something out that was oval, flat and white. A blue thread was wrapped around it like a fishing line, the hook already attached at the end. It looked like some fancy version of his needle-and-thread solution.

"Did you have fun, at least?" asked Cutler, grasping the bottle of alcohol that Keady had discarded on the floor after he'd dug out his first-aid kit. It was almost a liter of the stuff and promised more of a sting than anything the pretend Dom had done to him.

"Nope." It was humiliating, but strangely, it felt almost good to say it. It was the same as throwing something back in Cutler's face and slapping him the only way he could get away with. Keady had accepted his challenge, and he hadn't failed—not on purpose. *This is your fault as much as it is mine.*

"Good." Cutler nodded, dabbing the blood from Keady's arm before upending the bottle of alcohol over the cuts. Keady let out a hiss but didn't flinch away, closing his eyes and letting it wash over him instead. Energy bubbled under his skin, and he had to keep from squirming as every nerve prickled. There was lots of alcohol left—enough for Cutler to do that a hundred times with liquid to spare.

"You're doing so good," came Cutler's low voice as he dabbed the wounds a second time. "But I like that you didn't enjoy yourself. If you had gone back for seconds, they might've done some real damage."

This isn't real damage? Maybe the cuts weren't huge, but they were deep and stung something fierce. That, and Keady's pride, would never be the same.

"I don't have anything to numb you with." Cutler touched the oval cassette of suture material before pulling another instrument from his pocket that he used to grasp the needle with.

The guy was like a walking pharmacy. What else did he have in his jacket? A rectal thermometer?

Keady shook his head as he tried to focus on anything except the contrast of Cutler's gloved hands against his wrist. He wasn't in subspace, but he felt good—better than he had in a long time. "Make it hurt?"

He *needed* it to hurt. He'd done something terrible and dangerous, and he had to be punished for it so he could forgive himself. He'd never be able to look at the spots without bad memories dancing over his skin, but it was a start. Clint would think up something even worse once he woke up tomorrow, and when the news spread, his friends would descend like wolves.

"Piece of cake." Cutler watched him as he dug one finger into the smallest wound, blood welling around his gloved fingertip as he pressed so intimately. Keady let out a gasp, shuddering as he closed his eyes. His cock slapped against his belly, making itself known, even as he tried to hide it. *Oh God. Oh God.*

"Do you like pain, Keady?" asked Cutler, moving to the next spot and laying his finger against the wound. With simple pressure, he brought the edges together, the bleeding stopping in an instant. "I could make this hurt for you if that's what you need. But I'm not going to punish you for it... Even if I was your Dom, that's not my style."

Keady blinked, glancing around the fuzzy bathroom as his blood rushed through his ears. "No punishments?"

The idea of that was surreal. Even with Malone, his sweet and even-tempered Daddy—he'd still been punished from time to time — a spanking, some orgasm denial or his personal least-favorite, alone time to reflect his thoughts. Punishment was a part of the dynamic as much as praise and reward were.

Cutler gave him a long look, his lips twitching as if he were fighting a smile. "I've never needed to punish a sub. But they wouldn't dare step out of line in the first place."

Holy shit.

Between the first prick of the needle and Cutler's hands on him, Keady lost a part of himself. Subspace slipped over him like a veil, his adrenaline spiking as he started to float. He blinked it away, shaking his head. He'd already made enough mistakes for one night, and giving up control now was asking for something bad to happen.

Even as much as he needed it, Cutler was way too good with a needle to be anything but a serial killer. He wasn't *that* suicidal.

A neat row of stitches were slowly worked into his flesh, the tiny knots like nothing he would have been able to replicate. It was like something he'd seen on television in a late-night ER show or a flirty comedy. Everything slid into place in a heartbeat. "Are you a doctor?"

"Neurosurgeon," said Cutler, letting out a small sigh as he moved to the next slice. His hands were still steady, and he hadn't said a damn thing about Keady's erection. It was as if it didn't exist. "You doing okay up there?"

"Yeah." He didn't sound okay. His voice was breathy, his heart still beating hard as he fought against the pleasure thrumming through him, right along with the pain. At least the air didn't feel quite so cold anymore, but the bathroom lights were rather bright.

He wanted darkness and candlelight, the flame flickering as wax dripped against his skin, his Dom standing over him and laying a canvas of different colored beads. The veil chugged closer as he fought the images flitting through his thoughts.

He wondered if Cutler could hear his heart pounding against his ribs, so close to his face as he inspected his work. The smell of pre-cum was thick, along with his sweat and desire. Keady pushed away another shudder, looking away from the dried blood. The sight of it wasn't helping his state of mind.

"Why are you trying to fight it?" asked Cutler, his voice low but knowing as his gaze strayed to Keady's cock for the first time. He licked his lips. "I see you struggling to hold on, Keady. Are you afraid of me?"

Yes. No. I don't know.

"You should be afraid, but not right now." Cutler drew back. "If you were my sub, you would be *terrified* and so free that you'd never want to be any other way. You're safe…for now."

Cutler lined the needle up with the edge of the last cut, piercing the skin as if it were butter. Keady couldn't stop his whimper this time.

"Stop." He flinched as he said it, his skin prickling. Cutler instantly stilled, pausing as his blue eyes found Keady's.

"Are you scared?"

Swallowing, Keady nodded, gripping the edge of the toilet seat to try to hold onto the last threads of his sanity. Instead of the few stinging spots from the initial wounds, now there were dozens, each needle prick tingling and itching. "I don't want to end up in subspace — not like this…not with you."

Cutler didn't *look* offended, but Keady couldn't read him well. His lips hardly moved, the scar almost giving the appearance of weary heaviness. There were no laugh lines, as if Cutler's face had never seen a smile. He looked so fucking young.

"I don't want to end up in your freezer or something." Keady could picture it now, his body tucked between the neat rows of meat that Cutler probably had in his freezer. Clint would probably figure that Keady had gone off with another Dom again, never suspecting Cutler of a thing.

A lot of serial killers ended up being doctors, according to crime shows. How many of those were neurosurgeons?

Cutler snorted, covering his mouth with his wrist as he shook with laughter. His eyes sparkled, lighting up in a way that Keady hadn't thought possible. The man before him was rewritten in moments, until there was nothing to fear but a few confused memories.

"Clint mentioned that you thought I looked like a serial killer. I'll take it as a compliment." He pulled his wrist away, his lips alarmingly neutral. *He'd been laughing, hadn't he?*

Keady flushed, glancing away as his face flamed. *Of course*, Clint had told him that. He was such a gossip. But seriously? A compliment? He knew doctors had big egos sometimes, but that was beyond.

"Let me ask you something." Cutler tied the final knot, before snipping the edge of the thread. The spot throbbed, along with the rest of them. "You like pain and you certainly enjoyed me fixing you up. Does that mean you want an abusive relationship where you get shoved around, beaten and belittled?"

Keady couldn't stop his glare. He'd come up against that argument so many times before. Kink wasn't about violence or abuse. It was about trust.

"Just because Clint likes to play with fire, does that mean he'll burn your house down?" Cutler continued. Keady wasn't even sure how he *knew* that little tidbit. Clint usually kept that information close to his chest.

Swallowing, Keady looked to his shaking hands. That one hit close to home. He'd seen Clint after the fire that had disfigured him and had cost him his husband. He'd remembered wondering if he would lose two friends instead of one at the time, his chest aching as he'd watched the remaining one cling to life.

"No," he said softly, letting out a heavy breath. There was a reason that Clint refused to allow fire demos within his walls. Even wax-play was questionable, occasionally.

"I like to play a part," said Cutler, tucking his things back in his jacket and peeling off his gloves. He had to have been hot in leather, but he never made any move to remove it. "I like fear play and everything that comes along with it. That doesn't mean I'm going to eat your liver with fava beans."

Keady snickered, trying to hold steady as Cutler inspected his wounds one last time. The stitches itched something fierce, and his fingers twitched as he tried not to reach for them. A shower was going to be hell with them.

"I've never seen you smile. Even when you seem to enjoy yourself, it's like you don't know how." Without realizing it, Keady reached for the scar on Cutler's lip, hovering with his finger only an inch away.

Maybe it was the sudden easiness that made him ask, but the sparkle in Cutler's eyes instantly went cold and he jerked back, moving to his feet. He started the sink without a word, scrubbing his hands with soap before rinsing them.

"You should heal fine." Cutler reached for a fresh towel to dry his hands, grimacing when he noticed the bloodstain on the corner. Drying his hands on his pants instead, he stepped toward the door. "Did you need aftercare?"

What the hell just happened? The air had shifted, the brief warmth suddenly sucked from the room. The fear was back, tainting the soft thoughts that had settled his belly in a halo of warmth.

"I thought of a limit," said Keady. He shouldn't have tried to touch Cutler without permission, but he was in no state to fully blame himself. He just didn't want to be left alone quite so soon, with the blood stains on his floor still tacky and fresh.

"You really think that's enough?" Cutler held him with a steady gaze that could have frozen the sun. "There are at least four things that happened tonight that broke the rules of your community. You're dangerous, Keady, and you're going to get yourself killed."

Keady broke eye contact, slumping down and trying to cover himself with his hands. He wasn't hard anymore, but he'd never felt so exposed. There seemed to be blood everywhere he touched, some of it flaking, but all of it smelling like sickly copper. It made him want to gag.

He'd always walked on the edge of kink, trying things that others refused to. Breath play *was* dangerous, but the one time he'd convinced Malone to try it was the closest he'd come to subspace with him.

"I was desperate." His voice shook, tears gathering in his eyes. *And it's your fucking fault.* "You wouldn't understand." Cutler had his choice of subs, even with his reputation. He had an online following, for Christ's sake. He was attractive, too, and practically reeked of dominance. So what if he had a fast turnover. The more the merrier, right?

But Keady wasn't thirty anymore. No one wanted a sub his age, especially when he couldn't always tell them what he wanted. He *knew*, but he couldn't just say it. Not only was it against the rules, but he'd have to be brave enough to speak up to someone first. It had been so long since he'd felt brave enough to consider the dark thoughts of his fantasies.

The touch on his chin startled a gasp from his lips. He blinked away his tears, staring into Cutler's eyes as the man hovered close to him. They were so blue that they looked nearly like glass, his pupils just a touch bigger than they should have been in the bright bathroom.

"You assume a lot about me, Keady."

Fuck. Keady looked away, resisting Cutler's grip on his chin. That was his whole problem summed up in one small sentence. That's why he always chose the bad boy and ended up empty. "I don't need aftercare."

Cutler drew his hand back as if he'd been slapped, taking one last glance at the stitches before he turned away. "Goodbye, Keady."

Good riddance.

Chapter Five

Cutler

He hit his turn signal a touch too hard, the small plastic bar threatening to break as he took the gravel exit off the main road. Trees closed in around him almost immediately, a few potholes from the recent rain rocking his car. He couldn't remember them being that bad before, but they'd gotten a month's worth of rain in two days, the thunder vibrating the walls for hours earlier in the week.

Even if the holes blew his suspension, it would still be worth it. A half-mile of shitty road before Unkinked meant that it was private and near perfect. In the city, it had been different.

There were times when he'd wondered if someone he knew would see him heading into the club. He wasn't ashamed of who he was on any level, but things may have become difficult for him if he were recognized. The world wasn't as understanding toward kinksters as they were of other communities.

It was doubtful that any delivery trucks would agree with his appreciation of the new private setting. He'd heard a few grumbles from members when Clint had first announced the change, but if a short drive was a make-or-break decision, then those people weren't in it for the kink.

And those who spent most of their time drinking at the bar weren't worth his time.

The trees loomed even closer as he slowed and made the final turn on the single-lane driveway. The potholes rocked him slowly as he decelerated, threatening sleep with the gentle swaying of the car. Rubbing his eyes with the back of his hand, he brushed the feeling away like everything else.

In the last week, he'd lost two patients. Now there were two good people who had had loves and lives that he could never return them to. It had been a bad month for him — year, even. His hands were shaking from the last one, the scent of disinfectant and death still clinging to his skin.

Death had a very particular smell of its own, and it was unmistakable.

Sometimes it took a lot to make it fade, a shower doing nothing to strip his nose of it. It didn't matter how good of a doctor he was, sometimes cancer was cancer, and a fatal car accident was exactly that. He couldn't stitch together a brain that was mostly pulverized mush.

It was the trying that hurt him the most. With their hearts barely beating, and their breathing regulated by a machine, it was unimaginable how some managed to survive, while a bump on the head could kill another.

He'd poured everything he'd had to save them in both cases, but he didn't always win.

Gripping the steering wheel, he eased into the lot, frowning at the dozen or so other cars there. He'd hoped that he would be one of the only ones there, with the freedom to wander anywhere he chose. Sometimes all he needed was to just be among the implements to find his way back to himself.

He may not have been in this community for long, but it was by far the most understanding and welcoming that he'd come across. People were serious, and yet they didn't treat safewords like the end of the world. He'd stumbled across one place where if a sub safeworded on you three times, that was it. *And yet...*

He clenched his jaw as his thoughts turned to Keady. The dark-haired man had haunted his dreams for the past few nights. The sounds of his whimpers and the smell of his submission in stark vermilion droplets clung to his memory. He was so alluring, yet so fucking dangerous.

Dangerous for Cutler. The last time he'd started a relationship with a sub like Keady, he'd nearly gone too far. The last thing he needed was a prison sentence. His kinks weren't exactly mainstream, even within the kink community, so he needed someone who knew how to safeword. Hell, he relied on it.

Safewords were there to be used, in his opinion, and weren't some high and mighty standards that should never be uttered on pain of expulsion.

The front hall was quiet, along with the main stage area that promised one hell of a leather demo that weekend. Skipping the rooms, he pushed on to the open play area, letting out a sigh of relief at the whispered sound of conversation and pleasure.

The members who had left the fold didn't know what they were missing. This place was insane, with enough equipment and rooms that no kinkster would ever be in need. He'd even heard of the basement that treaded on the darker side of things, although the place was monitored a little more closely than Cutler would have liked.

He got it. The Dungeon Masters didn't know him well enough to trust him. It was probably a good thing. Some days, he didn't trust himself, either.

He caught Clint's eye across the floor, raising his hand in acknowledgment before he headed toward him. Without a drink or towel in his hand, Clint was almost unrecognizable. And the easy way he moved wasn't like anything Cutler had seen so far. Even during their scene, Clint hadn't really let go, just giving Cutler a taste to get an idea of who he was.

But he looked *good*.

"Slow night?" asked Cutler, sliding onto the seat next to Clint. There were a few couches spotted around the room, presumably for couples who didn't mind a bit of hustle during aftercare, or for those who wanted to watch. He was happy enough to take them up on the latter as often as possible.

Clint gave him a lazy shrug, looking around the room with a silly smile on his face. "It's Tuesday. Only lifers will be out tonight."

Shit. Was it Tuesday? Cutler looked around for the nearest clock. There had been a few emergencies that he'd needed to attend to, which had dragged out his shift from a twelve-hour to an apparent thirty-six. He was lucky that it was at the end of his seven-day rotation.

"There's an event on this weekend," said Clint, stretching his arms over his head. "I've got Gary coming in to show off his leather gear—everything from pants to panties and crotchless chaps. I know that's not your thing, but are you game? I know a certain someone will be there."

Cutler frowned, holding Clint's gaze steady. *Such a brat.* "Are you a matchmaker now?" Cutler hadn't questioned it when Clint had called him in the middle of the night to patch Keady up. He'd been awake anyway, and his place was closer. It had made sense. *Fucker.*

"Always have been." Clint grinned. "Just waiting for you two to get over your issues and get together. Everyone can see that you're made for each other."

That was the exact reason that Cutler didn't trust anyone's opinion but his own.

"Don't meddle." Cutler leaned against the couch, barely holding himself back from putting Clint in his place. A backhand probably wasn't acceptable outside of a scene. He must've been more tired than he'd thought to be pushing that close to the edge of his control. "I'm not going to play with someone who doesn't have any limits."

That gave Clint pause, his brows going up. "Keady didn't mention that part. He's always liked to play on the wild side, not that he gets the opportunity much. He's more of a dreamer. But no limits? That's insane. And that means that the punishment I handed out wasn't nearly enough."

Taking a deep breath to center himself, Cutler looked to the nearest piece of equipment. It was as simple as it was exquisite. There were so many things he could do with a cross that the possibilities were nearly endless. He wasn't going to offer to hand out the punishment, though. He didn't do punishments. *Fuck, maybe I should.*

"I think he had them for Malone and other Doms he's played with," said Cutler. He'd gotten that impression. "Keady is a hard man to read, but he said he's desperate. The problem is that he thinks he'll find something better if he gets rid of every limit. It already cost him once."

Clint inclined his head. "Speak of the devil." He motioned to the door where Keady was just making his way inside, casting his gaze about the room as if he were searching for something. He paused when he looked their way, his eyes going wide.

"He's been here every night looking for you. Well, that and cleaning every single piece of equipment top to bottom," said Clint, giving Keady a small wave, much to Cutler's chagrin. "I'll sit in on the first one if you're worried. You know I'm more than happy to do that for you. You look like you need a scene, man, and Keady needs a reminder."

Cutler grimaced, cutting off his reply as Keady came within earshot. He wasn't sure what he'd expected, but Keady dropping to his knees with his gaze lowered was not it. His throat momentarily closed off, his trembling hands going steady for the first time in hours.

Sometimes, that was all he needed. *Fuck, I'm going to make you hurt.* Cutler kept his face completely passive.

"Can I speak with you please, Cutler?" asked Keady, giving Cutler a brief look before he dropped his gaze again.

Cutler crossed his arms, then immediately uncrossed them when he realized what he'd done. Sliding his hands down his legs, he paused at his knees, holding on so he didn't reach out. He was usually so good at keeping calm and stoic, but Keady seemed to throw him off at every turn.

"Go ahead, Keady. I'm not your Dom. You don't need to ask for permission."

It must've been the wrong thing to say. Keady slumped, his eyes glassy when he looked up.

"I wanted to apologize for my behavior." Keady bit his lip, his cheeks flushing. "I was reckless and an idiot, and I ignored the advice of trusted friends, then took it out on you when I didn't get my way." It came out in a stilted rush, Keady's voice trembling. "And I'm sorry about what happened in the bathroom. I'm not sure exactly what I did, but I made you uncomfortable, and that's not fair to you, especially when you helped me."

Keady moved his hand to the spot on his arm where the blue Monocryl suture was still knotted. The area looked scabbed and well on its way to healing, albeit a little red from a possible suture reaction. They'd need to be removed soon.

"I—" Cutler stared, only to be cut off.

"And I have my limits if you'd like to hear them."

He fought not to roll his eyes. Keady seemed to have a one-track mind. But at least he had found a touch of a spine. He had honestly been worried that the conversation would have taken three times as long as Keady struggled to get over his shyness.

"You hoped that if you apologized, I'd give you what you want?" asked Cutler, finally giving in and reaching to tuck a strand of Keady's hair behind his ear. Sweat clung to his finger and Keady shivered from the touch. "Go ahead. Answer."

"Not exactly," Keady confessed, looking away. "I thought of a really good joke to tell you, and I wanted to see if I could make you smile."

Cutler cast a confused glance at Clint, who seemed just as clueless. What the hell did him smiling have to do with anything? The truth was, he hated the automatic reaction his face struggled through every time he found something funny. It was just a reminder of something he'd rather forget.

"When I feel bad, I try to make people laugh. I don't get out much." Keady trailed off, looking absolutely stricken at the look on Cutler's face. Cutler had to bite the inside of his lip to keep from laughing.

"How about this," said Cutler, tucking the same strand of hair that tried to escape again immediately. He smoothed it against Keady's head, hoping that it held. Keady leaned into the touch, so starved for attention and willing to please that it was nearly heartbreaking. But Cutler knew better.

He was also a reasonable man, and he could recognize when someone was trying to turn over a new leaf. It didn't happen often, and it was something worth cherishing.

"If you can make me laugh, I'll listen to your limits. If not, Clint here is going to give you a spanking in front of all these people. You okay with that, Clint?"

"Hell yeah," Clint grinned, rolling up his sleeves. "I owe you one, and I haven't beaten someone's ass in ages. I just bought a bunch of new floggers, too. They're bison hide, so they'll thud something fierce."

Keady was looking around the room, wide-eyed. There were only two couples there at the moment, but there could have been fifty for how nervous he suddenly seemed. "Here? In front of everyone?"

"Yes." Cutler stroked Keady's bottom lip once before he drew back. "So you better make me laugh."

"Or not," said Clint, sounding hopeful.

"Okay." Keady let his breath out in a rush, looking down to his fingers as he twiddled them. His nails were bitten raw, one of his nailbeds rusted with dried blood.

This was going to be way too easy. Cutler hadn't really laughed since the accident that had left him with a nasty scar and a partially paralyzed face. It would teach Keady not to mess with him, though, or try to manipulate him.

"Okay," Keady said again, closing his eyes and taking a deep breath. When he opened them, he had a new fierceness about him.

Should I be worried?

"So you said you're a doctor," said Keady, his voice suddenly steady as he gripped his own knees. It was like watching someone come into their own, leaving their life in the closet behind them.

"Neurosurgeon," Cutler corrected. He'd gone through enough schooling that he could afford to be arrogant about it.

"Sure. But have you ever done a prostate exam?" Keady bit his lip as he started to grin. He looked so much younger when he smiled, the worry and grimness lost from his features.

"Absolutely. After I completed medical school, I practiced for two years before I decided to go back to my studies. Besides that, I can make a man come with one finger." He held his finger up, waggling it as Keady flushed again and lost a bit of his momentum.

Not worried.

"I was thinking I could book a prostate exam with you on February second... That's Groundhog Day." Keady's eyes sparkled, and he bit his lip.

"Okay?" Cutler furrowed his forehead. "Did you have some concerns?" Work was the last thing he wanted to talk about right now, but he wouldn't pass up the chance to help Keady.

"No. No, not at all." Keady beamed. "But I was thinking... Since it would be Groundhog Day, while you're down there in my *hole*, you could tell me if we're in for an early spring or six more weeks of winter."

What the hell? Cutler snorted, slapping a hand over his face as a laugh burst from his throat. Clint cackled beside him, slapping his knee as he started to wheeze. It only made Cutler want to laugh harder. He'd heard a lot of jokes as a doctor, but that one was new.

Keady practically glowed, and his lips curved into a full smile that brought a new sparkle to his eyes. He was beautiful, his cheeks rosy as he laughed along with them.

"Sure," said Cutler when he finally got a hold of himself. He'd never paid much attention to Groundhog Day, but he certainly wasn't going to miss the next one. He grimaced as one corner of his lips weighed down as he smiled. Keady didn't seem to notice, though. "You deserve this one, Keady. What are your limits?"

Keady practically beamed. "Age play is a soft limit because it honestly didn't do much for me. Diapers are hot, but rashes are nasty." He ticked off one finger. "Let's call watersports one. I don't mind being pissed on, but being pissed *in* is just..." He shuddered, closing his eyes for a moment.

"What else?"

Keady hummed, looking around the room. "Aftercare!" He nearly shouted, drawing the gaze of one couple who was setting up for a scene. "I want aftercare. No aftercare is a hard limit. Oh, and nothing that could get me arrested, so let's say public sex scenes are off the table. I do *not* want to live out those jailhouse fantasies." Keady flushed, as if he'd just realized that he was nearly shouting. Cutler had to hold back another chuckle.

"No body mod." He said this one much softer, glancing to the healing cuts on his arm. "And that's it. Everything else is on the table, as long as we discuss it ahead of time."

It was much more practical than Cutler had expected. He was a devout believer in RACK, Risk Aware Consensual Kink, but he didn't fully trust himself for a total power exchange with no limits, especially if it was with someone who he couldn't trust to safeword.

Looking toward the open floor that had more options than he had time, Cutler let out a slow breath to calm his budding arousal. He was exhausted, sure, but Keady was beautiful and experienced. The art they could make together would be flawless. *If only I could trust him.*

"Cutler?" Keady asked.

Cutler sent him a false glare. "I said you could tell me your limits, Keady, but otherwise I expect you to keep your thoughts to yourself. You can make as much noise as you want to, and answer a direct question, but not a *word*."

Am I doing this?

Keady flushed, lowering his gaze. His jaw went tight as he opened and closed his hands a few times. What was Keady thinking? Cutler could already feel himself wondering and dreaming about peeling back the layers of his sleek shyness to the brat underneath, only to mold that part of Keady into the perfect sub that was deserving of his dominance.

There was no turning back now.

"I wish you had more limits," he mused, placing a hand in Keady's hair. It was just as soft as he'd hoped, but slick with sweat. The room was cool, but Keady's skin was almost fevered, the flush over his cheeks there every moment that Cutler recalled.

Malone had told him how shy Keady was, even after they'd been together for months. It must've killed him to approach Cutler and declare himself. If everything went well, it was something they could work on. Shyness didn't have any place near kink for him, unless they were diving deep into age play.

"My favorite thing to do is shatter a limit to pieces. I love taking something that someone hates most and shifting it so it's the only way they can come — until they desire it more than anything else and beg for it."

Cutler tried to ignore the way Clint inhaled sharply beside him. He'd given Clint a taste — a small one, of that exact thing. His proudest moments were when his subs conquered their fears and showed him a strength that he'd always known had existed.

In his single-minded focus, he'd almost forgotten Clint was there, though, along with the others around him. Breaking limits wasn't exactly something he wanted to advertise.

"If you had said no knife play, I would have edged you for hours until you were begging for a blade on your skin, only then letting you come while I drew it slowly across your flesh."

Or, in Clint's case, fire.

But what was Keady's fear? When was he at his most vulnerable and beautiful? Not bleeding with a needle through his skin, that was for sure. That had been a heady experience to watch Keady grow harder with each piercing of his needle.

But even a man without limits could experience terror.

It was during the first few minutes of discussions that most subs started to get worried with him. The bravado in their eyes would fade as worry crept in. RACK was one thing, but pushing limits was completely different. Some people stood by their limits as if they were engraved in stone, while others could be *convinced.*

Keady didn't look worried. Despite the flush to his skin, he appeared intrigued, his pants tight enough to give away exactly what he was thinking. Cutler remembered his cock vividly and every twitch it had given as he'd sutured Keady's wounds.

"Are you high or drunk?" asked Cutler, hoping that Keady's sudden bravery wasn't a manufactured one. "I won't punish you if you are. I know this was hard for you, and I would understand the need for liquid courage."

Cutler didn't mind a drink or two near a scene, but drugs were out of the question. There was nothing that could fuck up a scene faster than illegal substances — or even a few legal ones.

Keady shook his head, his eyes wide. "Never. I might be an idiot but I'm not suicidal."

"Good." Cutler tapped his cheek. They'd work on Keady belittling himself another time. There was only so much he could tackle in one day. "Clint offered to observe a scene today for us, and I think I deserve a little taste. If you're good, maybe I can go easy on your penalty." *Or maybe I'll tally it for later.*

"You didn't tell me your limits." Keady bit his lip, cringing as if he were waiting for a slap. Cutler was happy enough to let that one slide, too. He would make Keady pay soon enough.

He leaned in, placing a kiss on Keady's forehead. He couldn't resist his half-smile. "Limits? I don't have any."

Chapter Six

Keady

His heart was going to beat right out of his chest — that was, if he didn't sweat to death first. It was thumping so hard, like he'd run a marathon while he'd been kneeling at Cutler's feet. Clint wasn't helping, his knowing gaze burning into Keady and making his humiliation complete.

He hadn't decided if he was ever going to talk to Clint again or not. For being his friend, he sure was a dick sometimes. One hundred hours of servitude, and Clint didn't think that was enough punishment? Keady was a grown-ass man, but he was bussing kinky tables like a minimum-wage high school student.

He'd been so close to taking a shot of tequila to muster the courage to confront Cutler, but at the last moment, he'd bailed on the drink. *Thank God.* He'd given himself a dozen pep talks and had even talked with Malone and had run through a few scenarios each evening before he'd headed to Unkinked in search of Cutler.

He'd still been ready to keel over when he'd stepped into the open play area and had spotted him at last. Too many thoughts had run through his head, stealing his breath and every minute of prep work.

Malone hadn't thought his joke was funny, but Keady had always wanted to try it out on a real doctor. It was a touch crude, but so worth the payout.

Cutler's gaze was steady, as if he could see straight through Keady's clothes and skin to the weakness underneath. And fuck, he was a bastard, too. After he'd gone on and on about Keady's lack of limits, goading him and outright daring Keady, while having none for himself, Keady wanted to bite him, or maybe nip his cock when he got close to it for the first time. It would serve him right.

Grimacing with obvious displeasure, Cutler directed him to a set of restraints that hung from the ceiling. As opposed to uncomfortable manacles that could cut into his skin if he pulled too hard, these were leather cuffs that were padded and adjustable. The chains that connected them to the ceiling looked completely unforgiving, though.

Clint had gone a little overboard with everything, even thinking to dangle someone from the peaked ceilings like some kind of talisman. What had ever happened to promising to stay still?

"Have you ever been blindfolded and restrained in public?" asked Cutler as he secured the first cuff and tugged the chain tight. Keady had to stand on his toes so he didn't strain his shoulders too much, his calves aching from the angle. At least it distracted him from the crowd.

He bit back his automatic complaint. There was no way he was saying anything when Cutler was finally willing to play. He looked dangerous, too, with his gaze laser-focused on Keady's every twitch.

He'd been with Malone for too long, who had always put his comfort first. That was exactly why he'd been so fucking boring. Keady wanted someone who knew exactly how uncomfortable he was but didn't give a shit about it.

Masochism was his middle name, along with Tatum.

"No. Most of my Doms were into more private play. I did do one flogging demonstration with Derreck a few years back." *That* had been an exhilarating and overwhelming experience. His ass hadn't been the same for weeks. He didn't know how Maddy did it on the regular and still managed to show up to work not blissed out.

"What's your safeword?" asked Cutler, latching the other cuff into place as if Keady hadn't said a word. This one was just as tight, his arms and legs already aching. He'd be trembling in a matter of minutes. His skin prickled, the first bit of adrenaline starting to surge. He let it wash over him, soaking up every bit.

"I use the stoplight system. 'Red' for stop, 'yellow' for slow down and 'green' for 'I want more, please'." He shifted his feet apart as he wobbled, grasping the chains as he nearly lost his balance. It was harder than it looked to stay balanced.

"And when's the last time you used your safeword?" Cutler drew back to inspect his work, smoothing one finger across his mouth. Keady had seen him do it before, always touching the small scar there.

Keady chewed his lip as he racked his brain. Things were moving too quickly, sweat trickling down his back as his situation crept in and his gut throbbed. His answer was probably just going to get him in trouble again, which would set the scene early on. *Bring it on.*

Maybe he was more of a masochist than he'd thought.

"Before the other night...years. I can't remember exactly." He *did* know but he didn't want to talk about it. The scars on his back were a permanent reminder every time he cared to look at them in the mirror. Unfortunately, the lesson hadn't stuck.

Cutler let out a low laugh as he retrieved a blindfold and wrapped it around Keady's head, the thick fabric cutting off every ounce of light. He whispered directly into Keady's ear, his voice sending a shiver down his spine. "Let's see if we can change that, hmm? This is the part when I warn you that you'll probably be saying them...soon."

The blindfold was padded and uncomfortable, so hot against his skin that longed for cool air. The world seemed to tilt from the change, and he was already so off balance from being strung up that he couldn't tell he was falling until he'd already lost his footing. His jeans pulled tight, his cock throbbing.

He was so screwed. But Clint was watching, right? Cutler couldn't go *too* far. *Unfortunately.*

But what was Cutler even going to do? Keady was fully clothed in the middle of a kink club. On the other hand, Keady wasn't a hundred percent sure how many implements were at Cutler's disposal. He hadn't exactly had the full tour yet since he was between Doms, and Clint was the type of fucker who loved surprises.

His calf cramped and he lifted his leg, pointing his toes toward his knee to try to relieve it. It only made his other leg strain harder, his shoulders aching as he held onto the chains. His arms were going to be fucked tomorrow.

A murmur of voices passed by, and he strained to make out who it was. He panted when he realized that he had no idea how many people had come in since he'd lost his sight. It couldn't have been long, but being in the dark fucked with his mind. Unkinked could go from empty to packed within moments some nights.

The voices stopped right ahead of him, and he shuddered as he tried to make out what they were saying. His thoughts were sluggish, every word like molasses through his brain as his heart slowed. He couldn't have thought of a better position if it killed him.

"He *is* pretty."

Were they talking about him? The man said it the same way he would admire a puppy or a painting...as if Keady couldn't even hear them. Maybe they thought he was wearing earbuds? But that should have been obvious from how close they sounded.

Cutler must've planned it down to the second. First blindfold him, then invite a crowd to watch him squirm. At least he wasn't naked, then everyone would see just how turned on he was. Not that he was ashamed, exactly. He just didn't want every single person to know the shape and size of his dick.

He jerked a moment later when there was a touch of a hand on his hip. *Cutler?* He wasn't sure. The mystery male voice was close enough that it could have been him. And where the hell was Clint?

Panting, he clutched at the chains. Nothing had happened and he was already panicking. Maybe it was the darkness, but it almost felt like a nightmare — only the good kind that he didn't want to wake up from. He leaned into the chains, letting them take his weight.

Popping the button on Keady's jeans, they slowly pushed them past his hips, dragging his boxers down at the same time. His cock sprang free, bouncing so hard it slapped his belly. He wanted to wither away with embarrassment as someone laughed close by.

"What's your color?"

Fuck. Cutler's voice was far away. The hands weren't on his hips anymore, but it had only been a moment. There was no way he could have moved that fast. Who the hell was touching him?

Not knowing made it so much hotter. Malone never would have done this to him. Hell, there were few out there who would even consider it.

"Green." His voice was shaking to his own ears, but Cutler didn't make a sound in response. A hand touched his thigh, easing his pants the rest of the way off, one leg at a time. Keady bit back a moan as his cock pulsed.

There was no doubt as to how turned on he was, the air conditioning against his heated skin like a voidless caress. He always ran hot, but right now he felt close to boiling, the only thing keeping him from bubbling away, the padded straps around his wrists.

The strike came out of nowhere, the sound startling him almost as much as the hit. It was like a thousand needles across his skin, every strand of the flog probably leaving its mark across his ass. He cried out, the chains clinking as he jolted.

His heart pounded, blood rushing through his ears as he danced on his toes, trying to catch his footing as his shoulders ached.

Flushing, he bit his lip. The thud was morphing into a spreading warmth that made him want to touch the spot and look at it in the mirror. It hadn't even hurt that much. Cutler must've thought he was such a weakling, who was barely worth his time. *All talk and no game.*

He could even guess the implement that Cutler had used, picturing the shiny black leather strands as they glistened in the club lights.

Would he be swept away like the other subs who had taken Cutler for a trial run? It was no wonder they had safeworded. Mind fucks were on a whole different level in kink.

He took a deep breath, exhaling through his nose as he tried to settle. He could be stronger than them, especially if it got him what he wanted. He was done settling for second and third best. He wasn't going to give in so easily.

A second strike came as he let out a breath, his exhale morphing into a yelp as the crack of a paddle met his ears. Flinching away from the hit, he danced on one foot, barely managing to catch himself on the chains as his world rocked. The voices had blurred together, giving him no indication of which way he was facing or if he was spinning endlessly beneath the lights.

He could've sworn that it had been a flogger moments before. And *fuck*, paddles hurt so much more, the sting solid and intense in every place it touched.

"You want to call 'red' yet?" Cutler's voice was so steady and calm that it soothed the panic that had started to build in Keady's gut as he thought of what else would come his way. There were *so* many toys in the massive complex.

Fuck no, he wasn't ready to safeword. In fact, he was just starting to get comfortable. If there was one place he thrived, it was in the middle of terror. Cutler would have to do better to even get a yellow past his lips.

"Green light, boss."

Silence followed his words, even the one nearby whispering voice going quiet. Keady hadn't even been really conscious of how many there were until they cut off. Now he couldn't help but wonder if two onlookers had morphed into a dozen or fifty. Maybe they were lining up to beat him, each with a different implement to cause him pain.

Yes. His toes curled.

"If you drop this, I'll consider it a yellow," said Cutler. A moment later, someone was lifting Keady's shirt past his head, leaving it tangled over his arms and confining his movements even more.

A moment later they pinched his nipples hard. He hissed as something pressed against his buds one by one before the coolness of a thin chain was thrust against his lips. He opened his mouth, grasping the chain between his teeth. The taste of metal rolled over his tongue, clacking against his teeth as he bit down.

Nipple clamps were literally the worst. Even the ones that didn't seem to hurt in the beginning were brutal once they were removed. The longer they were on, the more pain he was in for.

He was so fucked. If he yelped, he would drop the chain. And it was tight enough that if he tilted his head back, it tugged at the clamps on his nipples. He tested it, letting out a keen when the clamps didn't budge from his skin.

The longer he held out, the more Cutler would fuck him over. And Cutler didn't have to lift a finger the entire time. It was all on Keady to decide when his torture would end.

A new flog slapped against his exposed belly, gentle enough to threaten and sting, but not risk any harm. He sucked in his stomach, using every bit of his stubbornness to make sure he didn't drop the chain.

He was more likely to crack his teeth on it at this point.

A moment passed before the real beating began, the stinging strands of a flog sparking over his ass and the back of his legs until he lost count of the strikes. There was no pause between them, just thud after thud, each one jolting his world until he was whimpering steadily and clenching his jaw so tight that it ached.

His ass hurt more than his nipples, but his calves were starting to tire. He sagged, his shoulders screaming at him as they took most of his weight.

"Good." Cutler's voice was still steady when the blows suddenly ceased. "I'm going to take the chain out of your mouth. Let it go, now." He almost sounded soothing as he touched Keady's cheek, rubbing at his jaw until he slowly released the chain. His nipples throbbed as the weight of the chain tugged them down, the movement promising agony.

Everything hurt, but Keady wasn't done. He could last.

Endorphins were rushing through him with each passing moment, sucking the hurt away and leaving a peaceful drunkenness behind. *So close.*

"How are your shoulders?"

That was a really stupid question, but Keady bit back his comments. His muscles were trembling, his eyes wet behind the blindfold. But he didn't want it to end.

"G-green."

"Hm." With a clinking sound, the chain holding his wrists suddenly went slack. Keady would have fallen if strong arms hadn't wrapped around his waist, holding him upright while his dark world tilted.

He'd been so wrong. His shoulders hadn't just been sore. The sudden movement was excruciating, pushing a weak scream from his throat. It felt like he'd been hanging for days, his muscles and tendons stretched beyond repair.

"And that's why I can't trust you," said Cutler, his voice a steady whisper against Keady's ear. "I don't want to harm you, Keady. Hurt you? Absolutely. I want to make you scream and writhe until you don't know which way is up and you don't remember what pleasure tastes like. But I want you to be able to lift your arms tomorrow...even if you can't sit down."

"Fine...yellow," Keady bit out as soon as he could speak. It was true. His hands were tingling, which he hadn't noticed before, and he wasn't sure if he could feel all his fingers or not. The cuffs hadn't been tight, but his weight must've cut his circulation off.

That didn't mean he wasn't pissed about the interruption. Instead of getting closer to subspace, Cutler just wanted to talk. Keady knew his way around restraints and cuffs and what he was feeling was not the worst he'd ever had. It was mild compared to one of his first Shibari scenes with an inexperienced Dom. That had been torture at its finest, and although he'd felt it for weeks, he'd gone *flying*.

"You know I won't break, right?" He was so fucking sick of people thinking he was some kind of fragile doll just because he was a sub. And fuck the other people listening in. They'd probably all wandered off because he couldn't hear their voices anymore. *Or it had all been in my head.*

"Yes, you will." Cutler's response brooked no question.

He was so sure of himself that Keady just wanted to slap him. He knew his own limits, dammit. He could have gone another ten — no — twenty minutes.

Growling under his breath, Keady tugged away until he was standing on his own, his arms at chest level in front of him. He was still connected to the ceiling with the chain, even if it had been loosened, and it jingled with every step. Forcing a smile on his face, he pulled the blindfold free, blinking until Cutler's face came into focus.

Oh. He'd thought he'd seen Cutler pissed before, but he'd been so wrong. He was approaching serial killer material again, the flog in his hand like a threat and a promise. The only thing that gave Keady pause were the people watching. There had to be at least a dozen, all seated and quiet. He looked away, shame burning through him.

"No." With narrowed eyes Cutler grabbed his chin, pinching the nerves until Keady winced. He was still calm, but his amusement was long gone. "If you want to see them watch you humiliate yourself, then be my guest. And as for the talking back? You should have mentioned that you wanted to scream."

Holding Keady's chin steady, Cutler reached for the chain on the nipple clamps, tugging them free with a hard jerk.

"Fuck," Keady screamed as the clamps came free. The rage of fire spread from the points and across his chest, digging deep and stealing his breath. They had to be bleeding, but he couldn't see through the rush of tears. He wanted to curl into a ball and let the pain wash over and through him until there was nothing left behind but Cutler's control.

He tried to reach for his chest, but Cutler released his chin and jerked the chain attached to his cuffs, bringing his arms back above his head. The shooting pain in his shoulders as his arms were stretched taut above his head was almost as bad as his nipples. *Almost.*

His world rushed away from him in a blanket of euphoria. *This is it* – The reason he would never leave kink behind. He'd never been harder in his life or felt more powerful. He was strength itself as he blinked the tears away and held Cutler's gaze.

"That's better." Cutler gave him an assessing look, his usual grimace back in place. He didn't *look* happy as he raised the flog, bringing the strands across Keady's chest.

The flared ends struck his nipples with a stinging thud that felt almost gentle against his skin but worse than torture against his already-abused buds. He couldn't hold back his scream that stretched out as Cutler landed a second hit.

"Much better. A little louder, Keady. They didn't hear you in the back." He reached for Keady's nipple, pinching it hard.

A sob burst through his throat as the agony overwhelmed him, only to be replaced by something so much better in an instant. It came on so quickly that at first he didn't recognize it, fighting the fog as it descended over his senses.

Oh. His thoughts drifted away into nothing, every ache transforming into something sweet that flared as Cutler touched him. He sagged against the cuffs, arching his chest out to meet the next blow. And when it fell, his orgasm rushed over him, taking everything along with it.

Chapter Seven

Cutler

Beautiful. Cutler had doubted himself on and off for the past thirty minutes, wondering how far he could push Keady until he broke — how far Keady would *let* him. Further than he could have imagined, apparently.

The first scream was laced with agony, but the second had a new tone that Cutler could have recognized anywhere. There was nothing sweeter than the relief of his sub giving in and diving into subspace headfirst.

Keady sagged, his shoulders straining against his bindings. Every muscle was pulled taut from his position, sweat dripping over his rosy flesh as he closed his eyes and let out a blissful hum.

Dropping the flog, Cutler reached for him, clinking the quick release on the cuffs and catching Keady as he slumped sideways. Cum soaked his belly, smearing on Cutler's shirt as he half-dragged Keady to the nearest recovery couch.

The crowd dispersed with a few murmurs and words of praise, one sub in particular looking a touch green about the gills. What Cutler had to offer wasn't for everyone, that was for sure. But Keady had taken it—and not just that. He'd thrived, fought it, demanded it, then let go.

"So perfect." Cutler cradled Keady to his chest, slowly untangling Keady's shirt from his arms before using it to wipe the cum from his chest and belly. Cutler's heart was racing, his cock so hard that it was bound to explode with a single touch.

He could count on one hand how many subs hadn't safeworded during a scene with him. And even though he'd pushed a yellow through Keady's lips, it barely counted as his chest heaved and he focused with single-minded intent on his sub.

Cutler didn't cover his mouth as he grimaced in an attempt at a smile. *Let them see.* For once, he didn't give a shit about the scarring.

"Was I okay?"

Cutler blinked in surprise. It should have been a few minutes yet before Keady found his words. Maybe he hadn't gone quite as deep as Cutler had thought.

There was a furrow in Keady's beautiful brow, his blue eyes glassy and bloodshot from his tears. His face was so pale, without a hint of the freckles that most had in the summer, or any sign of a tan at all, really. Cutler could imagine him bent over a computer screen, separated from the sun by thick panes of glass as the humid days passed him by.

"You were perfect," said Cutler softly, tugging Keady close to indulge in a much-needed hug. His own heart was still rattling in his chest as he struggled to keep his hands from shaking with the pure energy flowing through him. "I'm a surgeon, Keady, and I rarely give out praise or compliments, but I can't help it with you. I've never seen anyone so beautiful and perfect. You did so well."

Keady hummed, the furrow only going deeper as he narrowed his eyes. Cutler could almost see the veil of subspace slipping away before his eyes. "Are you sure?"

Cutler fought back a curse, wiping a hand over his mouth as the sensation of dragging numbness across his lips started to bother him. It wasn't often he really fucked up, but there was a line he must've been treading. Perhaps Keady didn't enjoy praise, or he'd missed something, just like the cry for help that all of Keady's friends had missed.

"Positive." Cutler let out a breath as Keady shifted and grazed against his cock. If Keady hadn't been so far gone, he would've suggested a fuck to go along with the impact and degradation scene. He wasn't one for fucking in public, but he was willing to stretch his own non-existent limits. "You trust your doctor, right? Six more weeks until spring and one perfect boy in his arms."

Chuckling, Keady closed his eyes, his face finally relaxing. "That was a good joke." He nuzzled against Cutler's chest, taking a deep breath.

"The best." It had been a *terrible* joke, but Cutler was going to do his darndest to work it into a conversation with his colleagues. Maybe he'd tell Jack while he was drinking coffee. It would serve the bastard right. Jack wasn't the only one more arrogant than him, but he hadn't earned it yet.

With the crowd dispersed, the regular sounds of the club started to creep into their bubble. There was the slapping of a belt close by and a laugh in the direction of the door. Clint was moving the temporary chairs back to their places, wiping down the cuffs and the toys. Cutler sent him a nod of thanks.

"You're still hard. Are you going to fuck me?" asked Keady, moving his hand from Cutler's chest to his groin and sloppily pawing him. Cutler sucked in a breath as he tried not to hump against the sensation. If it had been anyone else, he would have slapped them away. He wasn't sure why that rule didn't stand with Keady.

"Not today, Keady. The first time I take you, I want you to be absolutely aware and begging for it. It would be too easy right now. You would do anything I asked, wouldn't you?" Cutler kissed the top of his head, viscerally aching for more. It had been too long since he'd gone further with anyone.

"Yeah. I could still take more if you wanted, except for my nipples. They are almost in the red zone." Keady giggled, reaching for his own nipples and hissing as he touched them. "What kind of clamps did you even use? It feels like you ripped them off."

Cutler chuckled softly. "They had a bit of a bite to them, but they weren't the worst ones I've used — not by far."

"Ouch." Keady winced, looking around the room and blinking. His pupils were still too wide to be normal and he looked a touch dazed. Cutler wanted to put him right back into that state, until he was floating for *days*.

"How are you feeling?" Cutler grabbed for one of the water bottles that Clint had brought for them. He would have preferred a whiskey, but he wasn't going to ask for a more perfect day.

"Good." Keady grinned, giving him a goofy smirk. "I think I've decided to listen to you from now on, though. No talking out of turn and no calling you 'boss'. I don't think you liked that very much." He touched his nipples again, whimpering.

Now that just won't do.

"Where's the fun in that?" Cutler reached for one bud, giving it a quick twist. Keady responded beautifully by arching his back and crying out. His nipples were flushed bright pink — almost red — and they had to ache horribly. Cutler's cock throbbed, begging for release.

"What do you prefer for aftercare?" They really should have had that talk before, but Cutler hadn't planned any of this. He'd have to have a word with Clint after he leveled out himself. He planned his scenes with care because he liked to play near the edge. No planning could mean emotional or physical hurts that sometimes didn't heal.

He turned his attention back to Keady. "I can bathe you, or at least grab a cloth to clean you up better. Or we could spend some time together? Whatever you need, it's yours." He'd once had a sub whose idea of aftercare was jerking off with Cutler watching. That had always been an intense experience.

Keady's expression fell and he bit his lip, his lashes dropping over his cheeks. He locked his gaze onto Cutler's face and furrowed his forehead at whatever he saw. Cutler struggled not to rub at his scar that was suddenly aching.

"I'm good," said Keady after a moment. He'd gone tense again, tightening his grip as if he were terrified that Cutler was going to let him go.

"Another lie." Cutler leaned away to try to give Keady room if he needed it. His sub was a bundle of mixed signals, withdrawing and reaching out at the same time, but he wasn't sure which part to believe. "If you want to be alone that's fine, but don't lie. Aftercare is important to me, but I'm not going to force you into it. It was *your* limit."

He wasn't usually so snarky, but he was sorely in need of sleep and an orgasm. *And some answers.* Gritting his teeth, he bit back anything else he could say and regret. Lies pissed him off more than anything else, because for him, every part of kink was based on trust. *Maybe this was a mistake.*

"Would you like aftercare or did you need your space? That can be aftercare, too, you know. Time alone to reflect on a scene, especially an intense one, is sometimes the best thing."

Keady looked away, letting out a humorless chuckle. "Why would I need aftercare for a scene like that? You look like you hated it, and maybe it wasn't even that great. You can't even stand to touch me."

Fucking brat. Cutler stood, shoving his hands into his pockets and hunching down. A backhand was looking more imminent any second. He ignored Clint's concerned gaze from across the room. "Ouch."

The scene had been a bit spontaneous, but it had also been amazing. He'd thought Keady had been on the same page, but obviously not. He waited for the familiar guilt to sink in, but for once, it didn't. Maybe he was just too tired.

Keady flushed, shrinking in on himself and bringing his knees to his chest. There were tears in his eyes and a sudden paleness about his cheeks. "I didn't mean it like that. I'm sorry."

Maybe, he'd pushed Keady too far too fast. That was Cutler's fault and no one else's, even if it would have been easier to pin it on Clint.

"I'll be fine. I don't drop anyway, so it's not like I really need it." Keady scoffed.

"Okay." Cutler fought not to get defensive. *Too late.* The last thing he wanted after a scene was a bunch of fucking drama and dishonesty piled on top of other lies. "I'll ask you again, and maybe you'll pull your head out of your ass this time. What do you *need*?"

As much as he frustrated him, Cutler could imagine Keady as his sub. Oh, how he would revel in his brattiness, pushing him at every turn just to see Keady dig himself deeper. And he'd never needed to hand out punishments before, but maybe it was time to change that, too.

If only I could trust him.

"Maybe a smile," said Keady. "You said I'm perfect, but you've been scowling at me since I took off the blindfold. And that grimace of yours... I know I'm sweaty and maybe a bit smelly right now, but I can't help it. I can shower at home, so you don't have to bathe me." He crossed his arms, his eyes wet.

Oh fuck.

There were so many times that Cutler had cursed his injury, but this one took the cake. The scar still ached sometimes when it rained or when he stayed up for more than forty-eight hours straight. His face hurt almost constantly when he was awake, too, his good muscles weighed down by the paralyzed ones. Even in times when his life was light, things were still heavy.

"Keady." Cutler thrust a hand into Keady's hair, forcing him to meet his gaze. His grip was brutal and unforgiving, and it finally seemed to catch Keady's attention. "I *can't*."

Keady's scowl deepened, one tear escaping only to be quickly wiped away. He was beautiful, even when he was crying. "You *won't*, you mean."

"No." Grasping Keady's hand, he brought a fingertip to his lip, wincing as Keady touched his scar.

The simple sensation burned, and he jerked away. "I have partial facial paralysis. I literally can't smile." He gave a grimace, squinting one eye with the effort of what he'd been able to do before his accident. "This is the best I can do."

"Oh." Keady's mouth flopped open, and he slapped his hand over it, a small whimper escaping. "Oh *God*, I'm so sorry, Cutler. I just thought you were unhappy with me and that you didn't like it, and I got all defensive because it was really good but I thought you hated it—hated me."

"Breathe, Keady," Cutler caught Keady as he leaned in, pulling him tight until tears soaked his collar. Keady fit flawlessly against him—small, imperfect and beautiful, as if he were meant to stay forever.

"I'm sorry." Keady's voice rose, getting more desperate by the moment.

"Baby, it's okay. I've got you, and I'm not letting go." He couldn't remember the last time he'd called someone 'baby', but it seemed to work, Keady's sobs tapering off before he could work himself into a panic.

Clint had been circling them like a watchful hawk, eyeing Cutler a hell of a lot more than he was Keady. Although Cutler had passed a *test* of sorts, Clint still didn't trust him with those who were most precious to him. Cutler doubted he really trusted anyone, though.

Shooting Clint a nod, Cutler turned his attention back to Keady. He couldn't let his mind wander when his sub was so vulnerable and halfway between lashing out and sinking like a stone into a drop.

Cutler slipped back onto the couch, dragging Keady with him in a heap of limbs. Keady followed easily, his weight barely noticeable as he turned his face into Cutler's chest. He was still crying, tears soaking through the fabric of his shirt and staining it dark.

"I'm so sorry. I don't know what's wrong with me." He fisted Cutler's shirt as he started to shake, sobs racking his body and dragging a wail from him. It broke his heart at the same time his guilt eased. *This* was exactly what Keady needed.

"It's okay, baby. Let me take care of you." Cutler turned to Clint, who had stepped closed at the sound of sobs, concern etched on his face. There was a touch of fear in his gaze, along with surprise. *When was the last time you cried?*

"Do you have any candy? And maybe a blanket?" asked Cutler, drawing a hand down Keady's spine as he shook with another round of sniffles. It had obviously been too long with so many tears behind the now-broken barrier.

Clint returned a moment later with a handful of sweets and a thick blanket, which he threw over them. "You guys want a private room or even a quieter spot? Derreck is getting started on Maddy over there and things might get loud — really loud."

Cutler glanced across the room to where Derreck was stripping Maddy with skilled precision, revealing so many marks that they seemed impossible. There were a few fresh stripes across Maddy's ass, which Derreck caressed with reverent care.

"Yeah." Cutler helped Keady to his feet, draping the blanket around him before tucking it in like a cape. The last thing they needed were Maddy's screams right now.

Clint led them from the open play area to where Cutler remembered the new rooms, each stamped with an etched engraving. The hall was quiet and cool, each somewhat soundproofed like the last ones.

At the farthest point of the hall there was a single door that was propped open, the patrons able to come and go as easily and often as they liked. It was the one room that the bar had lacked. With implements and kinks filling up every square bit, there had only been public couches to come down after a scene.

How many times have I longed for something just like this? The further he pushed his sub — or they allowed themselves to be pushed — the more care they needed afterward. And the more Cutler needed it, too. He didn't want to ruin someone — not really, even if the illusion was beautiful. He needed aftercare as much as his sub did.

The flooring from the hall tapered away to a soft, plush carpeting, the room's lights dimmed until it looked similar to dusk. Four comfortable-looking couches sat around the perimeter, with only one occupied by another couple. They were sitting close to each other, their soft whispers barely audible.

Near the middle of the room there was an assortment of bean bag chairs along with a basket heaped with blankets, much like the one Keady was already wearing. The air conditioning seemed to be muted, leaving things warmer and a tad closer than the rest of the house.

Peppermint permeated the air, soft music tinkling in the background that reminded Cutler of something he would hear in a spa. The couple were in their own world, not sparing them a single glance. Cutler wasn't sure he really recognized them. He was still new, and he wasn't around often enough to remember every face. At first, he hadn't even tried to remember because he'd been almost certain that his stay wouldn't be long in the community.

"Nice room." Cutler nodded his thanks to Clint as he led Keady to the nearest couch. The team who had worked on the house seemed to have thought of everything. Sucking in a breath, he let the relaxing peppermint scent roll over him.

"With all of the rooms we had at the bar, we never really had a chill place to recover," said Clint, heading to the radio to adjust the volume a touch. It lowered a notch until it was just on the edge of Cutler's hearing. "So, this is *'Zen'*. I can't take credit for everything. Shelvin and Elliot did all the hard work and design." Clint headed back to the door, casting the other couple a soft smile.

"I'll let you guys be." He turned away, leaving the door propped open the way it had been. With the soundproofing in the rest of the halls, it was doubtful any noises would disturb them.

Cradling Keady close, Cutler couldn't help but agree on the name. Unkinked had been great for sceneing or chatting with other kinksters, but not ideal for recovery if you didn't have a private room. He closed his eyes, sinking into the calming scent and sounds, along with the steady breathing from his sub.

He could get used to shit like this. Cupping the back of Keady's head, he scratched over his scalp, losing himself in their internal rhythm and the steady beat of his own heart in his chest. He was still hard, but it probably wouldn't last much longer with the way his eyelids were drooping. He was so overdue for a good night's rest.

"What's your greatest fantasy?" asked Keady, pulling Cutler from his thoughts and half-doze. He hadn't realized that he'd started to drift, his cock long since soft as his exhaustion started to set in and his adrenaline wound down.

Rubbing his eyes with the back of his hands, he blinked the haze from his sight. The other couple in the room had disappeared at some point, leaving them alone with the music and warmth of their skin.

"What's that, baby?" The yawn cracked his jaw, and Keady shot him a small smile. His pupils looked normal again, his tears long since dried. He was probably mostly level, a drop a long way off. *Thank God.*

A sadistic bastard like himself, Cutler loved those tears, but not ones of confusion. It was like dealing with a newbie sub all over again, which was not his forte. He needed someone who knew what they wanted.

"Your greatest fantasy or your favorite kink—whichever one. Tell me what it is."

Cutler grimaced, half in a smile and half in an effort to stay awake. He must've been more off his game than he'd thought, because usually he was the one calling the shots and asking the questions.

"I thought you were shy." He caressed Keady's cheek, giving up on his attempt at a grin.

Maybe it was because he was so goddamned tired or maybe the air had shifted between them, but the words rolled out of Cutler's mouth. Words that he hadn't said to anyone before. *For good reason.*

"I guess it would be a TPE dynamic—total power exchange," said Cutler, scratching at his chin. "Practically, it would maybe last a weekend, or a few days at most, plus time for recovery." His stomach flipped, some of his sleepiness starting to fade. He hadn't confessed this particular fantasy because it was exactly that. A *fantasy.* There was no way it would ever happen for real.

"Tell me. *Please.*"

"Only because you've been so good." Cutler tilted Keady's face, bringing their lips together in a chaste kiss that immediately left him wanting more. "You'd be my prisoner—someone who I could control completely in every way, who I could take at will and do what I want with. You would be nothing more than an object, but you'd fight me with every breath. You would break for me and give me *everything*."

Warmth rushed over his skin, his fingertips tingling where he dug them into Keady's ass. He loosened his grip at the gasp in response, easing into another kiss that didn't last nearly long enough. Keady went stiff against him, his lips and tongue immobile.

It's too much. Cutler had always known it would be, which was the same reason he'd never entertained it. The kind of TPE he wanted couldn't be healthy for a person, even if they did consent.

"I'm sorry. It's a fantasy, nothing more. I would never ask that of you." Even as he said it, his stomach sank. He would never ask *anyone*. Even if Keady already felt like something special, it was still too much.

Keady leaned back, his eyes wide as he slowly blinked. The flush on his cheeks extended down his neck, a tremble going through his body as he let out a long breath. One hand disappeared under the blanket and between his legs. "Please don't apologize."

He grasped Cutler's hand with his free one, dragging it to his own groin. Cutler bit back a groan, turning his hand in Keady's grasp and grabbing him roughly. Keady was hard, so desperately hard that it had to be painful. He throbbed against Cutler's palm, his gasp beautiful as his eyes rolled back and Cutler *squeezed*.

"You like that?" He placed a kiss against Keady's neck, licking a drop of salt from his skin. Gasping, Keady rocked his hips in a slow wave, licking his lips until they glistened in the dim light.

"Yes."

Fuck. It was too much. He couldn't hold back another minute.

Where the fuck was a condom and lube when he needed them? Clint was usually so good at keeping every room stocked, but there was nothing in arm's reach. There was a suspect-looking basket on the shelf near the radio, but there was no way Cutler was standing up to get it.

Reaching inside his own pants, Cutler dragged his cock out and let it slap against his belly. With both hands, he heaved Keady into position until their cocks lined up with soft skin against soft skin. The blanket dipped to Keady's waist, leaving his chest and belly on display.

It wouldn't take much to fuck him like this. All he had to do was lift Keady a little higher and he could push his way inside, using his own pre-cum to ease the way. It would hurt without lube—for both of them—but that would make it so much better.

Keady's thoughts seemed to align with his own as he moved his hips, dragging their cocks together. The first stroke was pure sin, and when Keady moved his hips a second time, Cutler's restraint snapped and the sensation bloomed into heaven.

He couldn't remember the last time he'd been so turned on and so focused on a single goal to fuck and take. It was painful to hold himself back, biting his lip so he didn't come.

"Fuck." Cutler's voice was shaky as Keady ground down, bringing him close to the edge in seconds. "Would you let me do that? Tie you up and force my cock inside you, even as you screamed?"

Keady's body quaked, his eyes rolling back. Biting his lip, he nodded.

"So good, baby." Cutler gripped Keady's hips, urging him on faster. "You would be such a fucking slut for it. I'd catch you when you were sleeping and fuck you awake, covering your mouth so you couldn't yell for help. You wouldn't be able to stop me — and you wouldn't want to because you'd know exactly who you belonged to."

"Yes. Yes." Keady groaned, picking up his pace and grunting from the effort. Their pre-cum eased each movement, the sound loud in the quiet room. The soft music in the background did nothing to cover the slickness of their pleasure.

Grabbing the blanket that had pooled around Keady's ass, Cutler tore it away and tossed it to the ground. There was nothing that would get in his way now.

Keady's skin was flushed all the way to his cock, the head dark and wet. It bobbed as he writhed, losing his rhythm as he must've drawn close to the edge. Cutler wasn't far behind, gritting his teeth with the effort of holding back.

"You'd love every second of it," said Cutler, letting the fantasy wash over him for the first time with another man in his arms. "You'd beg for it, even as I hurt you. You could hate me all you wanted, but I wouldn't let you breathe without permission."

"I wouldn't hate you." Keady cried out, jerking his hips as he started to shoot. White pearled at the tip of his cock, dribbling down the shaft in a budding stream. "Anything. I would let you do *anything* — and I'd love you for it."

"Fuck. *Fuck*." Cutler bit into Keady's shoulder, scraping his teeth over the sensitive flesh as he started to come. *Fuck*. No one had ever said that to him. Where was the call of 'red'?

Heaving in a breath, he loosened his grip on Keady's hips, soothing the spots that must've been bruising already. Aftershocks sizzled along his nerves, dancing over his skin and trickling through his groin as his heart continued to pound.

"That was epic," Keady muttered into his ear, still twitching and rutting, only to whimper when he dragged their cocks together.

Cutler couldn't hold back his chuckle, drawing Keady into a kiss that probably gave too much away. His taste was addictive, and so was the smell of sex tainted with soothing peppermint. "Anytime, baby."

I mean every word. There's no going back now. You're mine, no matter what you have to say about it.

Chapter Eight

Cutler

It was early for him to be awake — far too early when he had three double shifts in the near future. Twilight hours had a certain smell to them and a taste that settled along his senses, threatening to cover everything in a fog that would drag him into his dreams.

There was no way he was sleeping anytime soon, though. He'd been wired for the last day, his high of adrenaline and serotonin refusing to fade.

It was the same feeling he got when an emergency rushed in with a bullet to the brain and he managed to extract it and mend everything exactly as it had been before. His hands shook then, too, from the energy-drink-laced coffee and the rush of saving a life.

Few scenes had ever left him in such a state — none if he were truly honest with himself. The people of his past were too rigid, too fragile and set in a solid state of rules and expectations...unlike Keady.

The halls of Unkinked were quiet as he moved through them, and dim with only a few nightlights to lead the way. There were few people that had early access, even among the volunteers. The only reason Cutler was among the select few was because of his degree. Clint was smart to keep a doctor at his beck and call for any accidents.

The open play area was dark, smelling vaguely like disinfectant. Every glimpse of Keady had been washed away, along with the memory of his screams.

Cutler moved past the room, heading for the sectioned-off space dedicated to Clint's private living area. It appeared to be an upgrade from his last place, which had mostly been the office of the bar, a cot for his bed and the 'Wet' room for his bath. Cutler had been told that it was rare to find Clint at his actual apartment and most thought that Clint had given it up.

Unkinked was big enough to get lost in now, and despite his wanderings, Cutler still hadn't managed to find the basement. Another time, he would go exploring for real and wouldn't give up until he'd found the place. There were rumors about it, too, and all of them were inspiring, in his opinion.

Reaching the unmarked door for Clint's quarters, he rapped on it three times, shifting from foot to foot as he waited. He couldn't seem to get rid of the vigor in his limbs, no matter what he did. Time in the gym certainly hadn't helped.

The knob turned a moment later, the door swinging wide to reveal the owner of Unkinked. Clint was dressed sloppily, as usual, with his pants hanging low and a shirt with three holes in it.

"Just in time," Clint grinned, pulling the door wider and beckoning Cutler inside. "Everyone is here, and

I've got the stuff all lined up and ready. The teddy bears are out, sans legs and all."

One perk about his new community was the close-knit relationships that Clint seemed to have with his patrons. Along with the new setting, he'd started up first-aid classes again and had invited Cutler along to assist during one. It just so happened to be at a ridiculous hour in the morning, so people could attend before work and before the bar opened.

The classes had gone by the wayside, like so many other things in the bar when Clint had become too overwhelmed with trying to run everything himself. Luckily, Maddy had helped turn things around, taking care of the books and almost everything else, according to Clint. The bar would have sunk without Maddy — and so would a few members, from the sounds of it.

The whisper of murmured voices reached him from the other room and Cutler plucked his jacket off, hanging it on a hook on the wall. It was humid and hot outside, despite the hour, but it had started to drizzle just before he'd left the house, so he'd donned the jacket despite the heat. He hefted his bag over his shoulder again, letting it settle deep into the muscle there.

Rounding the corner, Clint led him to what appeared to be the living room. It was surprisingly spacious, with three couches, all occupied by couples and a few solos. There were perhaps ten in all, and the low number lifted a bit of weight from Cutler's chest.

He could focus in a packed surgical room, gowned, gloved and brain-deep for sixteen hours, but he despised large crowds. Concerts were terrible and sometimes he struggled even in a farmer's market setting. With so many wandering eyes, there were always a few rude enough to stare, not to mention the questions from kids.

The area wasn't too full, leaving a little space and breathing room. The open patio door beyond helped, too, with damp air wafting through the open screen as rain pattered on the deck outside. There was a rumble in the distance as a thunderstorm rolled through.

The fixtures were a mix of minimalist and modern, but somehow fit Clint perfectly. And there were decorations of bamboo beams somehow fitted into the drywall. The view of the forest itself was beautiful, with a few mosquitoes buzzing against the screen.

"Good crowd." He sent Clint a single raised eyebrow.

The bar had always been packed, its seams bursting almost all the time. In recent months, it had become so bad that Cutler steered away most nights and aimed for early afternoons when there were only a few patrons.

It was so much easier in the massive house, where the same amount of people could fit among the rooms with privacy to spare.

Still, Cutler had expected more than ten.

Shrugging one shoulder, Clint sent him a knowing smile. "Don't worry about it."

O-kay. Cutler glanced to the couples, keeping his frown in place so he didn't give anything away. He knew Maddy, who was bouncing at the edge of the couch next to an annoyed-looking Derreck, and Philip, a sadist like himself who was currently without a sub. Maddy looked far too chipper for just having his ass beaten the night before.

Nikita surprised him, especially since he'd only met him once. He was one of identical twins and the polar opposite of his brother. Cutler had swapped a few ideas with Nikita one night at the new house, even if Nikita preferred the softer side of things.

It was probably best his brother Maxim hadn't attended. He was a hothead who didn't seem to give two shits about the law. Not that Cutler was intimidated... He knew his way around a knife.

Flickering his gaze over the rest, Cutler set his bag on the table in the middle of the area before opening it wide. There was over a thousand dollars worth of suture material inside, along with bandage material and gauze.

He'd find a way to write it off on his taxes.

"You all know why you're here, and it's too early for much of an introduction," said Cutler, tugging a few more things out of his bag. He was pretty sure he'd thought of everything. "Clint has been teaching first aid to you guys so far, but he invited me here to get into the gritty side of things."

Clint chuckled as he crossed his arms and leaned against the wall. "Thought it was about time for the real professional to show us his stuff."

Cutler quirked his lips. Now that was a joke. Clint had probably sewn up more people in his nursing career than Cutler ever had working in the emergency department during his early days.

"Any volunteers?" The room fell into a hush, Nikita's sub looking a touch green. Clint snorted and Cutler sent him a raised brow. "Why practice sewing on teddy bears when we have perfectly good pain-sluts?"

"I knew this was a good idea," said Clint, not trying to hide his grin. His cheeks had flushed and the look in his eye gave Cutler the smallest glimpse of the Clint he'd scened with.

Maddy squirmed, raising his hand as he bounced a little. "Oh, I will! Is that okay, Derreck? It sounds like so much fun." His smile was brilliant, and even Derreck seemed slightly less grumpy as he looked to his sub.

He must've still been feeling the high from his scene. Cutler had rarely seen Maddy so carefree and excited, usually manning the house with an attitude and a baseball bat.

"Only if I give them something to practice on first," said Derreck, crossing his arms and leaning into the couch. Maddy swallowed audibly, his demeanor never dimming, but taking on a slightly nervous edge.

"Sounds fair," said Cutler, grabbing an eighteen-gauge needle and popping it from its package. He handed Derreck an alcohol swab along with the needle. "If anyone gets woozy, call 'yellow' or 'red' and Clint will take you to the other room and get you some juice. If anyone gets turned on, well, by all means, I'm down for a show."

A few chuckles reached him, and Cutler zeroed in on one in particular. Malone was seated next to his boy on one of the couches. He was the singular reason why Cutler had agreed to run the show with Clint. Malone's new boy looked as sweet as he was tiny, the frilled edge of his underwear visible over the waistband of his soft-looking pants. They weren't going to be turned on by the bit of bloodplay Cutler had lined up for them.

"You're up next," said Cutler, sending Malone a look. His boy lost his fading smile, looking to his Daddy for reassurance.

"It's important, baby. Daddy needs to learn this stuff, okay?"

My teeth are going to fall out from all this fucking sweetness.

A gasp caught his attention, and he looked toward the sound, his groin going tight at the scene before him.

Maddy had taken a seat before Derreck on a small stool and had slipped his shirt over his head. His mottled skin was on display, with so many marks that Cutler knew he would never be able to count them. There were spots from the night before, too, some raw with an edge of purpling that must've been excruciating. Maddy let out another gasp as Derreck ran his fingers over the marks possessively.

Letting out a rare grin, Derreck drew the needle across Maddy's skin, the sharp point slipping through the top layer of flesh until blood welled, a tiny line dripping down Maddy's back. Maddy shuddered, licking his lips as a flush bloomed over his face. He let out a groan of loss as Derreck drew back, the vermilion line a mere three inches long.

Cutler pulled the sharps container out of his bag and Derreck discarded the needle inside before taking up an alcohol wipe and swiping it over the wound. Maddy's groan merged into a whimper as the alcohol soaked in. He didn't even need to see the tent in Maddy's slacks to know he was aroused.

Hot damn. The only thing that would've made it better was if it had been Keady kneeling before him, with the slice across *his* marred skin. He was probably bruised beautifully from the flogger, each stripe leaving its own mark. Cutler blinked the image away. He needed to focus.

"Perfect. That will give us some room to work with." Cutler moved closer, pulling on gloves before he visually inspected the wound. "May I touch you, Maddy?" He turned to Derreck, who gave him a slight nod before Maddy managed to answer. Maddy may have been too far gone to answer verbally, anyway.

"A wound this shallow wouldn't need stitches in reality, but it's perfect for practice. Anything that is gaping will need to be stitched, and it will most likely leave a scar, so be sure to talk about limits before attempting that. Also, take into account that something sharp like a scalpel or a needle will go a lot deeper with a smaller amount of pressure. Make sure your tools are sterilized, and that you wear gloves if condoms are a limit. Fluids are fluids."

Which was why Cutler always wore gloves for bloodplay and did his best not to lick at a fresh wound, no matter how tempting. There was nothing like the taste of fresh copper on his tongue and the sound of whimpering in his ears, but it was a treat he rarely indulged in.

Plucking a packet of suture material from his bag, Cutler showed it off to them. The material was a lot like a needle and thread, only it was safe to use on the skin, and the needle was conveniently attached to make one long strand.

One of the lone subs was looking woozy, their focus dazed and soft. Cutler sent Clint a look and Clint stepped forward, helping them from the room before they could pass out. First aid wasn't for everyone.

"I'll do the first stitch, and Derreck will do the rest. He's almost as much of a pro as I am, so don't feel bad if yours don't look as good."

Derreck looked at his hands, flexing his fingers ominously. "I've stitched someone up once or twice."

Yeah. The rest you probably buried. Cutler swallowed. Derreck even made *him* nervous, which was a feat when most people thought Cutler was some version of a killer. *I guess I am.* If losing someone on the table counted.

Shaking his head, he tried to ward off his thoughts before they could drag him down, focusing on the wound instead. The last thing he needed to think about was the number of people he'd lost when Keady had finally made him forget. At least, for a few hours.

Bringing the edges together, he grabbed a pair of forceps and picked up the needle, piercing Maddy's flesh and dragging the suture through with ease. "Don't try to grab the needle like this with your fingers because you'll just slice your gloves and your hands open. I've got a pair of sterilized forceps for everyone to use today, and I made little packages for you to take home."

Also, hopefully tax-deductible. It wasn't like he couldn't afford it.

"Thank you," Maddy murmured under his breath, not even flinching the entire time as Cutler knotted the suture in place and cut the stray end.

"Don't thank him yet, Maddy. You volunteered. That means everyone gets a try if they want. Maybe the doc has a steady enough hand to give you something that we can *really* stitch." Derreck's voice was a low rumble, even as he dragged his nail over the fresh knot.

I really don't want to die tonight. Cutler grimaced, not rising to Derreck's challenge. That was one bit of territory that he wasn't going to stomp on any time soon. "Your sub, your canvas."

Maddy turned, splitting his lips into a wide grin.

"I think I'm going to be sick," said Malone's sub as Maddy's grin turned downright lecherous.

Cutler looked toward the nauseous-sounding words, giving Malone a look of alarm when he noticed his sub, who looked to be close to puking or passing out. With one hand, he was clutching Malone, and with the other he held the couch, his knuckles nearly white. Malone was doing his best to soothe him, already moving to help him up and presumably take him from the room.

Clint was still gone, probably tied up with juice, and everyone else looked like they were in decent-enough shape.

"Here." Cutler passed Derreck the forceps and suture material before offering Malone's sub an extra hand. His was clammy to the touch, the middle of his palms slick, yet cold. "What do you think about some juice and a time-out, Malone? Everyone else should be fine without us for a bit. Derreck, you okay to teach? I have more material and a scalpel in my bag." A silent nod was his response.

The sleek hardwood of the living room gave way to gray-and-white tile and black cabinets with matching countertops. A small island with a few stools was the only blockade between the sinks and a few juice boxes that Clint must've set out.

The kitchen was a few degrees cooler than the living room, and Cutler shook off the shiver that raced over his skin. While Malone helped his sub into one of the chairs, Cutler grabbed one of the juice boxes. It was still cool with a touch of condensation on the sides. Clint and the other sub were nowhere to be found, so maybe they'd had to go to the bathroom to clean up. The air did smell vaguely like bile.

"You'll be okay, Oliver. We don't have to do this if you don't want to. We can make it a limit, baby." Malone crouched in front of the stool, clasping Oliver's hands in his own. Oliver pouted, his lower lip peeking out as he stared at the floor.

"I'm sorry, Daddy."

"Baby." Malone stood enough to kiss him on top of the head, before accepting the juice box from Cutler. "Did you want to do the straw, or did you want Daddy to?" He pulled the plastic straw from the box, pushing it out through its plastic wrapper.

"I can, Daddy." Oliver kicked his feet, some of his tension already seeming to drain from his small frame. He looked to be in his mid-twenties, but in a tiny and cute package, frills included.

That was one group that Cutler had rarely seen in the Unkinked community, or maybe he'd just been flirting with the wrong crowds. Littles were always the carefree smiles in the group, and without them, there was something missing.

"Here you go, baby. Just drink it slow and try not to make a mess." Malone kissed him again.

Too cute. He'd never been much into age play himself, but he had to admit that Malone and Oliver were perfect for each other. Oliver kicked his feet happily as he pushed the straw through the seal and started to suck. The smile on his lips had Malone beaming.

It's probably a bad time. "Oliver, can I borrow your Daddy for a second? We won't go far, just outside the kitchen."

Oliver nodded, sending Cutler a bashful grin. "Thank you for the juice, Sir."

"You're welcome." Cutler wasn't going to correct the cutie for calling him 'Sir'. "Malone, could I have one second?" He knew he'd made the wrong step when

Malone immediately looked torn. "It's about Keady," he added softly.

The last thing he wanted to do was talk about Malone's previous sub in front of his current one. Some relationships ended with as much drama in the kink world as they did outside of it, and he didn't want to drudge any jealous thoughts up when Oliver was so sensitive.

"You can talk about that here, Sir. That way Daddy doesn't have to leave when he's so worried, and I don't mind. Keady helped me find my Daddy in a way, and I know what they had together."

But sometimes that didn't make it any easier to hear from someone else. Cutler frowned, rubbing his lips where his scar ached. Thunderstorms always made it worse and the one rumbling in the distance seemed to be drawing closer, a few flashes of lightning visible through the window above the kitchen sink.

"Sounds good to me," said Malone with a hesitant smile. "There are no secrets between us."

Where the hell is the fun in that? No secrets meant no surprises, which was one of Cutler's favorite things on the planet. There was more than one reason Daddy Doms were insufferable.

"Did Keady ever safeword during a scene with you?" asked Cutler, addressing his biggest concern first. He cast a glance at Oliver, but he was still sucking at his juice. Well, he was more playing with it now, tonguing the straw and pulling it up and down with his teeth before blowing a few bubbles.

"No," said Malone, leaning against the counter so he was right next to Oliver's chair with their bodies touching. "And that was why I had so many limits for him. It wasn't long before I realized our kinks didn't match up well, but he wanted to honor his contract. I couldn't make him happy, but he was loyal to me and we became very good friends."

"He's Daddy's *best* friend," said Oliver, letting out a little burp. "Excuse me."

Cutler scratched his chin. He was well overdue for a shave, but he wasn't going to tackle that until right before his shift started. His hair grew way too fast either way, but he'd rather he didn't start out looking like he'd spent a weekend in the woods.

"What were his limits like?" Running his hands over his arms, he tried to rub the goosebumps away as the air conditioning kicked on again. Most of the cool air was probably being sucked out through the open door, making the rest of the place too chilly. "I just can't get a good read on him, and I'm worried about pushing him too far."

Malone nodded. "You aren't the only one. I never figured out what makes him tick, but his limits were pretty standard with me—no breath play, knife play or mummification. Anything that would break skin was out, but he did love a good beating. I usually had another Dom dole those out for him."

"Daddy's a sweetheart," said Oliver, sucking on the straw, despite the box being empty. The noise made Cutler want to grind his teeth, even if it was adorable. He would never be able to support a little in the way they needed.

"Fuck." Cutler gripped his hands into a fist. Oliver's eyes went wide, and Malone blinked in confusion. "When he first tried to negotiate a scene together, he told me he had no limits. It was only after I stitched him up from some asshole and refused to scene with him that he gave me a few…a bare minimum, really."

Oliver gaped, turning to Malone. "Can he do that, Daddy? That sounds so...dangerous." He hissed out the word, like he was spouting a secret between the three of them.

Malone winced before giving Cutler a pained look. "That might be my fault." He patted Oliver on the head, finally taking the juice box away. "I told him that he needed to go for it with his next Dom and not hold back as he had with me. I told him he needed to be brave. *Crap.*" He rubbed his forehead, letting out a sigh. "I didn't think he would take it so literally."

"What's wrong, Daddy? Is Uncle Keady okay?" Oliver kicked his feet, clutching at Malone's shirt as he pinched his eyes with concern.

Cutler already knew. He'd fucked up huge, even if he hadn't seen the signs. A sub like Keady was dangerous in the wrong hands, for himself and the Dom. Looking back, he never should have given Keady a choice in the first place.

"Keady is...different than you, Oliver," said Malone, cupping his sub's chin. "You give me your everything, baby, but Keady needs someone to *take* it. He wants to leave his limits and safewords behind and give everything to his Dom. He wants to be a slave."

Chapter Nine

Keady

Keady stared at the door from his spot on the bench, swallowing thickly as he read the signs. There were enough of them that it had taken him almost ten minutes to read. The biggest one was 'tattoos' in flashing neon green LEDs, where others were slapped to the door with brightly colored paper.

He knew he had to be eighteen, sober and have his ID on him in order to get any work done from the notice taped to the door. He had all of those, and the age, with room to spare. He couldn't find a smidge of fine print anywhere that would give him a reason that he didn't qualify to step inside.

Maybe just a piercing?

He'd considered getting one a few times. His tongue would be the best, but he didn't want to crack his teeth on the bar by accident—and what if it got infected? A nipple was out of the question in case he caught it on his shirt, and anything cock related was too much, even for him.

Glancing at his arm, he gritted his teeth. Cutler's stitches had helped the scars left behind by the other Dom heal into small lines in less than a week. The scabs had fallen off by themselves and Keady had cut the stitches, plucking them out with a pair of tweezers. It had itched terribly as he'd pulled the glorified thread through his skin and little drops of blood welled up as each came free.

The scars were the reason that he'd started looking up designs on the internet in the first place, and the same reason he'd booked an appointment the day before. Texting Cutler about it an hour ago had been the final nail in his coffin.

It was so much easier to be brave when he was on the other side of a computer screen in his quiet condo where the closest person he could see through the window could be squashed between his fingertips like an ant.

He had to do something, though. Every time he looked at his arm, he was assaulted by emotions that he'd rather keep buried. The one at the forefront was a brand of shame and regret that he didn't want to touch with a ten-foot pole.

A siren wailed behind him, the ambulance pulling into the hospital that was just across the street. Three more had passed him by in the short time he'd been sitting on the bench reading the same information over and over. There must've been a sale on heart attacks or something.

It may have been the reason that he'd picked that particular tattoo parlor. If he had a reaction to the ink, or worse, then they could toss him across the street and someone would be able to help him out.

Not to mention, he'd been envious of the tattoo parlor's website. Their designer must've been top-tier, because he was jealous of the simple, sleek design that made some of his mock-ups look like a kindergartner had done them.

But now that he was here, his heart was pounding as he glared at the glass window that had bars interlocking on the inside. He should have been brave enough to go inside himself, but when had he ever been brave? Since his last scene with Cutler, he'd withdrawn more than usual, shutting himself inside his condo except for a single grocery run.

His phone and laptop had been his ticket to the outside world, and they had been all he'd needed. *If I keep telling myself that, it might come true.*

As he stared at the barred door and thought about the conversation that would take place inside the shop, he wanted to shrivel up and hide under the wooden slats of the uncomfortable bench.

There was no way he could just stroll inside and *ask* for a tattoo, especially since there was no one else in there. He would be the center of attention, which was the last thing he needed.

I should just call him. He touched his pants pocket, feeling his phone through the tight denim. *Cutler.* He hadn't answered his text, but Keady knew that he was at work and only a few walls away. Maybe he was digging around in someone's brain...literally instead of figuratively.

Smiling to himself, he ducked his head. Cutler was sweet—terrifying, but sweet. Keady had noticed the healed white line across Cutler's lips but hadn't thought much of it until he'd touched it. The flesh had been just as warm as he'd expected, only smoother and without the shadow of scruff from the rest of his face closing in.

The disfigurement didn't bother him and neither did the grimace that looked nothing like a smile. It was that he felt so fucking guilty about calling Cutler out on not being able to smile — and maybe the serial killer thing, too. He should have noticed or guessed or *something*, for Christ's sakes. But he'd been so focused on himself and the scene that he hadn't even considered anything but Cutler's disappointment.

And he hadn't even gotten fucked. Maybe that was what bugged him the most, because it was pretty fucking irksome.

"You know, this is my neck of the woods."

Keady shot his head up, grasping the arm of the bench as he looked toward the voice. With the blue medical scrubs and dark lines under his eyes, Keady almost didn't recognize Cutler at first. It was only when he caught sight of the thick-rimmed glasses that he finally realized who had found him.

"Hey," said Keady softly, focusing on a dark spot on Cutler's scrubs. Was it blood? Or maybe just a coffee stain. Either way, he looked *good* – good enough that a tattoo didn't seem nearly as scary anymore.

"I think I like you like this," said Cutler, uncrossing his arms and strolling toward the bench. There was a fast-food bag in his hand, the top of the bag curled over and clutched in his fist. "Vulnerable, shy…beautiful."

A shiver went down his back and he sucked in a breath, casting his gaze up and down the sidewalk. There weren't that many people, but there were *some*. Surely Cutler could see them.

"What's wrong, Keady?" asked Cutler, his knee glancing against Keady's. "You look afraid. You've been sitting out here for the last fifteen minutes, and you didn't even notice when I walked by earlier." He held up his fast-food bag, giving it a little shake. The smell of onions and grease was strong.

Looking away, Keady bit his lip. His throat had seized up. The two people walking by may as well have been thousands when they looked his way. *I should have stayed in my condo.* He almost felt like a kid screaming 'stranger danger'.

"If you aren't interested, I can walk away now."

Keady wasn't sure if Cutler was talking about a relationship or a tattoo, but the answer was the same either way. He'd had lots of time to think about both.

"Just know that what I said during our scene, I would never ask of you. I would never ask *anyone.* It was just a fantasy," said Cutler, finally lowering his voice a touch.

No, it wasn't. It was a dream — a nightmare. It didn't matter which, because it had haunted Keady every night since Cutler had told him.

Being bound in chains, or in a cage, with every bit of Cutler's focus on him was thrilling and terrifying, twisting his belly in a way that he wasn't sure he liked or not. When he closed his eyes, he imagined it both ways, sleep eluding him until the first hint of the sun hit the city.

"I-I…" Someone moved behind the glass and a new sign appeared on the door. It was pink with navy block letters announcing a jewelry clearance. Maybe he would buy a stud, just to say he'd gone to the shop and tried it. He'd keep it in a drawer at home, taking it out every once and a while to watch the jewel sparkle.

"Talk to me, Keady." Cutler glanced at his watch. "I can call it for the rest of my shift. I only have a few hours left, anyway."

"Don't." Keady shook his head. Cutler *saved* people. Keady just designed websites, which was why he could bag off in the middle of the day and no one would even notice. That, and three a.m. was inspiration time.

"Last time I checked, you can't tell me what to do. Not unless you're looking for a fun time, that is." Cutler raised one brow, his permanent scowl deepening.

Fuck it. "Did you get my text? I have an appointment...in there." Keady looked at the shop, the new sign suddenly much more intimidating. He wasn't sure what it would smell like or how many people would be there, but he was certain that it would be terrifying.

"Did you want me to come with you?" Cutler asked easily and so damn softly that it almost brought tears to Keady's eyes. But he was a grown-ass man, and he could take care of his own shit. He didn't need a Dom to hold his hand. *Even if I do.*

"No." His chest constricted, even as he said it. "You don't have to," he quickly amended at Cutler's dark look. "It was a stupid idea, anyway. I don't even know what I'm doing here."

If he hadn't paid the deposit through e-transfer, he probably wouldn't have shown up to begin with. But flushing a couple hundred dollars down the drain just seemed wrong.

"Come on," said Cutler, reaching for Keady's hand and grasping it tight. His hands were warm, the pads of his fingers soft, despite the strength of his grip as he tugged Keady to his feet. Keady followed, his heart pounding and his stomach in his throat as the door loomed closer, the flashing sign like a beacon of doom.

"I don't think I can do this," Keady whispered, testing Cutler's grip. It was too strong to break. Cutler opened the door as if he hadn't heard, his paper bag crunching against the glass as the scent of fries and onions wafted Keady's way.

His mouth watered, even as his stomach flipped. It had been so long since he'd had a hamburger. The fake stuff had nothing on his memory of beef.

"Can I help you?" There was a lady behind the counter, her skin almost as covered with artwork as the walls. Some of her tattoos were colorful, like the roses on her wrist that shone with white-tipped red, while others were black like the lettering on the inside of her biceps. She only had four piercings, surprisingly enough.

Keady was frozen between running for the door and giving into Cutler's hands on him. He wanted to submit to that grip and feel Cutler on him and in him. The last time he'd done that, he'd been so fucking free.

"My sub here is looking for a piercing. He has an appointment."

The woman looked between them, raising one brow at the same moment Keady realized that he hadn't told Cutler what he had an appointment for in the first place. He must've just assumed it was for a piercing.

"That's hot as fuck," she said, her eyes sparkling as she leaned over the case in front of her that was packed with jewelry. "But the only appointment I have this afternoon is for ink."

He saw the realization dawn on Cutler's face and the way his eyes widened only a fraction before his grip tightened. "Then I guess we're getting both."

His heart was going to beat out of his chest, but he couldn't say a single thing to stop it. He didn't even like talking to people in retail stores, ordering online and donating items that didn't fit so he didn't have to go to the post office to return anything. But Cutler seemed to take it all in stride.

Cutler leaned into him, his breath hot against Keady's ear. "Color?"

Keady blinked in momentary confusion. What color was his tattoo going to be? He honestly couldn't remember a single detail about it. He'd sent a picture to the artist and he'd written a whole description, but he couldn't recall a damn thing.

Cutler's grip turned fierce, dragging Keady's gaze back. "What's your color, Keady?"

Keady looked from the woman who was grabbing a stack of forms, then back to Cutler. "Green, Sir."

Cutler sucked in a breath, his pupils dilating.

"I'll need him to sign," said the woman, motioning to Keady. Keady's hand shook as he skimmed over the form before reaching for the pen and scribbling out something that vaguely looked like his name.

"Relax, boy," said Cutler, dragging one hand up Keady's side. "Let the nice lady do her job and mark you up. If you're good, I'll give you a reward." Cutler kissed his neck, sending a whispered shiver over his skin.

"I'm not your artist," she said, a smile on her lips. "That'll be Scotland. He's gonna love you two."

Keady shifted uncomfortably, reaching for Cutler's hand again and meeting the paper bag instead. His stomach flopped as he started to move away, but Cutler seemed to sense his unease, catching him before he could retreat.

"Lead the way," said Cutler, his voice low and even. If only Keady could have been so calm. If he got one more whiff of beef and onions, he was going to puke.

She led them beyond a small hall to a curtained area with soft rock music playing in the background. There was more artwork on the walls, this time faces and animals glaring back at him. A padded table was in the middle of the area that smelled strongly of disinfectant, and it gave Keady another jarring slap.

He was going to be on that table in a few moments, a needle in his skin with Cutler looking on.

The last time Cutler and a needle had been in the same room as him, he'd humiliated himself completely. He glanced at Cutler's scar at the memory, ducking his head. He couldn't help but wonder how it had happened, but it was no time to ask.

The artist, Scotland, was bent over a counter, a lamp light shining onto a page that was strewn with scratched gray lines. His short hair hung over his forehead, the vibrant purple tips resting just above his eyes. Even as Keady watched, Scotland dragged his forearm over his face, knocking the hair away for a single moment before it settled back.

Keady's legs wanted to lock up, especially when Scotland looked their way, a smile on his lips that gave everything away. He was way too handsome for his own good, and that smile could only belong to a sadist who loved to poke people with needles for fun.

"Which one of you is Keady?" Scotland flicked the lamp off, shifting a blank piece of paper over his work before Keady could get a good look. All he caught was a masculine chest and an etching of hands before it was out of view, but somehow the features seemed vaguely familiar.

His handsome face, athletic body and the beautiful, inked art on Scotland's arms were enough for Keady to be able to stare at for hours, not to mention his eyes, which were so blue that they matched the violet bits of his hair perfectly. He may have been taller than Cutler, but it was hard to tell when he was stooped over on a stool.

Cutler cleared his throat pointedly when Keady didn't answer, pinching a bit of skin at his side.

"If I say it's you, would you roll with it?" asked Keady as he looked to Cutler, his words much too loud in the small room. His face flushed and he ducked his head, moving closer to Cutler.

Scotland chuckled, patting the chair as his eyes sparkled. "Nothing to worry about, little one. I won't bite."

No one had called him 'little one' since Malone, and Keady was surprised that he had actually missed it. *A teensy bit.* Still, he couldn't trust someone like Scotland...an obvious sadist if Keady ever saw one.

"Says the guy wielding a needle. I'm not worried about your teeth," Keady mumbled, squeezing Cutler's hand tight as he sighed and slipped into the chair. The seat was softer than it looked but the cover was cold, sucking the warmth from his skin.

Usually he was hotter than all hell, but he'd been blanketed in ice since he'd taken his first step inside the shop.

Cutler grimaced in a way that Keady was starting to understand was his version of a smile. His heart fluttered, a bit of calm seeping into his panic at the sight. *Maybe this wasn't such a terrible idea.* Anything was worth seeing Cutler's smile.

"I got your email and your pics and drew this design. You said your arm, right?" asked Scotland, suddenly flipping to business mode. He furrowed his forehead when he reached for a piece of paper among the many on the tabletop, handing it over to Keady.

Taking it with shaking fingers, Keady let out an unsteady breath. It was beautiful and intricate and exactly what he'd pictured in his mind. Scotland had even managed to capture the tiny details that he wasn't sure had even been in his email.

Cutler leaned over his shoulder, reaching for the design and touching it with his fingertip. "Exquisite. We might have to get more than one."

Keady's heart raced, his chest rising and falling as his pants suddenly pulled tight. Shifting on the chair, he tried to adjust himself without the two men seeing. He wasn't sure how successful he was when Scotland sent him a grin.

"Whereabouts do you want it?" Scotland grabbed the design, pulling up a screen on a nearby computer and printing it out.

Holding out his arm, Keady rolled back his sleeve, looking away from the mostly healed cuts. His skin prickled and he flushed hot and cold as Scotland touched him, the spots still sensitive.

Cutler dragged his fingertip over one of the pink lines as Keady shuddered, his lips twitching as his eyes went dark. Among the lines were the tiny pinpricks where Cutler's needle had pierced him, healed as slightly dark dots against his pale skin. If the knife had never touched him, he would have been able to pass the dots off as freckles or some slight imperfection.

"They healed well. Fast, too," said Cutler, pulling his hand back, even as he moved closer, his thigh pressing against Keady's arm. He was warm beneath his scrubs, the thin layer offering the scarcest barrier.

Scotland screwed up his face and he let out a hum before turning Keady's arm over in the light as he squinted at it. "They're fresher than I'd like, but I'll do what I can. You might have to come back a few times to get things touched up. Scars, especially fresh ones, are shit for ink."

Laying the stencil on, he checked in with Keady on the placement, even sending Cutler a look and asking for a second opinion. It seemed like only seconds later that a buzz hit the air as the machine started.

No going back.

Gripping the chair, Keady leaned into Cutler, closing his eyes as the humming needle touched his skin, the first line dragging over his flesh with a unique sensation he'd never forget. He'd expected pain and fire, but instead…*oh.*

Sweat dripped down his back as he opened his eyes, staring at the line that had appeared on his flesh like magic. It was better than a belt, and maybe even a whip, the subtle sting building into glowing ecstasy as Scotland wiped a paper towel over the weeping wound.

"You good?" asked Scotland, leaning back. His lips quirked as he looked at Keady's face.

With how flushed he felt, and with how his eyelids were quickly becoming heavy, he probably looked like he was ready to get fucked.

"Yeah." Keady sounded so much worse, his voice raspy like he'd just deep-throated a cock. Scotland seemed to take it as a compliment, chuckling as he shot him a wink. Cutler never moved, his solid thigh like a rock against Keady's arm. Maybe he was just as mesmerized as Keady was.

The buzzing resumed, the sharp prickle moving over Keady's skin. "So, I gotta ask. Are you guys together? Or are you just the supportive friend?" He gave Cutler a quick look before glancing back at his work and dragging the same paper towel over a new spot. The design wouldn't cover the scars, but wrap around them in a way that drew the eye away from the imperfections.

Biting his lip, Keady kept his response behind his teeth. Everything was so up in the air between them. They hadn't scened since the first time, and they'd had two brief calls and a handful of texts between Cutler's shifts. His work hours were more insane than Keady's, which was saying something.

The ball was in Cutler's court. Keady wasn't sure if it was a tennis ball or a basketball, but either way, he was going to get hit. *Not that I'd mind.* A hit would be better than the tentative tension that seemed to exist between them every time they were in the same room or even when Keady thought of Cutler when he was alone.

"He's my submissive," said Cutler, his voice completely neutral as his thigh flexed and the bag crinkled in his hand.

That was something Keady did not make a habit of telling strangers. He was kinky as fuck, but he was also private as all hell. Malone had called him shy but fuck that. He wasn't a kid...just an extreme introvert. *Who would rather stay at home for weeks at a time than talk to someone.*

Scotland let out a whistle. "Well then, thank you for letting me work on your sub, Sir." His composure seemed to change in an instant, his eyes lowering as he addressed Cutler. In a second it was over, and he brought the needle back to its place. "That's a new one for me. I've never tatted a sub as part of the dynamic before."

Keady shuddered, arching his back as the needle skimmed on the sensitive inner side of his wrist. The ache built, adrenaline rushing through him like a drug. He was so hard that he was aching, barely able to follow the conversation going on over his head.

"My boy is shy," said Cutler, carefully patting Keady's head. Keady glowed, leaning into the touch as much as he could while trying to keep still. "The ink was his idea, but so was backing out. I can't have him trying to make the decisions, though. He really can't handle it."

That's the spot. Why had Keady ever doubted this? He'd been so fucking stupid to even question their chemistry when Cutler always seemed to know what he was thinking. Cutler was obviously on board, slipping right into the impromptu scene and taking control while Keady felt himself start to slip.

It shouldn't have been so easy to lose himself, but between the sting and Cutler's gaze, the tattoo shop was getting further away.

"Fuck me, that's hot." Scotland grinned, wiping the excess ink before continuing. He adjusted his position, looming a touch closer as he squinted. His purple hair shifted from the move, the vibrant ends sweeping close to his face. The ends of his eyebrows were purple too, but so dark that they looked nearly black. He looked vaguely familiar, as if Keady had seen him on a distant floor of Unkinked before.

Keady needed one of them. Cutler or Scotland, he didn't really care—only he did. Scotland touching him—carving into him and leaving ink behind probably wouldn't have felt anywhere close to the way it did without Cutler.

"Sir?" Turning his head, Keady touched his face to Cutler's side and took a breath. He wasn't sure when Cutler had been replaced with Sir, but he couldn't think of him any other way right now. He wasn't supposed to call Cutler that, was he? Or maybe that was just a piece of his imagination.

His nose filled with antiseptic and blood, Cutler's scrubs still reeking of the hospital. He would have to get back soon and save someone's life. It was funny, really, that he was the complete opposite of what Keady had thought.

"Hmm?" Cutler dragged his hand through Keady's hair, tugging gently at the roots. "What is it? Too much? You can safeword if you need to, Keady. There's always the option to take a break."

There he was, trying to think that Keady was a weak pushover again. He narrowed his eyes, biting his lower lip to keep his whimper back.

No! "I'm—uh—hard, Sir." He shifted in the chair, unable to stop himself. Scotland gripped his arm, holding him still as he drew the tattoo machine back.

"Don't move unless you want this to be ruined," said Scotland, easing his grip once Keady had calmed. Whimpering as the pain flared again, Keady clenched his hand into a fist, fighting every muscle that begged to move.

"You okay with this, Scotland?" asked Cutler, slowly tugging Keady's hair until his head was tilted back and he was blinking at the lights that were much too bright.

"Go for it, Sir. I'm in the lifestyle myself."

That explained why he looked familiar. Keady avoided busy nights, so it wouldn't be impossible for him to miss someone like Scotland.

"Perfect," Cutler grimaced, his grip going fierce on Keady's hair. "I don't think you deserve to come, Keady. Not for a long time. Don't think I've forgotten that I owe you a punishment. The other night was just a taste. I usually don't have to punish my subs, so it ought to be interesting."

Keady whimpered, biting his lip hard enough to make it bleed. Cutler pulled his lips from between his teeth before slowly pressing his finger inside the cavern of Keady's mouth. Soap and blood soaked into his tongue just as the needle passed over the very edge of a scar, nerves zinging over his flesh.

"I can't help it." His voice was muffled against Cutler's finger, saliva slowly gathering in his mouth. His cock was dripping, the inside of his boxer slick and uncomfortable, like he'd been edging himself for hours. Any more and he would come against his will. He didn't need a hand on his cock.

"I know you're a slut who gets off on pain and humiliation, but you're also too dumb to look after yourself. Let me do the thinking." Cutler twisted his finger, adding a second and grasping Keady's tongue. If you're good for the rest of this and you keep from coming, then I promise I'll scene with you this weekend."

"I can't. I can't," Keady begged, drool slipping from his mouth and running down his chin. Tears prickled in his eyes as Scotland wiped his skin again, every drag of the damp paper towel like fire against his skin. He needed it to end almost as much as he needed to swallow or come.

"He's not so shy when he's begging for cock," said Cutler, quirking his lips. "It's something I've noticed. Do you have a Dom in the area, Scotland? I don't think I've seen you before, but I'm fairly new to the community myself and there have been a lot of changes lately."

You've got to be kidding me. They were not going to shoot the shit while Keady was about to explode. That was completely uncool. Not to mention the mess of drool that was making its way down his neck.

"I've been a part of the Unkinked community for a few years myself," said Scotland, dabbing at the ink before stretching out his back and starting a new section of the outline. "Haven't found a Dom that I'm a huge fan of yet, but maybe that will change with Clint's new place."

Cutler reached for his abandoned paper bag with his free hand, the smell of greasy fries overwhelming as he opened it. "I hope you don't mind if I eat. I'm just on my first break in the last twelve hours." He stuck a French fry in his mouth, chewing as he glanced around at the art on the walls.

Motherfucking bastard. Keady tugged his tongue free, wiping at his chin.

"I don't mind." Scotland shrugged. "But keep your sub still, please."

Keady was about to break. His hand was aching from where he held the chair. He didn't even want to think about how much his cock hurt. Blue balls didn't come close to the fierce ache that was probably going to be permanent at this point.

"It sounds like we are part of the same community, though," said Cutler. "Clint brought me into the fold recently, but I was active in other communities before then. Have you been to the new house? It's surreal."

The machine paused as Scotland adjusted his chair and shook his head. "Not yet. I'm working on the nerve to get out there. I've got my eye on someone, but they haven't given me the time of day."

Cutler made a thoughtful sound before eating another fry. "Then they aren't worth your time."

Keady agreed, even if he did want to strangle both of them. Scotland was smoking hot in a rugged and dangerous kind of way. It was crazy to think that someone would toss him aside. Maybe their limits didn't line up?

"This guy is." Scotland smiled when he said it, his eyes lighting up. "Okay, Keady, the linework is done. Let's give it five minutes so I can stretch out my back, then we'll continue if you're good."

The lines were perfect, permanently inked and so dark against Keady's skin that they looked like they would never fade. He could only imagine what it would be like when it was complete, the embarrassing scars wrapped in a design that would turn them into something beautiful.

He didn't look up when Scotland stepped out of the room and Cutler knelt next to him, too engrossed in the design.

"You feeling good?" Cutler asked, his hand hovering inches over the fresh ink. Keady longed for him to touch it, but at the same time, he was terrified that it would somehow smudge.

"I want more."

Cutler quirked his lip. "Are you going to be good and sit as long as Scotland needs you to? Coming is off-limits."

"I'll be good." Keady humped the air, even as he said it. He was absolutely squashed in his pants, but he'd played a bit with orgasm control, and the payout was always intense.

"Good." Cutler grabbed his bag, before crumpling the rest and tossing it into a nearby trash can. "The next time I see you, you're mine. There's no backing out of it this time, Keady. Text me your limits, and I'll send you my address and the time. Don't be late."

Cutler turned from the room, Keady's hands sweating as he swiveled in the chair. "Not at the club?"

Clint had spared no expense, and there were spots that Keady hadn't even checked out yet, like the notorious basement which hadn't been part of the tour. And even though he was starting to understand Cutler better, he was still terrifying.

"No." Cutler shook his head before drawing a finger down his lip. "You need someone to take you and put you in your place for longer than a simple scene. If I left you chained up at the club that long, someone might notice."

Holy shit.

"Goodbye, Keady."

Chapter Ten

Keady

Cutler was fucking loaded, that was for sure. Keady swallowed as he stared at the house, the spotlights on every part of the soffit like dollar signs down the drain. And there was a *yard*, which in itself was insane. Yes, it was on the outskirts of the city where there was still farmland and a few cows, but land was *expensive*.

The trees were a nice touch, along with the grass that was so green that it must've been painted with something to make it look that way. It shifted to something darker as the sun disappeared behind one peak on the massive roof, the lights around the house like a beckoning angel...*or devil*.

His own upscale condo amidst the bustle of traffic was modest in comparison. He'd never been hard up for money, but he wasn't sure if he'd ever met someone with quite so much of it—at least, someone who flaunted it like Cutler did.

Keady stared at his phone one last time, just to make sure he had the address right. His list of limits was at the top of their last conversation, every glaring word like salt in the wound.

He could see the point of some of them — like aftercare — even if he'd hoped to be done with the whole goddamn list. Apparently, a Dom like Cutler, who balanced on the edge, still needed some kind of guidelines.

Cutler had taken a full day to reply to Keady's text with the time and his address, and Keady had spent nearly the entire time pacing his condo and checking his phone over and over. A call to Nav hadn't helped, seeing as he was recovering from an intense scene with his Dom Trick, and Maddy had just told him to be patient.

It was easy for them to say.

The nearest house to Cutler's was almost a full block away, the lawn stretching behind a black gate with little rolls and dips separated by only a few trees. Someone had done the gardens up and must've taken care of watering the little pink flowers that seemed to blossom in almost every bed.

But the gardener was nowhere in sight, and the neighbor's house looked empty from a distance.

No one would hear him scream. If he happened to go missing, Nav and Maddy would eventually notice that he hadn't dropped by Unkinked, but he was like that. Sometimes he spent weeks away before he mustered up the courage to brave the potential crowds.

Work would notice eventually that his tasks weren't being completed on time or that he wasn't answering his email. He'd finished up his latest project by staying up until four a.m. the night before, and the next one wasn't due for twelve days.

That was plenty of time for Cutler to chop him into pieces and bury him in different parts of the city.

He's a good guy. Still, it was never silly to be safe.

Closing the last text from Cutler, he brought up Clint's contact, shooting off a quick text.

Sceneing with Cutler for a few days. If you don't hear from me, he's definitely a serial killer. Take care of Sassafrass, my goldfish.

Chuckling, Keady powered off his phone. Clint had fucked with him enough lately, so it was only fair that he turned the tables. They both knew that he didn't have a goldfish, but they'd used codewords before to keep members of the community safe.

Locking his car, he took a step toward the house. *Fuck, it looks bigger already.* His foot slipped on the stone walkway as he stepped into a small puddle that must've been left over from a recent dousing with the sprinkler. There wasn't a brown blade of grass to be seen, despite it being the middle of summer.

With Keady's condo, anyone could tell it belonged to him the moment they stepped inside because it was so open and desolately lonely at the same time. With Cutler's house, anyone could have lived there. *Anyone rich.* It was modern and new, with a fancy metal roof that looked like old terracotta tiles. With siding that was a replica of real stonework, and the deep red door that could welcome a giant, it reeked of money.

The red was a nice touch, though, the black designs across it showing off just enough personality that it could almost be considered character.

Taking a deep breath, he hopped onto the porch, his heart pattering in his chest. Every time he saw Cutler, he got a little more comfortable with him, but it wasn't that long ago that he had turned his nose up at the man.

The moments between their meetings, when there was nothing he could do but wait, unnerved him the most. He'd never been the most patient person in the world, either.

He rapped his knuckles on the door, cursing a moment later when he noticed the very obvious doorbell. It was one of the ones with a camera in it, and it was probably hooked up to Cutler's phone. Snickering, Keady covered the lens with his finger as he rang it, the dark shadow of his fingerprint hopefully blocking the view.

My final act as a brat.

"Come inside, Keady." Cutler's disembodied voice came from the direction of the doorbell and Keady flinched back, dropping his hand. "You can leave your bag and your clothes at the front door. You won't be needing anything once you're inside. Come find me when you're ready."

Nodding, Keady swallowed and grabbed for the doorknob. He'd half-expected it to shock him as he touched it, but it turned easily under his hand, the door swinging wide with a quiet groan.

If he'd thought the outside looked rich, it was nothing to the inside of the place. Everything was white except for the black painted beams that lined the ceiling. What he'd taken for a two-and-a-half-stories was instead a massive main floor with a peaked roof that stretched far beyond any ladder's reach.

The heating and cooling bills must cost a fortune.

It was almost entirely open concept with the huge kitchen and living room visible from the door and leather couches sitting in front of a television screen that was probably great for some kind of sport that Keady was never going to watch. There wasn't a speck of dust out of place and the cupboards looked completely organized through the glass doors.

It was complete and utter sterility, like a surgical suite without the patient and aftermath. It didn't *look* like anyone had been dismembered there. *But looks can be deceiving.*

Keady dropped his bag and set his shoes on the mat, taking one step before he paused. Cutler had asked him to leave his bag and clothes at the door, but he hadn't exactly told Keady to get naked.

It may have been a test already, or Cutler was setting him up to fail. Well, Cutler had another thing coming if he thought Keady would back out so soon. They were away from the public eye, and there were no onlookers to be seen. There was no need to be shy.

Just keep telling yourself that.

He popped the buttons on his shirt one by one, sliding it from his shoulders before dropping it to the cold floor. It was a simple dress shirt that he'd spent entirely too long picking out. The slacks completed the look, giving way too much formality for the way they felt coming off. The fabric was smooth and soft, but too restricting for what he needed.

Perhaps it was a good thing that he was stripping so early, since he'd dressed up as if he were getting ready for a goddamn job interview.

It was almost too cool as he rubbed at his legs where his skin was prickling. He'd never been comfortable with his own body, not even after forty years of gradual changes. He'd always been a touch too soft, never developing the abs that seemed to come so easily to some men. And once thirty-five had struck, he'd inexplicably sprouted gray hairs in the middle of his dark ones.

There were almost more grays than dark hairs now on his chest, giving him a speckled appearance. Who knew what Cutler saw in him.

Most Doms in his community looked for lean subs who were flexible, young and outgoing. No one wanted someone his age who hadn't managed to land himself a steady partner and who still screwed up enough that Clint had to keep him in check. It was a wonder Cutler even wanted to see him, let alone naked.

Maybe he'd misinterpreted everything? He reached for his pants, holding them against himself without pulling them back on. They offered little warmth and protection, a weak shield against his own insecurities. It was time to leave it all behind and really go for it.

Letting out a shuddering breath, he let them fall to the floor.

He was keeping his boxers on, though. Cutler would just have to deal with it.

"Cutler?" Keady called into the house. The ticking of a distant clock and the gentle roar of central air were his only answer.

In a house this size, there must've been thousands of places to hide, but there was something very off about the feel of the place. There was no breath, no life, and despite the lights and furniture, there was an emptiness to the place.

Slipping off his socks, Keady stepped off the mat again and made his way through the kitchen and living room to the white door along the far wall. The shiny tile transitioned to cool hardwood at the threshold, the dark stained wood setting the mood for the room beyond.

He wasn't sure if he'd ever seen a bedroom so large. It was like something out of a castle, with sprawling dressers and a bed he could get lost in. He let his gaze linger on the bed for a long moment. How much time would it be before he was under those sheets with Cutler's arms wrapped around him?

A shiver ran along his spine. Ten minutes wouldn't be soon enough.

There was no sign of anything kinky at all, though. It was massively disappointing. Where were the handcuffs on the four-poster frame? Or the choke-chain dog collar tied to the headboard? The hunter green sheets and a few oversized pillows were almost domestic.

It was less disappointing that he hadn't found a murder room yet.

Letting out a frustrated sigh, Keady reached for the nearest door of three in the bedroom, revealing a closet that was approximately the size of his living room. There were suits, casual clothes and scrubs hanging from every hook, along with a rack of nearly identical dress shoes. At the very bottom of the rack there was a single pair of running shoes that looked brand new.

Keady stepped back out of the closet, heading for the second door. A pristine white bathroom greeted him, the tile under his feet like blocks of ice. Fuck, it felt good against his skin that was slowly growing hot. The empty rooms led him closer to Cutler, the anticipation rising in his gut like a sickness.

With every step, his nervousness built, his heart pounding as his hands trembled with adrenaline. Had he missed somewhere?

He glanced behind the door of the bathroom, just to make sure that Cutler hadn't tucked himself behind in the hopes of scaring him. A black housecoat swung on the hook, the space too small for anything else, including his Dom.

Only one door remained, the textured paint like the worst kind of promise. It *had* to be a playroom — or something a bit more nefarious. Keady swallowed as he glanced at the doorknob, the brushed nickel calling to him.

"I'm all for the haunted house feel, but can you not jump out at me?" His voice echoed as the sole sound of life in the house.

He actually loved haunted houses, but they were a touch awkward. People were supposed to freak out in them, but he just got hard, which made the wandering hands of the staff so much odder. And jerking off in a corner to the sound of startled screams was pretty frowned upon, too.

"Cutler?" Keady spun, marching back to the closet. He could have sworn he saw something out of the corner of his eye. His breathing came in quick bursts as he clutched at the door frame, skimming the bottom of the clothes rack for a hint of feet. There was no place to hide.

Darkness plunged around him as every source of light suddenly cut out. It was as if he'd been blindfolded, unable to even see his hand in front of his face. The small emergency blue nightlight to his side gave off less light than a star in the dead of night.

Fear gripped his gut, his groin pulling tight as his heart raced. His breath trembled, barely filling his lungs. "Cutler?"

Oh fuck. Maybe it was just a power outage. It was so dark, even as his eyes started to adjust. He reached for the rack of fancy suits that he could've sworn was right beside him, but his hand met empty air. *Am I even in the closet?*

"C-Cutler!"

A hand clamped over his mouth, cutting off the scream that burst from his throat. His face met the wall as he was pushed against it, the heat of Cutler's body smothering him from behind. Something hard pushed against his ass, and he moaned into the hand over his mouth, regretting keeping his boxers on with everything in his being.

"Gotcha, Keady," said Cutler, his voice low and utterly calm against his ear as he cut off Keady's breath. Keady wriggled in the hold, testing Cutler's strength and trying to get any sort of pressure against his oversensitive cock. Anyone else would have let him go as he thrashed, but Cutler held tight, Keady no match for him. *Oh God.*

"Do you remember what I told you?" Cutler spread his fingers and Keady sucked in a sharp breath, his head swimming as he filled his lungs. Cutler bumped against his ass, pushing him into the wall. The pressure on his cock was almost enough to make him come, but he held back with a halting whimper.

Keady shook his head. He couldn't even remember who he was. It was better just to forget.

"You're my prisoner now, Keady, and you've been keeping something from me. I've tried to get you to fess up before, but you're just too stubborn. I like that you don't know what's good for you because I can *teach* you." Cutler nipped his ear before dragging his teeth over the lobe. Keady let out a groan, relaxing into the grip as Cutler moved a hand to his throat.

Firm, steady pressure made his head throb, his breath noisy as he tried to fill his lungs. Cutler's control was monumental, giving Keady just enough room to keep from passing out but not a single gasp more.

"The thing I really want to hear from you is your safeword," said Cutler, moving his free hand to Keady's chest and pinching his nipple before rolling the bud between his fingertips. "I'm not going to rest until I hear it on your lips, your voice cracking from screaming for me. I can stay awake for forty-eight hours. How long do you think you'll last? You look tired already, Keady. So precious and so delicate."

It was like he could read Keady's mind. After he'd finished off his work in the early morning hours, he couldn't get to sleep, their scene the only thing on his mind. He'd imagined so many scenarios, but none of them had prepared him for the real thing—the pure fear that was driving him straight into subspace.

"I'm going to do everything I can to get you to say that word, and once you do, I can give you aftercare, baby. You'd like that, right? You want me to take care of you, not brutalize you until you give up that little word."

"Fuck." Keady struggled just so he could feel Cutler's hands on him, holding him tight and not budging an inch. Cutler clamped down on his neck, probably digging the first bruises into his flesh and not stopping until Keady was almost lost in the darkness of his mind.

"We're going to practice first, Keady, just so I can make sure you know what you're getting into. What would you say if you need me to slow down?"

His throat clicked as he swallowed and dragged his nails over Cutler's wrist. He hadn't released Keady's nipple yet and was slowly applying more and more pressure, the pain like a memory of the clamps. "Yellow."

"And when you need to stop? When you finally accept that you can't be my prisoner for another moment?"

"Red."

"Perfect." Cutler chuckled before sucking a spot on Keady's neck. "And I'll give you a choice in just one more thing. If you aren't ready, go back the way you came. Put your clothes on and leave now...right now. If you want more, come downstairs to the basement." He scraped his teeth over the same spot, Keady's skin prickling as he whimpered. "Choose wisely."

As fast as Cutler had grabbed him, he retreated, releasing Keady and leaving him a panting mess against the wall. Shivers racked his body as the cool air swept in and silence greeted him a second time.

Keady clawed at the wall before reaching behind him and swiping at the empty air. There was no one there, not even a whisper of a breath.

"Cutler?"

The lights flicked on overhead and Keady stumbled back, slapping his hands over his eyes as his vision swam. "Fuck, that's bright." LEDs were the worst.

He blinked as his eyes adjusted, turning and pressing his back to the closet wall. He hadn't moved that far from where he'd thought he'd been when the lights had gone out, but he was definitely alone. Without the throbbing bruises on his nipple and neck and the damp kiss on his neck, he would have wondered if the last few minutes had been a figment of his imagination.

Keady touched his neck, dragging his finger over the stinging mark where Cutler had dragged his teeth. His skin was ridged with the impression of a bite, just another spot where Cutler had marked him. *Like the tattoo.*

He may have finished the tattoo on his own, but it was Cutler who was stamped in his flesh, the healed dots from his needle circled by swirling designs that elevated them to art.

Palming his cock once, he dragged his hand away before pushing from the wall. His legs were weak, trembling and barely able to hold his weight. Sweat dripped down his body, even as he shivered in the air-conditioned space.

The front door called to him, his bag sitting there and completely packed for his stay. His clothes were still piled beside it, his socks just barely off the mat where he'd left them. It would only take a moment to put them back on and head home.

He could text Maddy and Nav to tell them that he'd made a mistake and that he was in over his head. Maybe he could convince them that the risk wasn't worth it before he dragged himself to the bar to check in with Clint. Would they believe him?

Rubbing his hand over his face, he stepped to the front door, glaring down at his discarded clothing. The dress shirt that he'd painstakingly ironed was crumpled, one of the buttons stretched and barely hanging on.

He slipped one finger under the waistband of his boxers, tugging them off and tossing them next to the rest. His cock bounced as soon as it was given freedom, the wet head matching the patch on his boxers from when Cutler's hands had been on him.

"Now to find the basement." For the first time in his life, it was time to be brave.

Chapter Eleven

Cutler

Cutler ducked around to the basement steps, keeping one hand on the wall so he didn't fall. Keady lingered on his lips and in his nose, everything pinpointing to the man he longed for. His cock was rock hard, making it awkward as hell to rush down the steps as fast as he dared.

As he reached the landing, he brought his phone out of his pocket, clicking the button to light up the screen. At the same time, he opened the electrical panel tucked in the wall at the base of the stairs. Using the light from his phone, he found the main breaker and flipped the switch back on.

Upstairs, everything was probably beeping back to life, his microwave and bedside clock included. There were probably more than a dozen digital clocks that he would have to reset in the house, but every single one of them would be worth it. So had nearly falling up the stairs in the darkness as he'd rushed to capture Keady as soon as he'd flipped the breaker off. The camera app on his phone had seen to the rest.

He'd gone back and forth with himself as he decided what their scene should look like, sucking down a dozen energy drinks as he'd tossed out plan after plan.

Restrain Keady in the basement and flog him? They'd basically already done that. Going primal and stalking him in the house? Close, but not perfect. He knew what he wanted, but…

He'd bitten his lip as he'd finally hardened his resolve. Keady hadn't been the only one holding back, and it was time for one of them to be honest. And if he waited on Keady to be the honest one, he would be waiting an eternity.

But Cutler wasn't going to let things get out of hand. Just because Keady was his prisoner didn't mean he couldn't earn certain privileges.

That was, if he decided to stay.

Cutler pulled up the cameras on his phone again, his heart dropping as he watched an image of Keady as he strolled toward the front door. His heart picked up when Keady pulled off his last layer of clothing, tossing his boxers with the rest.

This is going to be good.

Cutler headed to the room in the basement that he'd converted into an impromptu dungeon for the weekend. What had been an eternally unused guestroom had been easy enough to change into something so much better. He didn't have a lot of tools, because he rarely brought a sub home with him, but that didn't mean he wasn't creative.

He'd left the mattress but had taken the bed frame down and had shoved the box spring into another room. A trip to Walmart had supplied him with a metal dog crate that was large enough that Keady would be able to lay down in it but not stretch out all the way. Without the brand name stickers and dog, it looked more like a tiny version of the prison Cutler so desperately wanted to emulate.

When he'd had the house built, he'd left the basement partially unfinished but had put large rugs over many of the surfaces. He'd rolled the rug in the room away and had tucked it in a closet, leaving the concrete cold and bare. It even had a convenient drain in the middle, although the attached bathroom would be the desired place for any unfortunate accidents.

He had everything ready to prepare Keady to get into the right mindset that would set their entire time together. It was time for both of them to leave their uncertainties behind.

He could see the potential they had and how far they could go. *Too far*, if he wasn't careful.

Cutler pressed his back to the wall, tucking his phone away and leaning casually as he caught the sound of Keady's footsteps at the top of the stairs. Despite the size of the house, the layout was so basic that it wouldn't take long for Keady to find him. It had really been by chance that Keady had left the door to the basement where Cutler had been hiding for last.

Keady stepped into the room, his eyes straight ahead as he padded his naked feet across the floor. He didn't seem to notice the chill, or Cutler, as he walked over to the bare mattress before turning a glare on the cage and putting his hands on his hips.

His cock gave him away, though. It twitched when he looked at the cage, the flushed shaft dark and beautiful. He was perfectly proportioned, and he'd obviously taken the time to trim himself.

"Put this on," said Cutler. Keady startled, spinning toward him before flushing at the sight of the collar in Cutler's hand.

It was expensive, leather and rich with fresh polish that Cutler had painstakingly applied after watching a dozen videos on how to condition it properly. He'd never given much care to leather before, but he'd never considered getting a collar before, either.

There was a solid metal ring at the front of it that gleamed in the light. It was perfect for clipping a chain or leash on it, but instead, he'd adorned it with a simple tag.

The lady at the pet store had been so helpful when Cutler had asked for the engraved tag. She'd helped him set up the machine and had even suggested the color while she'd asked him all about his new puppy named Keady. *Poor girl.* She'd been so oblivious.

Simple had been best. Keady's name was on the front of the tag with Cutler's information on the back. That way, if Keady was ever lost, they'd know exactly who to call and where to go.

Keady trembled as he took the collar, playing with the buckle as he wrapped it around his neck. Cutler made no move to assist as Keady pulled it tight and slipped the metal peg through the punched hole.

Too tight. Maybe Keady didn't know that every move was a test between them, and Cutler had no qualms about correcting him. Either way, he was nervous…or asking for it.

Cutler was going to choose to believe the latter.

Reaching for Keady's hand, Cutler brought it right back to the buckle as he adjusted it to a looser setting that would be more comfortable. "Feel this spot here?" He smoothed Keady's finger over a spot that was nearly hidden beneath the solid layer of leather. "This is the safety latch. If you feel you can't safeword or you need the collar off, just pull that and it will unravel. If there's ever a time you can't verbally safeword, just do something twice — snap your fingers, clap, pinch me. It will all mean the same thing."

Cutler adjusted the collar until the metal ring was at the center of Keady's neck and dipping into the hollow of his throat, practically begging for a leash. "Any questions?"

Keady shook his head, his eyes wide. He seemed to be trembling less and was just a tad calmer now that Cutler was visible. It was too bad, really. His fear had been incredibly addictive.

"First rule. Every answer is a verbal one. I want to hear your voice tremble." And Cutler would hopefully be able to tell if Keady were lying. He wasn't exactly a good liar, but Cutler had to hear a few truths to be able to know for sure.

"Yes, Sir." Keady shifted as he touched the collar, running his finger over the safety latch before tugging at the metal loop. A smile played over his lips that made his eyes light up. The smile changed something, not just about his face, but the entirety of him. It made him look softer somehow, like a weight had been lifted from his shoulders.

"You look good in that collar." Cutler hooked a finger through the metal loop alongside Keady's, tugging him off balance. "I think your cock agrees with me. But let's find out."

Dragging Keady along with him, he moved to a section of the wall that he'd covered with a curtain. With one tug, he pulled back the thick material with his free hand. Keady had probably expected a window or something, his mind already forgetting that they were underground. Cutler had hung a mirror for that very reason — a very large mirror. *You can't forget when you're looking yourself in the face.*

Flushing, Keady turned his face away, but Cutler touched his chin, dragging him back to the mirror. Self-esteem was a big thing he had to work on with Keady, and he was more than glad to do it.

"Don't look away. I want you to watch how much of a whore you are for it, and I want you to enjoy looking." Cutler slapped Keady's cock and it bounced, the rigid flesh smacking against his belly from the momentum. "Admit that you like it."

Keady stammered as Cutler released him, only to circle behind him, watching every movement in the mirror. It wasn't hard to imagine himself as a predator. It was certainly who he saw when he looked at his own reflection. "Well?"

"I-I don't like to look." Keady dropped his gaze, his face flaming. "I'm not very attractive." He touched the patch of grays on his chest that were so light they looked nearly blond. "There are much nicer people to look at than me — better subs."

"Are you calling me an idiot or a liar?" asked Cutler, growling and tugging Keady's chin until he was staring into the mirror again. His patience was usually infinite, but Keady was so wrong. Why couldn't he see how beautiful he was?

"Neither, Sir." Keady swallowed as Cutler dropped a hand to his neck, caressing the throbbing pulses just above the collar. The marks where he'd choked Keady softly before were blush red, with darker crescents where he'd dug in his teeth. The collar covered some of it, but not enough to hide it completely.

"Well, it must be one of them," Cutler mused, sliding his finger under the edge of the collar and tugging the leather. It creaked as Keady swallowed, the band momentarily going tighter. "I have a PhD, so I'm not *stupid*. It must be the liar part, then." He paused, trailing his fingers over Keady's shoulder. His skin was pale and so perfect for biting that it made him salivate. "I guess you aren't going to enjoy this next part."

Cutler stepped back, moving through the door to the adjoining bathroom. He'd left everything he'd wanted to use out on the counter as he'd finally come to terms with their scene. A new beginning meant a fresh start, and he needed Keady to be *clean*.

He filled the silicone bag with warm water and a few added surprises, making sure that the attached tube and nozzle were closed tight so nothing could escape. He'd intended for Keady to use them solo, but his humiliation was too beautiful to miss out on.

"This is for you," Cutler returned, handing the nozzle to Keady as he hung the bag on a hook above the mirror. He'd placed it there just in case he wanted to pull the restraints out, but it worked even better for this.

"I have lube as well." Cutler rifled in his back pocket, tugging out the single-use packet. He had a larger bottle of slick only a few steps away, but he wanted to watch Keady struggle to open the foil, flushing the entire time.

He wasn't disappointed. Keady stammered as he looked over his shoulder to where Cutler had hung the bag before staring at the nozzle as if it would bite him. He had to know what it was. You didn't have to be kinky to recognize it, and Keady was one kinky man.

"I told you I don't usually do punishments, Keady, but I will if I have to. You don't have any choice but to listen to me." He dropped the packet into Keady's hand before strolling to the mattress and taking a seat. His view of Keady's ass was perfect, showing off his pert cheeks and the fuckable crease between them.

"I already did one," said Keady, looking to the bag and back to the mirror with a flush spreading down his chest. His cock throbbed, the head wet and gleaming as he clenched his ass. Their gazes met in the mirror, and for once, Keady didn't look away. "Before I came over, I got ready for you."

"That's nice," said Cutler, plucking an invisible piece of fuzz from his pant leg. He'd gone with track pants for comfort, even though he usually hated the things. He could lounge in slacks any day. "Let me know when it's all in and I'll start the timer. Let's say, fifteen minutes?" If it had just been warm water, fifteen minutes would have been a breeze, but not with what Cutler had added to it.

"Okay." Keady let out a soft sigh, tearing into the lube packet and squirting some onto the nozzle. Reaching back, he slipped one finger into himself before replacing it quickly. He unlocked the line until water rushed through it, starting to fill him. It was obviously not his first time, even though he screwed up his face and closed his eyes.

"Eyes on the mirror. I won't remind you again." Cutler rubbed the scar over his lip before letting out a hum. "It looks like you must do this a lot. Back arched, legs wide, you look like a fucking slut for it. If I would have known that, I would have grabbed the bigger bag."

Keady shifted, furrowing his forehead as concern crossed his face. He bit his lip, meeting Cutler's gaze in the mirror. The reflective glass seemed to give him just a touch of bravery, and Cutler soaked it up. "Sir, it feels—uh, ah—something's wrong. It's too hot."

Cutler hid his lips behind his hand as he chuckled. The temperature had been perfect when he'd filled the bag. If anything, it may have been a tad cool now. "I checked it myself. It's not too hot."

Shifting again, Keady brought a hand to his belly, his hand just above his groin. His cock was nearly purple now and dripping a steady pearl of fluid, his balls heavy and full. *Only a little bit left now.*

It wasn't enough to bloat him, and barely more than a routine clean, but to Keady, it was hopefully monumental.

"Almost done. You can shut it off if you like." Cutler scratched his chin and crossed his ankles before leaning back on his hand. Keady clenched his ass again, the muscles in his back straining. "Relax."

In Cutler's experience, that word always invoked the opposite.

Keady panted, shifting his feet as he let out a low groan. His flush spread down his belly as the first bit of sweat broke over his skin. The muscles in his legs flexed, his lips pressing into a firm line as he reached for the hose and shut off the flow before the last could drain into him.

"You took that like a pro," said Cutler, resisting the smile that wanted to burst from his chest as pride overwhelmed him. *That's my boy.* "Not that that's surprising. Do you think your ass is tight enough to keep it inside or do I need to plug you up?"

"I'm...I'm. Sir, *please*, it's hot!" Keady panted, his mouth dropping open as he touched the mirror and dragged his fingertips over the surface.

"That would be the ginger oil," said Cutler, leaning his chin on one hand as he tried to get more comfortable. His cock was freaking uncomfortable, even with the track pants.

Keady's skin rippled as he danced, his muscles flexing and sweat dripping along his skin. The discomfort on his face was mixed with a bliss that Cutler had seen before. They were getting close.

Keady really had no idea how gorgeous he was.

"Sadistic bastard," said Keady, letting out a breath before he moved his hand back to his belly. "That shit fucking hurts." His tune changed a moment later. "Ah, fuck. *Please.* I don't want to make a mess."

Cutler hummed. "And you don't want to find out what will happen if you do. Do you think ginger is the only thing I have up my sleeve?"

Cutler flexed his wrist as if he could conjure something from thin air. In reality, he only had lube and one dildo close enough to do that sort of magic trick.

"It's getting worse. Fuck, it burns." Keady moved his hands to the edge of the mirror, leaning his forehead against the surface as his gaze went dark. His swallow was audible, as was his gasp a moment later.

It was exquisite perfection. Cutler was almost disappointed when his watch vibrated on his wrist, marking the fifteen-minute mark.

"There's a bathroom through that door. Go relieve yourself."

Grabbing the bag from its hook, Keady rushed for the bathroom, clutching between his cheeks the entire way. Cutler chuckled to himself as Keady slammed the door, cutting off the sounds from the other room. That wasn't his kind of torture, anyway.

Keady looked even more flushed when he returned a few moments later, his hair in disarray and his chest completely red. There was a fire behind his eyes that seemed to have burned his shyness to ash and dust. "It still hurts, you sadistic bastard."

"Good." Cutler raised an eyebrow. *Like it wasn't supposed to?* Subs were so innocent sometimes.

Without being asked, Keady took his place in front of the mirror again, his gaze going straight to Cutler's. Pain and humiliation were doing wonders for his boy. It was like a whole new man in front of him — a man who he'd only caught a glimpse of through an enveloping shroud. "I like the new title by the way. It's very suitable."

He'd been called worse than a sadistic bastard in the OR. Hell, he'd been called worse in kink clubs before. "I would even be fine with 'SB' for short. It almost has a ring to it."

Keady glared at him through the reflection, his eyes narrowed as he gritted his teeth.

"Now, are you going to put up another fight about instructions, or do we have to clean the front as well?" Cutler opened his legs wide to give his cock space. He should have forgone his boxers as well. The usually comfortable material was restricting as hell at the moment.

"The front? Oh hell no." Keady turned, grabbing for the head of his cock as he shook his head. "I don't want to get a bladder infection because you want to sound me with ginger-laced lube."

Cutler frowned, dragging himself from the mattress. Perhaps he shouldn't have sat down at all if Keady thought he could take control or be a brat.

Keady shrank back, his shoulder touching the cool mirror as he paled. There was that fear that they both longed for, and the completeness settled something between them immediately.

Wrapping a hand around Keady's collar, Cutler tugged until Keady was facing the mirror again, landing two sharp slaps on his ass as he settled. His hand tingled, his palm unused to the assault. His hands were strong, but he didn't have a callus to his name.

"I'm a doctor. Placing a sterile catheter is child's play." He grabbed Keady's cock, strangling it in a tight grip. Keady whimpered, his eyes wide. "It would be fun to watch you try to hold it in, clutching yourself because you couldn't make it to the potty on time. That would *really* make you dance."

He moved his hand to Keady's balls, kneading them one by one. "But I'll let it slide this time. I think I'd rather take you to dinner first."

That seemed to give Keady pause. "I thought we were staying here?"

Cutler tapped him on the forehead. "And that's why you leave the thinking up to me." Letting Keady's balls go after one final squeeze, Cutler plucked at a nipple instead. Ever since he'd mentioned getting Keady pierced, he hadn't stopped imagining silver barbells through his delicate nubs.

"I have to get you all dressed up first," said Cutler, digging his nails in just for a moment. "I have a reservation at a four-diamond place. Their reputation is second to none, so I wouldn't want to get turned away for not meeting their dress code." He gave Keady's nipples one final tug before he released them. They were flushed, hard, practically begging to be kissed.

"Get on the bed with your ass in the air."

Cutler headed for the closet where he'd stashed the toys he'd picked up for their weekend together. He'd picked out every one with Keady in mind, so many possibilities blooming within one adult store.

When he turned around, he found Keady on his hands and knees on the bed, his ass in the air and his legs spread. His ass cheeks were parted from the position, showing off his hole that looked a touch pinker than normal. It was probably still burning from the ginger.

"Another position that you seem to be a pro at," said Cutler, adjusting the plug in his grip. It wasn't overly large, but it had a few surprises to it. The first was the wicked curve that would line up directly with Keady's prostate.

"Any lube left from before?" Cutler mused as he approached before lining up two fingers and pushing them into Keady's hole. Fuck, he was tight, and warm, clutching at Cutler as if his life depended on it. Keady let out a cute yelp, arching away.

"Not enough for what I want," said Cutler, twisting his fingers. The tiny bit of lube was long gone.

Cutler grabbed the bottle from beside the mattress, lubing up the plug just enough so he could get it inside, but hopefully not enough that it would slip out unexpectedly. Pressing it to Keady's hole, he slowly eased it in, rocking until Keady's hole spread wide.

He held it at the widest point, teasing Keady's rim until his sub whimpered. Giving it a final thrust, he let Keady's body suck it deeper, his rim clamping over the narrow neck just above the flared base.

Keady groaned, fisting his hands in the bed as a drop of pre-cum leaked from his cock.

"Looks like that's all lined up there. Now to keep it inside." Cutler pulled the specialized tube from his pocket for the toy—the very reason he'd spent a ridiculous amount on it. It attached to a spot at the base of the plug, allowing him to pump air into the flexible body of the plug. It was detachable for when he was done, and he could always reattach it if he needed to put in that little bit of *extra*. The neck remained narrow and sleek, barely any consequence at all in his opinion.

He pumped the bulb once, pausing as Keady let out a questioning noise. He didn't move, though, except to twitch his hips as Cutler pumped the plug larger.

"There. Now you have a knot keeping it in there. It goes with the collar." Cutler detached the pump, making sure everything was secure. With the twist of a valve, he could release the air, but he wouldn't be doing that for quite some time. "Comfortable?"

"Not really," said Keady, turning his head to the side and placing his cheek on the mattress. His eyes were heavy and half-lidded, his pupils blown wide. "Feels fucking huge, SB."

"Don't be so dramatic." Cutler patted Keady's hip. There was plenty of room to grow. He hadn't even purchased the largest model. "Now for your harness. You'll like this one, my little animal."

Cutler dug the modified harness out of the closet. It was almost like a pair of underwear, only made of intricate leather straps instead of cotton. One strap went directly between Keady's cheeks, holding the plug in by the base. At the front, it cradled his cock and balls, with a few spots for Cutler to clip on an attachment if he wanted to. It made Keady's cock jut straight out as Cutler tugged him to his feet.

"Excellent. Now, to take care of these little distractions." Cutler pinched Keady's nipples before pulling out a set of clamps. He had been looking forward to this part the most.

The clamps weren't nearly as harsh as the ones he'd used at the club, but they had some bite to them. They were also more discreet and almost unnoticeable under a loose shirt. *Almost.*

"Perfect." Oh, the sounds Keady was making, his eyes wet as stimulation of every kind appeared to overwhelm him. "I hope you don't think that I'm done." Cutler circled Keady's cock with his fingers, jerking him a few times. Keady went rigid, a moan pushing through his lips.

"I want to make sure that you enjoy yourself tonight. I know fancy dinners can be so boring sometimes, so this should keep you occupied." Cutler pulled a silicone cock ring from his pocket. It had two loops, one for Keady's cock and another that stretched over his balls and gripped them tight. Settled between the two was a textured vibrator, the remote resting in Cutler's pocket.

All wrapped up nice and neat.

"I ordered some clothes for you. I hope you don't mind." Cutler moved to the closet again, plucking a shirt and a pair of pants from their hangers. He'd guessed Keady's size, but it looked like he had gotten pretty close. "Put these on."

The shirt was pink and *thin*, the metal nipple clips just visible through the material. Cutler was confident that no one would be looking close enough at his chest to notice, not when Keady's loose pants gave so much away. His arousal would be clear to anyone who glanced his way, and they would probably be a little envious, too.

The pants were perhaps an inch too short, but maybe that was because all the slack at the crotch was being used up by Keady's cock.

Yeah, no one would be looking at Keady's top.

Chapter Twelve

Keady

Cutler was a motherfucking sadistic bastard. 'SB' wasn't nearly long enough to express every emotion he wanted to hurl at Cutler like a sharp blade. By the end of the weekend, he was going to have a dozen acronyms, and none of them would be close to describing the intimate agony that was engulfing every inch of him.

At least my ass doesn't burn anymore. That had been a surprise, for sure. He'd tried figging before and had loved the burn that had tingled and spread as he had squirmed, but ginger *oil* had been a whole different animal.

"Anything to drink, Keady?" asked Cutler, turning the page of his menu. He looked entirely too comfortable in his dress shirt and slacks, sipping at a glass of ice water that the waiter had rushed to their table moments after they'd been seated.

He kept his automatic reply to himself, casting his gaze at the couples around them instead. 'Shove the drink up your ass' probably wouldn't go over well. Cutler was *cruel*. He had to know Keady hated public places. Unkinked was different — it was kinky — but a restaurant?

It wasn't so bad now that Keady's cock was discreetly hidden beneath the tablecloth, but that hadn't been the case when they'd arrived.

Keady hadn't managed to convince his ringed cock to go down by the time Cutler led him through the entrance, announcing their arrival by clearing his throat loud enough to draw everyone's attention. *"Sorry... I had a tickle in my throat"* had been the piss-poor excuse.

There had been four people waiting at the front desk, not including the maître d', who had given Keady a look that spoke volumes. Keady had almost died. Every person had reacted the same way. Their gaze had settled on his chest for a brief second, only to zoom to his groin, their eyes going wide at what they found.

They all knew he was a solid seven inches, and from the way he walked, they could probably tell there was a plug up his ass, too — unless they had thought that he'd just been fucked in the car and Cutler was packing a sledgehammer in his pants. But no one could see that one. Cutler wasn't even fucking *hard*.

The plug. Keady gripped the edge of the table as the feeling of fullness descended over him again. It came and went like the flush that settled over his face, only to flicker away when he got distracted. It was stretching him in beautiful and wonderful ways and dragging over his prostate every time he shifted in his chair.

Which was why he was holding himself uncomfortably still. The spot of pre-cum on his pants had started to dry, but a few nudges and it would be wet again.

At least he wouldn't come. His SB Dom had seen to that.

"Water is fine," Keady replied, gritting his teeth as Cutler's eyes practically sparkled. Fancy restaurants were the worst, because they were so quiet, even when they were full. Everyone would hear him if he let a moan slip. A packed bar would have been preferred.

"Doctor, it's good to see you again, sir," said the waitress as she approached their table. "And it's good to see you with someone. It's been a while."

That improved his mood in an instant. Keady snickered when he caught Cutler's scowl, instantly regretting it when it somehow made the plug shift inside him. He had to take the bait, though. "Years, probably."

Cutler shot him a look but Keady only grinned. *Fuck it.* If Cutler wanted to humiliate the hell out of him, then he wasn't going down alone. This was a two-man plane, and they were both crashing.

"Do I need to remind you what happens to boys who don't behave?" asked Cutler, his voice deep enough to cut straight through Keady. His humor drained away as the waitress laughed, raising one eyebrow.

Oh hell no. She had to be in on it. Was she a Domme? Keady didn't recognize her, but there were a few communities in the city, and he only ever stuck with one.

"I think I forgot." Keady slapped the smile right back on his face. They weren't in a private house. Cutler wouldn't do anything here. *And I'll be happy to collect payment later.*

"You'll have to remind me— *Fuck*." Keady nearly jumped out of his seat as the plug in his ass buzzed to life. He yelped, leaning forward to try to pull away from the sensation that battered his prostate and pushed him right next to the edge. The harness kept it buried deep despite his efforts, nudging it harder against his prostate as he shifted.

Slapping the table, Keady dropped his head next to the fabric napkin. "Motherfucker."

He was going to come. The cock ring had no chance of stopping this one. He fisted the tablecloth, a tremble shooting through his limbs.

Seconds from the edge, the vibration cut off. Keady collapsed, his muscles going lax as he trembled. He hadn't come, but his pants were wet again, the sticky pre-cum clinging to the fabric and making everything uncomfortably tacky. He heaved air into his lungs, shutting his legs tight as his cock throbbed. *So close.* All he needed was a little nudge.

"Let's make that medium-well. And a whiskey for me. My boy can have a glass of milk." Cutler finished their order, the scratch of the pen loud as the waitress presumably wrote it all down. Keady had missed the entire order except for the goddamn milk.

"Wine would be better," said Keady, huffing against the tablecloth. He waited an extra moment before he tried to sit up, going slow to avoid any other surprises.

Cutler leveled him with an even look. "If you insist on acting like a boy, then I'll treat you like one. Milk for now. We'll see if he earns a ginger ale."

Fuck, I hate ginger ale. But it would be better for him than the milk.

"Very good, sir." The waitress scribbled out another note. "And if I can say so, sir? I like this one." She sent Keady a wink before she turned away.

"You are the worst," said Keady, wiping the sweat from his forehead. His shirt was sticking to him in the worst ways, and he was in desperate need of something strong to drink. He was going to need a shower soon if Cutler kept this up.

But now that the threat of his orgasm had passed, the throb in his nipples came ever clearer. Cutler had given them a 'break' on the way in the car, which was another way of saying a moment of agony followed by thirty minutes of throbbing before Cutler had put them back on. Keady had sobbed when the clamps had bit into him a second time.

"I am," said Cutler, his typical grimace in place. It was a mystery how he could look so goddamn good and moody at the same time.

Well, I'm happy that you're happy.

"I wondered if you knew about this place," said Cutler, picking up one fork to inspect it. It was probably worth more than Keady's entire set at home. "I came here for munches in one of my previous kink communities. One of the Dommes in the area runs it, and she is very open to play in her dining room."

That sounded wrong in so many ways. Was that a health code violation? Or was it okay to fuck someone with a banana while you ordered the soup du jour?

"How many communities have you been a part of?" asked Keady, his curiosity overwhelming sensation. He really didn't know much about Cutler, other than his sadistic tendencies and that he was a neurosurgeon.

Cutler rubbed the scar over his lip, letting out a hum as the waitress returned with their drinks. He waited for her to leave again before he answered. "I became involved in kink during university. A boyfriend asked me to tie him up, and it wasn't long after that I went to my first munch. Unkinked will be my fourth community...and is my favorite so far."

Keady grinned, pushing the milk carefully to the side before reaching for his water. *Bleh.* It must've been tap water because it tasted as if it had been rolling around in the city too long. "Clint does have a lot of toys. There isn't a kink club around that has better equipment."

"I prefer the view," said Cutler, giving Keady a slow look. He seemed to see straight through Keady's clothing to the nipple clamps under his top. They were more apparent with Keady's shirt sticking to his skin. "Did you need another break from the clamps? You can take one now until our food arrives."

That sounded both glorious and terrible. When they came off, Keady was going to scream. And the thought of putting them back on again made him want to shudder and cry. But leaving them on would be so much worse if he put it off any longer.

"I'll take them off in the bathroom," said Keady, slowly moving to push his chair back. He looked down at the tent in his pants, remembering the very reason why he didn't want to walk past all those tables again.

Just because the owner was kinky didn't mean the patrons were. He'd already had enough embarrassed and concerned looks for one day, thank you very much.

"You can take them off here or not at all." Cutler calmly took a sip of his whiskey.

There were so many names Keady had for his Dom right now and none of them were restaurant appropriate. He leveled him with a glare, pouring every bit of his grumpiness into that look. Cutler couldn't punish him for glaring, right?

"Come on, Keady. There's no reason to be shy. No one is watching us now, and the waitress just slipped back into the kitchen to grab some plates. I'd say you have a thirty-second window to get those clamps off."

Keady checked for himself, eyeing up the closest table, which had just emptied. Everyone else seemed to be engrossed in their meals and conversation, and there were no waitstaff on the floor. *He's not a liar, but he's still a sadist.*

"Yes, Sir."

Keady slid one hand under his shirt, his stomach warm and sticky with sweat. When he touched the clamp, he couldn't hold back his whimper. They hurt so much, especially when he was focused on them. Cutler was insane if he thought Keady could stay quiet. He was going to get them kicked out.

He pinched the end of the clamp, the instant relief overshadowed by the wall of absolute agony. The clamp dropped from his fingertips, and he tore the second one free before biting into his arm to muffle his scream.

Fuck. Fuck. Fuck. His nipples had never hurt so bad. The ache washed over him, going straight to his gut and throbbing through his cock. He was on the edge in seconds, the cock ring the only thing holding him back. *I'm gonna come.* He hadn't realized how much of a true pain slut he was.

"You really are beautiful, Keady," said Cutler, reaching across the table and taking Keady's hand. His grimace had disappeared, replaced with a look that was almost serene. "You suffer so well for me."

It wasn't so bad when Cutler was looking at him like that—something soft that Keady wasn't sure belonged. Keady dragged his gaze away, despite the butterflies in his stomach.

"Here we are, gentlemen," said the waitress as she approached, seeming to ignore Keady's distracted state. "Atlantic salmon with mushroom risotto and the tenderloin special."

Keady swallowed as she placed the steak in front of him. The smell was overwhelming—and not in a good way. He'd gotten sick from beef so many times that it was almost an ingrained response in his brain. He tried to avoid steakhouses and grills at all costs because of it. Even backyard barbecues were strictly out, not that he was invited all that often.

"Everything okay?" Cutler asked as he reached for his fork and knife. There was a furrow between his brows that Keady just wanted to smooth away. Everything had been going so well.

"I'm sorry, Sir. I can't eat this."

Cutler's concern morphed into confusion, then realization. "I'm sorry, Keady. I hadn't considered that you were a vegetarian. I should have asked."

Keady's relief was almost palpable and eased the extra sting of his throbbing nipples. "I have Alpha-gal Syndrome, have since I was a kid and got one too many tick bites, I guess." Keady shrugged.

If anything, Cutler seemed more alarmed now. "The milk?"

Keady was lucky in that respect, but he wasn't a big fan of the taste of milk or the film it left on his tongue. While every type of mammal meat under the sun was out, he *could* still have milk and Jell-O. It was nice to be understood, though.

It was crazy how many people reacted badly when he told them he didn't eat meat. Some wanted to argue with him, while others went on rants about humane treatment of animals. Few considered that it wasn't a choice on his part, but an actual allergy caused by a tick bite during his younger years.

"It's fine." Keady flushed, ducking his head. "No Jell-O or milk, though. That's just because I hate them." He shuddered. It was a texture thing.

"Here then. You must be starving." Cutler stood, swapping their plates. Keady blinked at the salmon before him, his mouth watering. Now *that* was an animal he could eat in spades.

"But, Cutler, this is your plate." Keady shook his head, ready to give the salmon back. He couldn't just eat his Dom's food. The tiny smidge of service sub in his blood wouldn't allow it.

"Are you questioning me?"

"No, Sir." *That settles that.* Keady grabbed his fork, stabbing a piece of salmon and shoving it into his mouth. The flavors burst over his tongue, his stomach grumbling in response. He must've moaned out loud, because Cutler's eyes were dark when Keady finally swallowed the bite.

"Any other allergies?" asked Cutler, slicing his steak and slipping a piece into his mouth. He was too good with that knife. Instead of being the bad kind of scary, his cock pulsed harder. He'd never been so turned on in his life, especially not in public.

"Nope." Keady shoveled a second forkful in. God, he was starving. He hadn't been able to eat well all day, too nervous about his scene. "I should tell you that I get migraines with loud noises, so maybe keep shouting to a minimum."

Cutler raised one brow. "I don't *need* to shout. I speak and people listen."

Keady snorted, choking as he inhaled another piece of his fish. He pounded his chest, yelping as he struck one of his nipples. Sipping his water, he sent Cutler a grin. "Sure."

"Time to put those clamps back on, boy. I gave you a reprieve."

Oh shit.

Chapter Thirteen

Keady

His opinion on Cutler was changing so rapidly he couldn't keep up. On one hand, he was almost sweet? But in an evil asshole kind of way. He was smoking hot, too, and only seemed to get more attractive the longer Keady looked.

He'd pay Keady a compliment, only to turn it around a moment later and make him flush, slapping Keady with a side of humiliation that got better each time. He couldn't remember the last time he'd been so comfortable with so many strangers, even in Unkinked, where everyone had a sort of mutual understanding.

"You're very cute when you blush," Cutler would say, leaning over the table to cup Keady's chin. "Your face will look even better when I paint you with my cum." Keady had nearly choked on his own spit at that one, the image sticking in his mind until it was all he could see.

He seemed to love Keady's tears, too. He'd started sobbing halfway through dinner, unable to take the pressure of the nipple clamps any longer, even with some of the best food of his life before him. Tears had rolled down his cheeks as his forkful of risotto had hovered inches from his mouth. If he'd opened his lips to let it in, he would have screamed.

Cutler had merely given him a careful look before the plug in his ass had thrummed to life. The pleasure was enough to turn the ache into something so much better, making his cock weep as they both continued to eat. Cutler finished every bite, even when Keady faltered a second time, his anticipation too much to fit another morsel.

Keady's plate had been left half-full, but they'd packed it up in a small takeaway container for him as his sobs started again, despite the vibrator. Keady clutched the package tight as they'd walked to the car slowly, people's faces blurred by his tears. He couldn't bring himself to care what they were thinking.

Cutler's arm was looped in his, guiding him along to the car as every part of him throbbed and pulsed. He needed to come so bad, but being on the edge was the only thing that was keeping the pain from ripping him apart. Cutler seemed in no rush, and only tugged him to a stop once when a car had pulled into the parking lot across their path.

"Cutler, please. I-I can't do anymore." Keady trembled, nearly dropping his food. Sweat poured down his back, soaking into his shirt until it stuck to him like a film. He could barely see where they were, and it was so dark that it must've been close to midnight. It was the time when his mind was usually at its best, but he could barely think.

"Two more steps, Keady, then I'll give you some relief." Cutler leaned in, placing a kiss on Keady's cheek. It wasn't nearly enough.

Keady let out a groan of loss, grabbing the closest thing he could reach and tugging Cutler to him. Their lips touched, a fire like no other engulfing him. His takeout fell to the ground, completely forgotten and unimportant next to his Dom. Cutler was soft and addictive, even if he barely moved to meet Keady's kiss.

Cutler jerked back, shaking his head despite his look of desire. "Nuh-uh, boy. I don't want any kissing until I've brushed and gargled. I won't have you getting sick because I ate steak."

What a terrible, considerate bastard. Keady wasn't sure if he was in love or just in subspace. In his haze, he dropped his gaze to his leftovers. The container had upended and the lid had popped off, spewing the salmon and remaining risotto over the tarmac. *What a waste.*

"Leave it." Cutler popped the locks on his Lexus, suddenly moving fast. "*Now.*"

He helped Keady into his seat, seemingly ignorant to his whimpers and moans as everything shifted inside him. The plug felt bigger somehow, and he tingled as if the ginger oil was still fresh.

He was going to break. He was absolutely sure of it.

Slipping around the front of the car, Cutler lowered himself into his seat, instantly reaching for Keady's shirt and tugging the front open. One button survived, but the rest were torn free, pinging about the car before falling into nooks and crannies, likely never to be seen again. His shirt tangled about his arms as Keady flailed, just as desperate as Cutler.

"Take it off."

Keady shrugged the shirt from his shoulders, leaning forward to keep his sweaty back from sticking to the leather seats. The toy shifted inside him, dragging over his prostate and making him leak.

"Deep breath, boy."

Cutler pinched the clamps, releasing both at the same time. Blood rushed to the area and Keady let out a shriek, grabbing for his chest as he bent double. His prostate was pounded by the toy, the vibrations jacking higher as Cutler reached into his pocket.

"Take your pants off," said Cutler as soon as Keady could breathe again.

The words sounded like they were coming through a fog, the throbbing of Keady's chest and cock the only thing that mattered. He was so close, but the cock ring held him tight, refusing to let him release. He was sure he'd come with a cock ring on before, but this was so different.

"Your pants, boy."

Sobbing, Keady reached for the button on his slacks, shifting in his seat and arching so he could slide them past his ass and toss them to the floor. The harness haloed his cock with black straps that were dark with sweat, the head of his shaft purple and dripping. His balls had pulled up, fighting against the grip of the silicone rings.

"What's your color?" asked Cutler as he started the car with the push of a button before pulling toward the exit. Keady shuddered in his seat, cupping his pecs and trying to soothe his nipples. His *bruises* had bruises, and he wasn't sure if they'd ever stop throbbing.

"I'm at yellow for my nipples, and my ass is getting close, Sir." The vibrations seemed to intensify, even though Cutler hadn't touched the remote. "The plug, it's so big, and I need to come so bad. Please let me come."

"Soon." Cutler hummed, keeping his eyes on the road as he moved his hand, taking them somewhere that Keady couldn't see. "If you reach under yourself to the base of the plug, you'll find a valve. Twist it counter clockwise and the air will release. Seat belt first, though."

Keady snapped his seat belt into place, before he propped his legs up on the seat, spreading himself as wide as he could in the space. It wasn't too hard to reach between his cheeks and find the little nub tucked just next to the strap that was holding the plug in place. With a hiss of air, relief washed over him at the same time a terrible emptiness filled him. He wasn't sure which was worse.

"Good boy. You *can* listen. Let me know if the vibrations become too much. I plan on fucking you more than once tonight, so I don't want you too sore."

Well, how considerate of him. Keady struggled not to roll his eyes as he panted against the seat. He was well and truly stuck to the leather but couldn't bring himself to close his legs and lean away.

He was already way past sore, but he had to admit that the vibrations made the rest of his body feel so much better, especially his nipples. He touched one, reveling in the sharp ache.

"In the glove box you'll find some cream that will numb your nipples." Cutler reached over the center console, popping the drawer open. "It will only last about an hour, but I think you'll be too distracted after that point to really care."

Too distracted? Things couldn't get more intense than the last few hours—or maybe Cutler *was* just getting started. His body throbbed at the thought as he looked from Cutler to the small purple tube tucked next to the owner's manual.

"Or not." Cutler snapped the door shut again, a grimace on his lips. "I love this part of you, Keady." He stroked Keady's cock twice before he pulled his hand away. "You're so desperate to find out 'what if' that you don't even worry about being shy. That's what I want for you."

Swallowing, he couldn't quite get past the lump in his throat. No one had ever said that they loved *any* part of him. His stomach flipped, and he gripped the leather seat tighter. The car was dark except for the displays on the dash, but Cutler's gaze didn't seem to miss a thing.

"Now I feel bad for not getting you dessert at the restaurant, since you are being so beautiful for me. I'll give you a different treat instead. Wrap those pretty lips around my cock and keep me warm and hard all the way home. The second we get in the door, I want to be ready to take you."

* * * *

Cutler

Shit. Keady's mouth was like a dream—a very good dream that was just barely in his control and stepping on the edges of reality.

Cutler struggled to keep his hands on the wheel and his eyes on the road as wet heat engulfed him. Maybe he'd overestimated himself and underestimated

Keady. No one could have control with a mouth like that on them.

Slowing to the speed limit, he turned off the highway, taking the back route instead. Others wouldn't care if he was driving slow there, unlike the two people who had flashed their lights when he'd gotten too distracted to keep up with traffic. The only ones to complain about the slow pace on the back road were his balls.

Two minutes in and he already felt like he was going to explode. He'd managed to keep calm and cool throughout an epic dinner, even when Keady had been reduced to a perfect sobbing mess. *My mess.*

"Don't suck. Just hold it in your throat and choke on it. Keep me wet." Cutler dropped one hand from the steering wheel, squeezing the back of Keady's neck when he didn't listen right away. They were both pretty far gone.

His movements immediately softened, drool dripping to Cutler's balls as Keady lowered himself, gagging as the car rocked over a bump in the road. "Just the head now, baby."

He tugged Keady higher, until he was mouthing at the tip. If the little brat thought he could make Cutler come that easily and get off the hook, then he had another thing coming.

"Are you going to behave or do the clamps need to go back on?"

Keady shuddered, his mouth instantly going slack. Resting his head on Cutler's thigh, he turned, fitting about half of Cutler's cock into his mouth with the new position.

"Much better." Cutler reached between Keady's ass cheeks, keeping his gaze resolutely on the road as he toyed with the base of the plug. The vibrations still felt fairly mild against his fingertip, although he was sure it was a whole different story with the toy jabbing directly into Keady's prostate from the inside.

"Comfortable?"

Keady nodded, adjusting the seat belt which he'd moved from his shoulder so he could lean into Cutler's lap. It was just another reason to drive slow.

The drive seemed to last closer to an hour than the thirty-eight minutes that passed on the clock, the road dragging by in a sea of darkness that was probably ripe with wildlife. Every time Keady tried to close his lips and swallow, Cutler pinched his cheek, reminding him exactly what his purpose was.

"Keep me wet."

He was soaked, the seat and his balls coated by the time he pulled into his driveway and hit the button for the garage. He parked in record time, slamming his brake on at the last minute when Keady gave him an unexpected suck as he presumably tried to resist swallowing.

Closing his eyes, Cutler leaned into his seat, letting himself feel for just a moment. Keady's ass was slick with sweat under his free hand, like every other part of him, but his skin was so damn soft at the same time...and firm. Cutler gave one ass cheek a squeeze, relishing in the tautness.

Keady hummed in response, and the vibration went straight to Cutler's balls. He'd never been so frustrated in his life, and he had the patience for hours of intensive surgery. He was supposed to be edging Keady, not himself, but the tables had turned.

"We're home, Keady," said Cutler, forcing his stubborn eyes open. Keady only whimpered, trying to suck him deeper. *So fucking good.* "Be good. Let go now, and I'll fuck you... Remember?"

He still had to brush and floss his teeth and gargle like crazy. There was no way he was putting Keady at risk because he had a bit of something stuck between his teeth. And there was no way that he wasn't kissing his sub.

Keady leaned back, and Cutler nearly lost his breath at the sight. His face was streaked with tears and drool, his eyes bloodshot and distant. He must've been floating almost all the way home to look so fucking good.

Cutler almost cursed himself for missing that moment when Keady finally dropped into subspace. He'd been hovering near the edge in the restaurant as far as he could tell, but he wasn't sure if his sub would go there with him watching—too worried about everyone except himself.

"What's your color, Keady?" Cutler threaded every bit of sternness he possessed into his question. He needed to be sure that Keady could still answer him.

"Green, Sir. Can you fuck me now?" He blinked slowly, the sloppy smile on his face loose and light. He was so fucking stunning.

"Of course, baby." He cupped Keady's cheek. "Go to my bedroom and lie in the middle of the mattress. I'll meet you there in just a few minutes."

"Okay. I'll be good, Sir." Keady nodded before reaching for Cutler's hand and squeezing once. "I promise."

Something fluttered in his gut at those soft words, his chest aching as Keady stepped from the car without wiping the drool from his chin. Cutler remained in the car long after Keady had disappeared through the garage door and into the house. *Fuck,* that boy was going to be the death of him.

Chapter Fourteen

Cutler

He gargled twice, brushing so hard that he may have shredded one spot on his gums. The mouthwash stung as he gave it another swig and spat it into the sink. His cock hadn't softened in the least, but Keady's spit had dried to a sticky film. He ran a cloth over himself, cleaning every inch and wiping away any sweat that had gathered.

Keady was waiting in the middle of the bed when he stepped into the room, his ass in the air and the harness pulled tight over the plug in his ass. His cock hung between his legs, purple and hard. Cutler tapped the remote, watching as Keady flinched and let out a long moan before fisting the sheets.

"Such a slut for it," said Cutler, kneeling on the bed and grabbing for the harness. The straps were made of thin, supple leather, and strong enough that he could tug Keady off balance until he flopped to the side. He was completely pliant as he floated, his gaze distant. Cutler wanted to keep him that way all fucking night.

"I think I could have your ass any time I wanted. You're practically trying to give it away, waving it around like that. This, though..." He touched Keady's cock, slowly pulling the silicone rings free. It was the best thirty bucks he'd ever spent. "You keep trying to hide this pretty cock from me."

Keady rolled the rest of the way over until he was on his back, his legs falling wide. Cutler didn't hesitate to lean in, swiping the head of Keady's cock with his tongue.

"I'm going to come," said Keady, arching off the bed at the first touch. He was overwhelmingly salty with sweat and dried pre-cum, but he was still one of the best things Cutler had ever tasted.

Cutler released him, watching as his cock bobbed and twitched at the loss, his swollen balls tight to his body. "Not until I'm inside you, Keady."

Keady furrowed his forehead, so innocent in his confusion. "Then what the fuck are you waiting for? I've been ready for like three hours. *Please.*"

Christ, he loved this Keady. He'd meant what he said in the restaurant. His shyness had shattered, leaving the opinionated brat open and exposed — a brat that Cutler could tease all he wanted — a brat that was all his. He doubted anyone had ever seen him like this, even Malone, who had been with Keady for nearly a year.

"If you had been ready, you would have bent over the table in the restaurant with your pants around your ankles." Cutler reached for the buckle on the harness, releasing in with a tug. The collar was staying on, though. "I don't think the owner would have minded.

The tips might have gone up, too, so the staff would have appreciated it. Or maybe someone would have slid a bill right under this collar and waited for their turn."

"Oh. Fuck. *Fuck.*" Keady grabbed at Cutler, his nails clawing deep. "I'm coming."

Cutler grabbed Keady's leg, holding him wide so he could watch as cum pulsed from his cock in thick ropes, painting Keady's chest and belly. His balls twitched with every wave of release as Keady's eyes rolled back and his mouth dropped wide. As he wound down, every muscle went slack, his eyelids drifting shut until only slits remained.

Is he even conscious?

Cuter pulled the harness the rest of the wall off, easing the plug from Keady's hole as he soothed up his inner thigh with one hand. His rim was shiny and red, with hardly any lube left over at all. It must've rubbed a bit from all their movement, chafing him from the inside out. He'd be oversensitive for days, maybe longer because of the pre-treatment of ginger oil.

Grabbing a condom and lube, Cutler covered and slicked his cock, shoving two fingers into Keady to spread the lube around. There was no need to stretch him.

He pressed himself between Keady's legs, hovering chest to chest as he lined himself up. Keady hardly stirred from his state, too fucked out and pliant. It was exactly what Cutler had hoped for.

"What's your color, Keady? I need you to answer."

Keady blinked slowly as he licked his lips before swallowing dryly. He'd left one of the bedside lamps on, and his sweaty skin glistened in the artificial light, mesmerizing in its perfection. "Please fuck me, Sir. Green."

It was barely above a whisper, but it was enough.

Cutler guided himself inside, cupping the back of Keady's head and bringing their lips together as he settled deep. With the stretch from the plug, Keady was soft and smooth around him and hotter than anything he'd ever felt. It was nothing to the sweetness of his lips, the touch of his tongue like a static shock.

He didn't give Keady a moment to adjust, diving into his mouth as he pulled back until he rocked his hips to bury himself again. He didn't have time to linger, with his own cock so hard that he was ready to burst.

The faint taste of dinner rolled over his tongue as Keady slowly responded, digging his hands into Cutler's hair and holding on as he picked up the pace. Cutler felt him flex, his hole snapping tighter as he clenched his abdomen.

Usually he disliked kissing people, avoiding it as much as he could. With such close proximity, melding two people as one, his flaws were so much more apparent. He could only truly kiss with his tongue and one side of his lips, and he'd been told before that his technique was off-putting and unbalanced.

Keady didn't seem to care, dragging Cutler closer and arching, even as he whimpered. He writhed with every thrust, his voice gaining pitch until he was yelping as Cutler slammed his prostate. Wrapping his legs around him, Keady brought him closer and deeper, and Cutler took every inch.

So fucking close. Cutler dropped his mouth to Keady's throat, biting the pale column above the collar that tasted of sweat and sex. His cock throbbed, his groin going tight as he reached his limit. He needed Keady to again come first, even if it killed him.

Moving fast, Cutler dropped one hand between them, jerking Keady's cock wildly, and matching his hips with every thrust. With the other, he reached for one swollen and bruised nipple, pinching *hard*.

Keady screamed as he clamped down and milked Cutler's cock for all it was worth and Cutler's ears rang from the sheer pitch of the sound. Fresh cum joined the drying film on his hand as Keady peaked for a second time, looking as if he were giving everything he had left.

He couldn't have held back if he wanted to. With one last thrust, Cutler emptied himself into the condom, his arms trembling as he tried to hold himself over Keady's nearly comatose form. He sucked a breath in through his nose, placing one last sharp bite over Keady's collar before he slowly eased back.

Keady was lost, his expression so far gone that he looked to be on another planet. His poor nipples looked almost purple, his cock finally returning to normal as he breathed slow and deep.

Grabbing a warm cloth from the bathroom, Cutler cleaned every bit he could reach, swiping the come from Keady's belly before gently cupping his cock and balls. He pulled back Keady's foreskin, making sure he was fully washed there before he scrubbed the lube gently from his ass. He was open and wet and so fucking warm, but not too red that Cutler wouldn't be able to go again.

Once he'd gotten his breath back, though.

Giving himself a cursory scrub, he trotted to the kitchen, grabbing a water bottle and Gatorade from the fridge and plucking a metal straw from one of the drawers. Keady hadn't moved an inch by the time he returned, the smile on his lips the only thing that told Cutler that he wasn't asleep.

"Drink this, baby," said Cutler, holding the straw to Keady's lips. Keady sucked back the blue Gatorade as if he'd been lost in the desert for days, downing half the bottle before Cutler eased it away.

He took a few swigs from the water himself before he slid next to Keady in bed, pulling the top sheet over them. Keady was like a furnace against him, but he had finally stopped sweating. A shower would do them both good, but he had a feeling they weren't moving any time soon.

"Do I have to sleep in the cage?" Keady asked after a long stretch of silence interrupted only by their breaths and a few murmurs. He'd turned into Cutler, his head resting against Cutler's pec.

Cutler chuckled, fighting his own high that was still simmering beneath his skin. He'd almost caught his breath, his desire starting to flood him. "Not tonight, Keady. Tonight, you're in this bed so I can take you anytime I want. You could be sleeping in the middle of the night when I need your ass, but I could just roll you over and wake you up with a kiss before I take you."

Keady grinned, placing a kiss to Cutler's chest. "Or you could just let me sleep. You can have me anytime, always. If it's anything like *that* just was, I'll spontaneously orgasm in my sleep. No awakeness required."

If only it were that easy. "I'd need your consent first, so you'd have to give me a green before you go back to sleep. I'll be gentle so I don't keep you up."

When was the last time he'd promised he would be gentle? Probably on that first experience when he'd tied a man to his bedframe. Gentle was sexy, but not always the most exciting.

"Good." Keady snuggled in closer, slotting his leg between Cutler's thighs. "Now can you carry me to the bathroom? Either I have to pee or my prostate exploded."

"Sure." Cutler fit an arm behind Keady's knees and another behind his head, grunting with the effort of tugging Keady on top of him, then getting to his feet.

Keady squealed, flailing his arms as he kicked out. "I was joking! I was joking! Put me down!"

Cutler chuckled, burying his face into Keady's hair as he filled his lungs. "Too late."

* * * *

Keady

He was never moving again. Someone could dangle a chocolate bar and a million dollars and the end of the bed, but he was certain he wouldn't even twitch. He wasn't even sure if he *could*. He'd never simultaneously been so uncomfortable and content, muscles aching and his mind numbingly empty.

The soft tick of a clock that didn't belong to him sounded somewhere over his head, the glow of the bedroom peeking through his eyelids. It wasn't enough to wake him.

The hand on his waist, however, *was* enough to drag him from one of the best dreams of his life. And the hard cock against his ass was another story. He'd dreamed about that thing and how much it had stretched him, even after the fucking plug.

Cutler. Keady snuggled deeper into the blankets, nudging his ass into that hard beast. Every muscle from his stomach to ass strained from the move like he'd run a marathon the day before. If sex marathons counted, then he had. Stranger than all of that, was the tightness in his chest.

He dreaded the moment that Cutler called an end to their weekend. He couldn't just go home to his empty apartment and back to work like nothing had changed, when everything had.

It had been *years* since he'd floated in the bliss of subspace, but Cutler had put him there and held him under for hours. Every time Keady had started to slip out, Cutler had pushed him right back into the veil. *Hours* of torture and bliss—enough for Keady to question his sanity. He could have called yellow or red at any moment, but it had been bliss, pure and simple.

He was waiting for the crash.

Keady twitched as Cutler passed a hand over his belly a second time before playing with his chest and tapping one nipple. Whimpering, he turned his face into the pillow, breathing in the deep scent of Cutler. He could stay in this bed for the rest of his life.

"You awake, Keady?" asked Cutler, tapping his nipple a second time when Keady didn't answer.

"No." Keady pouted into the pillow. "Don't make me wake up." He snaked his arms under his head before stretching out his toes, letting out a contented hum.

"You only have to wake up for a second. You know what I want, and I need a color first. Then you can go back to sleep, baby."

God. Those hands... They would be the death of him. Cutler had such long fingers that he could touch almost every part of Keady's chest at once. And he never stopped moving his fingers, caressing, twisting and pinching simultaneously.

"You can fuck me, Sir. I'm all green." *Now let me sleep.*

"Sweet boy." Cutler kissed his shoulder before scraping his teeth over the bony knobs there. "Go to sleep, then. If you wake up, I'll consider it a yellow and I'll stop."

He was up for that challenge. It was hard not to move with every touch lighting up his nerves and pulling him farther away from dreamland, but he was so relaxed he could ignore it. An itch on his foot prickled into awareness, and he struggled not to twitch.

Cutler touched his cock and Keady almost jerked, smothering his face with the pillow and fisting his hands. He wasn't going to make it. He couldn't pretend to sleep through it when everything about Cutler made him come alive.

"Let me tell you a bedtime story, sweetheart," said Cutler, stilling his hands for a moment and placing a kiss to the back of Keady's neck. He humped his hips, dragging his hard cock between the seam of Keady's ass.

"Once upon a time there was a little sub who learned to listen to his Sir." Cutler chuckled, beginning to roam with his hands once again, softer and slower like the sound of his voice. "He closed his eyes and went to sleep, letting his thoughts drift and his dreams take him. He slowed his breathing, only listening to the sound of his Sir's voice because he was such a good boy who would do anything to please him. His arms and legs grew heavier, and he was so comfortable and still that he never wanted to move again. He had his words and he knew he could stop his Sir at any time, but mostly he just wanted to be good."

"Keady?"

Something weird had happened as he listened to Cutler speak, each word mesmerizing him and pulling him deeper to somewhere unknown. Cutler's hands were so distant that instead of bringing him to life, they pushed him closer to sleep. He knew that Cutler had asked his name, probably looking for a color, but most of his senses were overwhelmed and dulled.

His nose was full of Cutler, though—the scent of his sweat and cum and the aftershave that he'd applied before they'd snuggled together in bed. There was the sweetness of his laundry detergent, too, and something almost floral about the room. Perhaps there had been lilies in the kitchen, because that was what it reminded Keady of—lilies sitting in the window in the spring's light.

"G-green." His voice was fucked, but he could talk, move and probably roll away, not that he wanted to.

"And Sir's little one got everything he ever wanted." Cutler turned his head and kissed Keady slow and deep, Keady's neck aching from the angle. "Now sleep."

Every muscle that had had an ounce of tension left went slack, the sudden burst of energy from waking, leaving his body on a wisping breath. His eyelids dragged down, lower and lower until he couldn't imagine staying awake any longer.

Cutler moved his hand along Keady's ass, squeezing one cheek, then the other before he dipped one finger along the seam. Finding Keady's hole with unerring accuracy, he rubbed at the furl, making it go slack under the pressure.

He was already fucked out, open and empty from earlier, but Cutler took his time, sliding one slick finger in at a time, slowly, as if to not startle Keady. He didn't seem to want to give Keady an ounce of pleasure, simply feeling instead of aiming for his prostate.

By the time the third finger slid home, Keady almost was asleep, drifting and separate, even though he could feel everything. He let out a little snore as his rim zinged once before it fizzled away to pleasure.

"You look so peaceful when you're sleeping." Cutler kissed his cheek as he pulled his fingers free. "I'll do my best not to wake you."

He must've had the condom and lube ready, because before Keady could catch up to what was going on, Cutler's cock was against his entrance, the thick head nudging him as he tried to get inside.

Normally he would've arched his back, or pushed out, anything to welcome the intrusion. He let it wash over him instead, allowing Cutler's presence to ground him and his mind to go blank.

Cutler rocked and a sharp sting crept up Keady's spine as the broad head pierced him. He didn't react, not even by sucking in a sharp breath or clutching at the sheets. He reveled in it as Cutler forced him wide.

It didn't matter if Keady was awake for it. His Dom was taking what he needed, and everything about that was perfection. He didn't need to respond or even be conscious to please him.

Slowly and steadily, Cutler moved deeper, until he was all the way in, with his hips settled against Keady's ass. He felt so much bigger from this angle, as if the plug were back and splitting him wide.

Whimpering softly, Keady waited for the fog to roll over him again and to suck the ache and fullness from his core.

"You must be having a nightmare, baby. I've got you. Don't be scared."

That was all it took for Keady to let go, plunging back into a dream that was half in his mind and half reality. In his dream, his Cutler smiled as he slowly rocked his hips, nudging no more than an inch in and out in a rhythm that made the bed creak delicately. In the dream, Cutler was *his*.

The hands on him were very real, though, clutching his hips and stroking along his back. There was no grin in the darkness, only sweet whispers of unhurried breaths as Cutler never strayed from his slow beat.

Keady moved in his mind, kissing Cutler's mouth. But he was frozen, trapped in the weight and contentment of his drifting, his muscles beyond his reach. One blink, and he could have woken, but he wanted to stay forever where Cutler was the only thing that mattered.

A soft gasp against his neck and a scrape of teeth marked Cutler's orgasm, and his hand tightened over Keady's hip for a split second. Holding himself deep, the minutes stretched, until Cutler let out a contented hum and finally withdrew.

Empty. He ached to be filled again — to be completed. The dream grasped him tight and pulled him under.

He roused slightly when a cloth wiped beneath his cheeks, streaking a path of warmth followed by soothing coolness. His legs were parted for him and a finger pieced him for a moment, only to withdraw before the cloth made another pass.

Shivering, he groaned as the sheets were pulled the rest of the way down, exposing him to the cool of the room. It felt so sweet against his overheated skin, but he couldn't stop the shudder that went through him.

He was rolled onto his back and his legs were pushed wide, the bed shifting as Cutler settled between them. Keady could feel him hovering closer and the whisper of his breath against his cheek. He wanted the kiss that the dream had given him, but he didn't want to interrupt whatever Cutler was doing.

Cutler must've been staring at him in the low light, and Keady wasn't about to stop him. If he did, he would have to face what it meant.

"Are you still asleep, baby?" Cutler asked softly, his lips ghosting over Keady's neck as he asked. One hand settled over Keady's groin where his cock had gone soft. It firmed up in a few strokes and he felt the grimace against his skin as Cutler smiled in the way only he could.

No. I'm still asleep for you.

Letting out a heavy breath, Cutler moved lower, kissing down Keady's chest and belly until he came upon Keady's cock. He licked the head, swirling his tongue before he sucked Keady to the base.

Oh fuck. Keady had never imagined Cutler giving head. He had seemed like the kind of Dom who would take more than give — and never one to be found on his knees. But there were a lot of things about Cutler that Keady hadn't expected.

Like the gentleness.

Cutler swallowed around his cock, one finger straying and slipping inside Keady's body. It wasn't nearly enough, but Cutler curled his finger, striking his prostate dead-on.

He barely managed to keep still, digging his claws back into the dream and begging it to take him. If he woke up, he would move, and he never wanted the moment to end.

"Color?" Cutler asked as he pulled back, his voice strangely unsteady.

Keady tried to move his lips, but they refused to listen. He shouted, yelling green as loud as he could, but the sound only echoed in his head and no further.

"You really are asleep." Cutler's voice was shaky as he placed a sloppy kiss against Keady's hip. "Fuck, baby. You make me so fucking hard."

For a moment, Keady lost him in the night, until warm lips were on his. Cutler bit his lower lip, plunging his tongue into Keady's mouth as he sucked in ragged breaths.

"Fuck, Keady. Tell me if you're green. Please fucking tell me. Kiss me back — something." Cutler kissed him again and Keady was almost swept away. He tossed off the fuzziness, kissing Cutler back with everything he had.

"Good. Good. *Stop*. Go back to sleep." Cutler sucked Keady's lower lip into his mouth. "Go back to sleep for me, baby."

Easy. The next kiss, Keady didn't respond, even as much as he wanted to. Cutler devoured his slack mouth, moaning as he lined his cock up with Keady's hole, pressing in dry.

There were still some remnants of slickness from before, but Cutler had wiped most of it away, his cock dragging as it speared him deep. It nailed his prostate dead-on, pulling a sleep-filled gasp from Keady's lips.

"You're so innocent like this, Keady," said Cutler, presumably only speaking to himself. "I know what you need, and you're taking it so well. You're so fucking good for me. I won't last long."

It was a good thing that he wouldn't last long because Keady was barely able to keep his struggles locked away. He was *sore* and Cutler wasn't exactly being gentle anymore, snapping his hips and folding Keady in half to drive himself in.

No one would be able to sleep through something like this unless they'd taken one hell of a sleeping pill. Keady bit his lip, fighting his instincts with everything he had because it was so fucking good to be *used*.

"Wake up, baby. Fight me." Cutler held himself all the way inside, releasing Keady's legs and grabbing at his arms instead. "Show me what you're made of."

Kicking out to the side, Keady tried to roll, his heart suddenly pounding as he came all the way awake. Cutler was so much bigger and heavier, but Keady could be a squirmy fucker if he wanted to be.

Every wiggle dragged inside him as Keady broke his arms free and tried to push Cutler off, pawing at his hips, then his chest. He bit his nails into Cutler's skin until he was sure that his Dom was bleeding.

A low chuckle sounded as Cutler leaned into him, pinning him to the bed with his weight alone. With all his flailing, Keady had never managed to get Cutler's cock from his ass, and as he bore down, it only slipped deeper.

"I want to make you come. What do you need?" asked Cutler, biting into the lobe of Keady's ear.

"Fuck." Keady tried to kick, but his heel dug into the bed, completely useless. His cock was hard, throbbing and he was so fucking close. "Just fucking tell me to come. That's all I need. Make me take your cock and call me a good boy."

Cutler chuckled, leaning away only far enough that he could grab a fistful of Keady's hair, twisting and holding him to the bed. "If you wanted me to force you, you only had to ask. Here I was asking your color the whole time, and you've been green all along. I should have known you were a slut. Good thing you're *my* slut."

"Ah, fuck." Keady tugged against the grip, just to feel a few hairs break free. Cutler picked up his pace, slamming into his prostate with every thrust. "Say it again."

Sinking his teeth into his neck, Cutler bit him hard, sucking a bruise into the delicate skin. His breathing was ragged and loud as his pace started to stutter. "You're my slut, and I'm not letting you go. You're stuck with me now, Keady."

As Cutler sank his teeth into him for the countless time that night, Keady came, shooting between them and coating their already filthy bellies with his cum. His body clamped down and everything suddenly felt too big and too rigid inside. *Fuck, it hurts.*

Cutler pushed him straight through it, until he was soaring and slipping under the veil as if he'd never left. Time slowed, and all that mattered was the sensation of Cutler coming inside him, his cum like fire over his frayed nerves. There was no condom between them, and as Cutler eased out, his cum dribbled from Keady's hole.

"You're mine, Keady." Cutler kissed him, fierce and soft at the same time. "*Mine.*"

Chapter Fifteen

Cutler

"As you wish," said Keady, mumbling along with the television. Cutler couldn't remember the last time he'd watched this movie, even though it was one of his favorites. It was unexpected, fun and beautiful, at the same time it was absolutely ridiculous.

"Do you want takeout?" asked Cutler as he scrolled through his phone. His lips were pressed into a line, and to anyone else, he probably would have appeared upset, but he hoped Keady knew better. With Keady reclined against his chest, it was impossible to be anything but content.

Work had messaged him a half-dozen times. He wasn't on call and it certainly wasn't an emergency, which he'd already replied to the head nurse with. Apparently, that wasn't a good enough response, because the messages had kept coming.

"Nah. Make me something." Keady's hands were the only part of him peeking out of the small burrow they'd created, and he hadn't stopped moving them in an hour. He'd fiddle with the edge of the blanket, only to sweep down Cutler's body a moment later.

Raising one brow, Cutler silenced his phone as it vibrated again, setting it on the side table next to him. He was hungry, seeing as it was already close to noon and they'd had nothing more than pancakes and OJ, which Keady had prepared. It was only fair that Cutler did lunch.

"If you want to avoid food poisoning, you'll let me order," said Cutler, sliding his hand down the back of Keady's neck and tucking his finger under the collar. It looked good, the strap wide but soft enough that they'd only taken it off to shower. The whole time in the shower, Keady had kept touching his neck, as if he'd wondered if Cutler would put it back on when they were done.

Cutler had dried Keady's neck first, placing the collar on before toweling the rest of him. Keady had asked for a pair of boxers, shooting Cutler a shy look that he answered with a raised brow. He was fine with blankets, but Keady wasn't wearing a thing that Cutler didn't put on him.

"The great and powerful doctor can't figure out how to make mac and cheese?" asked Keady, rolling his eyes as Cutler glared.

"Don't be such a brat. Your ass must still be sore from this morning." Cutler smoothed one hand over Keady's ass under the blankets, squeezing and pinching the red-hot surface. Keady squirmed, letting out a tiny whimper. There was more than one reason they were so hungry.

"But you like that I'm a brat," said Keady, tucking his head under his chin and placing a kiss on Cutler's scratchy neck. He didn't seem to mind the extra scruff that had grown in.

"True." Cutler hummed, landing a swat before settling back again. "I can make you something if you want, but you'll be puking later. Consider yourself warned."

It wasn't his fault. It didn't seem to matter what recipe he tried. Nothing turned out for him. Even the barbecue had let him down. Ordering was so much easier.

"I'm just surprised you want takeout. Isn't that against doctor's orders? You said I need to reduce my sodium intake and stay more hydrated." Keady's voice was all innocence, but Cutler narrowed his eyes.

He *had* said that. He'd been finger-deep in Keady's ass in the guise of checking him for damage after their rough round the night before, when Keady had started to complain he was thirsty. And later, he'd trashed the eggs Keady had made after he saw how much salt he'd poured onto them.

"I think you're confusing fast food with takeout." Cutler reached for the remote, turning the volume down as the music picked up. His surround system was a blessing and a curse.

Keady giggled, pulling the blankets tighter. He was like a furnace under them and there was sweat beaded on his forehead and his skin. *My shy boy.* There was no better time to boost Keady's confidence than the moment.

"Before I order for you, I have a question." Cutler reached for his drink, sucking back his straight coffee. He'd needed double the amount as usual after what little sleep they'd gotten.

"Okay." Keady blinked, his eyes wide and innocent. How no one had snatched him up before Cutler was a fucking mystery. The boy was a pleaser as long as he was kept in his place.

"Do you think I should allow you blankets today? After all, I want to see what's mine, not watch you hide it."

A flush rose over Keady's cheeks, and he ducked his head. "Sorry, Sir."

"No need to apologize, but don't let it happen again." Cutler's phone vibrated, and he struggled not to convey his annoyance. He was not answering. If they really needed him, they knew how to find him.

The blanket dropped away from Keady's shoulders as he sat up, pooling around his waist in a way that covered the essentials. Grabbing it in his fist, Cutler tore it the rest of the way free before tossing it behind the couch.

Now that he was seeing Keady in the light, he realized that he may have gone a bit overboard. Keady's nipples were dark and bruised and there were enough bite marks that Cutler had to focus to count them all and not lose track. The blush on his ass completed the look, and even without seeing his hole, Cutler knew it would be red and soft.

"Do you know what you do to me?" asked Cutler, grabbing Keady's hand and thrusting it against his groin. He was hard, like he always seemed to be around Keady, his cock tenting his sweats.

"You're hard," said Keady, flushing brighter and looking away. Playing with the string on Cutler's sweats, he went to dip inside, biting his lip as he grinned. Cutler stopped him with a hand on his wrist.

"No. If you can prove to me that you understand how beautiful you are, then I'll let you do something about this." He squeezed his cock once, hissing at the sensation. He'd never been so turned on after coming so frequently. "Now let me call in an order. Anything you're craving?"

Keady leveled him with a determined look, moving his hands to his thighs. "Chicken. Cooked, please."

Fucking brat. "I'm not ordering you something that you can't eat. Pick another movie, and I'll be right back."

When Cutler came back from the kitchen after ordering, he paused against the door frame, biting his lower lip as he gazed at the couch. Keady had sprawled on top of the blanket, hooking one leg over the back of the couch while resting his head on his arm. It all looked very posed and anything but innocent.

"You find something?" asked Cutler, crossing his arms as he took in the view. Keady grinned, reaching for the remote that he'd left on his belly.

"Yes, Sir." He hit the play button, his grin going wider. He must've found something good to be so fucking jolly about it. Cutler couldn't think of what it could be. He had a lot of documentaries and a few comedies. Maybe it was one of the latter?

Fondling his cock, Keady stretched against the couch, arching his back as he moved. He'd firmed up while Cutler had been in the kitchen, and apparently, he'd lost his shame in the last few minutes. The lube bottle next to the couch was new, too, and it wasn't even one of Cutler's.

Narrowing his eyes, Cutler pushed away from the wall, circling so he could see what was on the television. Keady hit something on the remote as Cutler reached him and sound blasted through his high-quality speakers, loud enough that it could probably be heard outside. With the cheesy music and breathy moans, Cutler knew what it was in a second.

Porn?

Keady chuckled, his eyes locked on Cutler as he presumably waited for some sort of reaction or outburst. Cutler did neither, sliding onto the end of the couch before bringing one of Keady's feet into his lap with the other still resting on the cushion behind Cutler's head. Palming the sole of Keady's foot, he gently dug his thumb in, caressing the tense muscle.

"Uh, fuck. Do that again." Keady's leg twitched, the muscle of his stretched inner thigh going tight. The pose was perfect, giving Cutler a view of that tight little hole that he'd spent the weekend loosening up. It was already inflamed, but Keady could probably take a bit more. He was asking for it, after all.

Digging his thumb in again, Cutler slid his other hand along Keady's thigh, pausing as he reached his balls. They were heavy and swollen from repeated abuse and edging, but they weren't bruised like his nipples were. He bypassed Keady's cock, going straight for his hole, before dipping between his cheeks and pushing one finger in dry.

"Ow." Keady scrunched his face, shooting Cutler a glare. "I brought the lube out, SB."

"I see that." Cutler pushed deeper, finding Keady's prostate and rubbing. It was a touch swollen, so he gentled his movements, circling around before tapping it. Keady jerked with every touch, his eyes fluttering shut.

"Watch your movie, Keady. I'll let you know when the food is here." Cutler settled against the couch, leaning his head back against Keady's leg. Keady was going to regret that position in a few minutes when his muscles started to strain, if they weren't already.

"You aren't watching." Keady pouted.

"I'm not a needy sub, begging to be fucked and filled, even though he already came three times today," said Cutler, slowly easing a second finger inside. He tried not to move too much, conscious of the lack of lube. There was a touch of sweat that helped, but not much.

Keady winced, training his gaze on the television. His eyes went wide at whatever he saw, and he clamped down, helping Cutler slide deeper.

"Pass me the lube?" asked Cutler, casually flicking his gaze to the screen. *What the fuck?*

He'd been expecting bondage, and maybe a little roleplay, but not something so hardcore. *Is this mine?* He didn't remember having this in his collection. His half-hard cock pulsed, firming up in moments.

"You want me to fist you, baby?" asked Cutler, splitting his gaze between Keady and the screen to try to catch his reaction. "Did I not stretch you out enough already?"

Keady's leg started to tremble, his breathing picking up as he reached for the lube and passed it over. Cutler immediately slicked his fingers, before putting them back where they belonged. On second thought, he slid a third and fourth inside consecutively, reveling in the tightness.

"Ouch, *fuck*. I'm really sore." Keady furrowed his forehead but he didn't look away from the screen, just as drawn as Cutler was.

"Is that a yellow?" Cutler tapped his prostate, spreading his fingers wide without withdrawing.

"Fuck, no. Things are just starting to get good."

"Then answer the question." Lacing a threat into his voice, Cutler pushed, butting his knuckles against Keady's rim. The voice worked well on nurses, interns and subs alike, and Keady responded wonderfully.

"Yes. Maybe? I don't know. I never thought I'd be into you fucking me while I was asleep, but you changed my mind on that pretty quick."

What a dirty name for the beauty we created. "I prefer the term consensual non-consent," said Cutler, not easing up, even as Keady whimpered. The television caught his gaze again and he almost lost his rhythm. "Look at that, Keady. Do you think I could go that deep? I have long fingers, but my arms are so much bigger than his."

He pressed harder, until Keady yielded around the bump of his knuckles. Tickling Keady's perineum with his thumb, he eased in and out slowly until Keady was whimpering and moaning non-stop.

"Ah, fuck, it hurts." Keady tried to close his legs, but one was still trapped behind Cutler's head, with the other pinned easily enough.

"I think that's why you like it. You love being my little pain slut. It's too bad the food is here." Cutler pulled out all at once, standing from the couch and heading back to the kitchen.

"What?" Keady sat up, his eyes wide. He couldn't seem to stop himself as he reached for his ass, touching his rim. "Why did you stop? I didn't safeword."

"You're going to grab dinner from the delivery person and I'm going to get washed up." Cutler chuckled as he stepped into the kitchen and started the sink, drowning out the sound of Keady's stutter with the water. He wasn't going to remind Keady that he wasn't allowed to put clothes on, and Keady didn't have to know that Cutler had instructed the driver not to knock and to leave their food on the porch. His hearing was good enough that he'd caught the car coming and going a few minutes before.

"No way, SB." Keady called from the other room as he paused the porn. "You are out of your mind. You don't want me to answer the door naked. What if the delivery guy thinks I'm the tip?" He laughed, starting up the porn again.

"What makes you think I'd care?" Cutler dried his hands, peeking around the corner. Striding to the television, he hit the mute button that was tucked away on the side. "You're a horny slut, and I don't feel like fucking you right now. I'm more than happy to share your ass."

Keady's mouth flopped open. "You can't be serious. You *can't*."

"Unless you're safewording, get to the door. That cage downstairs hasn't been used yet, and I'm looking for an excuse right now."

That seemed to sink in quick. Keady shot off the couch, wincing and grabbing for his ass as he jogged to the door. Glancing over his shoulder one last time, he tested the knob, paling as he found it unlocked. He cracked it, peering around the door and using it as a shield.

The next look he turned on Cutler was a glower as he threw the door wide. Their food was waiting for them in neat little packages, the driver long gone with no one in sight. The sun hit Keady as he stepped outside to retrieve them, surrounding his pale skin like a halo.

"You're an asshole, SB."

* * * *

Keady seemed to perk up a bit when he opened his food to find an assortment of different pasta — all meat-free, of course. Lining them up on the table, he grabbed his fork, shifting on the blanket as he bit his lip.

Cutler could have cleaned him up, but no. It was much funnier to watch Keady squirm, especially when there was no way he was asking Cutler for help. He was still pouting too much for that.

"How long have you been a part of Clint's community?" asked Cutler, reaching for his own meatless wrap. He didn't feel like gargling again if he wanted a quick kiss.

"Unkinked?" Keady asked around a mouthful of pasta. "Not quite since the beginning. Clint and his husband started it together, and I joined shortly after from another community. It was just a bar at first, for like-minded people to talk shop. After the neighboring business went belly up, they leased the extra space, smashed down some walls and added the rooms and open play area. I won't tell you how long ago that was because I'd be dating myself." Keady grinned, before reaching for another forkful of pasta from a different dish.

"Did you know Clint's husband well?" It had been eating away at Cutler, ever since he'd put on a little scene with Clint. No one really seemed to know much about him, even when Clint seemed to know everything about everyone.

"No one really did," mused Keady, licking his lips. "He kept mostly to the books. Rarely saw them together even. Maybe that's how Clint wanted it. Some Doms are like that." He shrugged.

Some Doms? Cutler blinked, nearly choking on his wrap. "Clint isn't a Dom."

Keady stared at him like he'd suddenly grown two heads. "I know, he's a switch, but he prefers to Dom. Well, since his husband passed, he prefers to watch, really. I'd rather not say anything too personal because Clint is a good friend, but he's lost. He's never been the same since the fire."

Cutler wouldn't have been the same either. He could fix nerve endings and a brain, but emotional damage was something else altogether.

"You know I scened with him, right?" Cutler asked, setting his wrap on his plate. If Keady didn't know, it was best to get that tidbit out of the way. "When I applied to be part of the community, I offered a scene to show him that I wasn't some abusive psycho."

Keady's eyes turned stormy as his lips went tight. *Jealous little thing, are we?*

"That was before I knew you existed, Keady," said Cutler, refusing to give in to the smidge of guilt. He'd scened with too many people to be guilty about one. "Cool it."

Flushing, Keady looked at his food. "Sorry, Sir. Sometimes I forget how new we are at this. I feel like..." He trailed off.

"Like we've been dancing around it so long that it's like we've been together for some time?" Cutler asked, resting his chin on his hand. "You're cute."

He took another bite, chewing slowly so he could drag out the meal and observe every reaction. He ordered out so frequently that most of the places knew his order as soon as they saw his number come through. They'd seemed a bit surprised about all the changes today.

"I was just curious about the community. Since I've been a part of it, you've had an open house, but not one munch. Seemed strange is all." His last community had been ripe with munches, which were a great thing to talk and meet prospective partners. Cutler usually sat out on the talking part, waiting for his subs to come to him.

Shrugging, Keady grabbed a napkin, wiping his mouth. "We have a few a year. There were a couple of people in the community who ran all that stuff, but Clint and his husband slowly took over all the planning as people moved on. When Ross passed, stuff like that just stopped, for the most part. It was fine by me. I rarely went, and I never talked to anyone, anyway."

"Of course you didn't." Cutler could imagine his shy boy sitting at one of the booths at the club, watching the chatter around him but never joining in. If someone had approached him, he probably would have ducked his head and flushed, not saying a word.

"But you could now. You just opened the door naked with the intention of getting food from a stranger. It's a step down from there to talk to someone new," said Cutler, ignoring Keady's glower.

"I don't like talking to people."

"Which makes it perfect." He let out a sigh, setting the rest of his wrap aside and leaning against the couch. "I like to push people — it so happens to be my crack — and you like to be pushed. Do you think I'm bluffing?"

Keady shook his head, wincing as he shifted. "No, you don't seem like the type to bluff."

That was pretty fucking laughable. Cutler was an excellent bluffer when the payout was a good mindfuck.

"I would never put you in harm's way or ask you to do something that could get you arrested, but everything else is on the table. Fuck safe, sane and consensual." Folding the paper package over his wrap, Cutler tucked the rest back into the bag. He spied the twitch of Keady's cock from the corner of his eye.

A knock at the door cut off his train of thought and Cutler looked toward it, reaching for his phone. He hadn't expected anyone else, and there would be no delivery drivers on a Sunday.

Flicking the app open, he pulled up the camera for his front door, raising one brow as he saw who was standing there.

"Let me guess," drawled Keady, "it's the delivery driver for dessert." He rolled his eyes. "Not falling for that one again, SB. I'll get it."

Cutler's lips twitched, and he almost didn't notice the numbness along his scar. He tended to forget about it around Keady, which was strange, since he usually thought about it most moments when he wasn't alone. "I can't pull the wool over your eyes, Keady. You got me."

"Uh-huh." Keady waved his fork as he stood from the couch. The blanket stuck to his ass as he moved and he flushed bright red, tugging it free before grumbling under his breath.

"Sorry... I didn't catch that," said Cutler, closing his phone and setting it face down. There were a handful of notifications to address, but he'd take care of them later...or never.

"Nothing." Keady smiled sweetly, batting his eyelashes. "Just said that I would be happy to get the door, SB."

Cutler turned in his seat, leaning back so he could enjoy the show from the front row. Keady strode to the door, turning the handle and pulling it wide. The fork tumbled from his hand, clanging as it struck the tile. He looked to Cutler, his mouth dropping open in horror.

Chapter Sixteen

Keady

"Hey. You aren't dead," said Clint, his arms crossed as he impatiently tapped his foot on the front porch. His shirt had three holes in it and his track pants had seen better days, the dark circles under his eyes making everything look so much worse. "Be a dear and let me in."

He couldn't move. Every muscle had seized the moment he'd realized that there was a person on the other side of the door after all—and not just any person...*Clint*, the one he'd been talking about while trying the world's most delicious pasta dishes.

"Come in, Clint. You'll have to excuse my sub. He's a little fuck-dumb at the moment."

Cutler. What an asshole. He must've known. Keady clenched his jaw as Clint chuckled and moved past him, turning so he slipped by sideways so they didn't touch. At least *he* was a gentleman.

"Clint!" Keady shouted as he suddenly came alive. Slapping a hand over his hard cock, and another over his chest, he backed himself against the nearest wall, pushing his ass against it. He had no way of covering up the lube that trickled down his thighs or the dried cum in a few places.

"Keady." Clint inclined his head before toeing off his shoes and stepping toward the couch. Cutler patted the spot beside him, flinging the blanket out of the way. *Fuck*. There were lube and cum stains on that blanket that Clint would smell, if he hadn't seen them already.

Why was he so upset? Clint saw naked ass literally every day and didn't judge anyone. Hell, he'd seen Keady's naked everything and had seen him at his worst. That didn't make it any easier, though.

"Close the door, Keady," said Cutler before murmuring to Clint and offering him a second sandwich wrap that he hadn't touched.

Shaking his head, Keady pressed his back into the wall. He was too busy covering himself to reach for the door, despite the hot and humid air floating in.

"Suit yourself." Cutler shrugged, rubbing at his chin where a small piece of lettuce clung. "But the neighbor usually goes for a walk around this time and will be able to see you from there. Maybe that would be good for you. If you saw yourself plastered over the news and every porn site, maybe you'd finally understand how beautiful you are."

Oh fuck. He didn't have a choice. Waiting until the two men looked away from him, Keady reached for the door, slamming it shut. He darted for the blanket a second later, grabbing it and wrapping it around himself.

Lube and other slick things stuck to his skin, and he wrinkled his nose, stepping back. He'd just had a shower that morning, but they hadn't exactly been doing innocent things since then.

"Did you want a drink, Clint?" Cutler passed him a napkin. "And Keady, what did I say about wearing things in this house?"

Ah shit. 'Sadistic bastard' didn't describe Cutler well enough. Squinting his eyes shut, he dropped the blanket, letting it flutter around his feet. Cool air prickled against his skin, and he could imagine a thousand eyes looking at him.

"It's good to see you, Clint, but who's running the club?" asked Cutler, continuing as if he were discussing the weather.

Un-fucking-believable.

Peeking his eyes open, Keady let out a breath, trying to convince his heart to stop pounding quite so hard. They weren't even looking at him, just eating and chatting as if he weren't there. *Thank goodness.* He could do invisible. He was *great* at being invisible.

"Keady, grab Clint a Sprite, please. There should be a few in the fridge," said Cutler without looking up. He was frowning at his phone again before he tossed it back to the couch, giving Clint his full attention.

"Maddy's watching things until I get back," said Clint, laying a napkin over his lap. "I swear, that kid does a better job than I ever could, and nobody messes with him, even when Derreck isn't around." Clint shoved the wrap into his mouth, chomping loudly. "This is fucking good. Where the hell did you get this?"

"McGuinty's. Have you heard of it? Maddy actually recommended it, and they are fine doing custom orders and deliveries." Cutler turned a look on Keady, who hadn't moved. "I don't ask twice, but since you insist on being a brat, you get to crawl. Take any longer and see what happens."

If he hadn't been hard before, he would have been now. Keady grabbed his cock as he went to his knees, releasing himself and bringing his hands down before he could fall. One thing was for sure, his knees were not meant for floors like this.

Crawling to the kitchen was probably the single most humiliating moment of his life, and it made him so hard that he left a little trail of pre-cum along the way. It was worse when he looked over his shoulder to see them watching from their spots on the couch.

"You guys look like you've been having some fun," said Clint, clearing his throat as his gaze dropped to Keady's ass. "*Lots* of fun."

Cutler grimaced, covering his mouth with his hand as Keady watched. He only ever seemed to cover his mouth when there were other people around, but he hadn't done it all weekend with just the two of them. *What does that mean?*

"I had him up to four fingers. It would have been a fist if lunch hadn't interrupted us. I'm stretching him out for the upcoming show."

Keady perked up, straining his ears as he crawled into the kitchen. He couldn't hear shit over the sound of the fridge as he pulled the door open, standing briefly to grab a bottle of Sprite from the top shelf.

At least it wasn't a can. But how in the hell was he supposed to carry it? A thought worked its way into his mind. If Cutler wanted dirty, then that's what Keady would give him.

He had no idea where his newfound confidence was coming from as he put the top of the bottle into his mouth, locking his teeth behind the ridge of the cap. It swayed as he crawled, a bit of drool escaping that he wasn't able to swallow.

Knees aching by the time he returned, he deposited it on the couch, backing away and licking his lips. Clint didn't skip a beat, wiping the drool off with his shirt before popping the cap. Cutler's eyes were dark, though, his jaw clenched as he watched.

"Here." He pointed to his feet and Keady scrambled to comply, sacrificing his sore ass so he could sit on Cutler's feet and rub at his knees as he settled. He was going to bruise, especially at the ridges of his knees where he'd always been extra boney.

On the bright side, Cutler was getting lube from Keady's ass all over his bare feet. Keady grinned, wiggling his ass to spread it around. At least he wouldn't be the only filthy one.

He yelped as Cutler slipped his big toe against Keady's rim, pressing inside. His breath caught as he stilled his hips. *Ow.*

"I appreciate the visit, Clint, but I don't think you're here on a purely social call," said Cutler, wiggling his toe until Keady whimpered.

Clint hummed under his breath. "I got a funny text a few days ago."

Keady's stomach dropped as Clint shifted on the couch, producing his phone from his pocket and handing it to Cutler. Glaring at the floor, he tried to ignore the prickle of his tears as they washed over him, his high and the toe in his ass completely forgotten.

He hadn't remembered about the text he'd sent, but he did now.

Sceneing with Cutler for a few days. If you don't hear from me, he's definitely a serial killer. Take care of Sassafrass, my goldfish.

"Okay." Cutler read over the text before handing it back to Clint. "Keady already made it abundantly clear that he thinks I'm some kind of *Dexter* reincarnate." He wiggled his toe, but Keady barely felt it as he slouched, wrapping his arms around his legs and bringing them to his chest.

"Sassafrass is one of my established safewords with Clint," said Keady, mumbling against his knee as he tucked his head. "Mandatory forty-eight-hour check-in. Any scenes going on are full-stop if he doesn't hear from me."

The silence was deafening.

Glancing at the clock, Keady ducked his head again, unable to face the two men beside him. Cutler withdrew his toe, and he wanted to sob from the loss.

"Sorry I'm late," said Clint. "I didn't actually get your text until around this time the next day, and when I realized my mistake, I headed straight over here."

Cutler still hadn't said anything, and Keady bit his lip as the first few tears rolled over his cheeks. He would never be able to make it up to his new Dom. His intention had been to play safe, but the fact that he hadn't checked in, belittling his own safeword, was worse than the lack of trust he'd had in Cutler.

Subs had been dismissed for much less.

"Do you want me to go?" he asked softly, peeking out from his legs to glance toward the door. The couch was in the way, blocking his view of escape and freedom.

"No," Cutler said softly. His voice was completely void of emotion, even for Keady, who had gotten so good at reading him. "But I would appreciate it if you stay for a moment, Clint. I need to step outside for a breath."

Cutler tugged his feet from under Keady's ass, padding to the front door where he grabbed a pair of sandals and let himself out. The door shut softly, the central air kicking on as the heat finally overwhelmed it.

"He's pissed," said Keady, letting out a sob before he tried to clamp down on it. "I fucked up."

"You sure did," said Clint, speaking through the piece of wrap in his mouth. "I don't know what's gotten into you lately—throwing out your limits, making a fool of yourself and nearly getting killed by a Dom outside the community, getting tatted out of *nowhere* then sending me a text like that and not checking in? Your consequences don't seem to be sinking in."

Shaking, Keady finally looked up. Despite still munching on his wrap, Clint looked fucking pissed.

"Is it too late for an apology?" Keady asked, sinking his nails into the bruises forming on his knees. "It *is* too late."

He had a feeling that a few months ago, the thought of leaving Unkinked wouldn't have gutted him nearly as much as it did now. But over the past few weeks, he'd realized that the community housed his only friends, even if they were few and far between.

When he needed help, advice or a shoulder to cry on, there was only one place for him to go. But he'd backed himself into a corner and lit a match.

"I haven't decided. I imagine that will be up to Cutler more than me now." Clint shrugged. "But your membership is on the line, that's for sure." He met Keady's gaze, wincing at what he found. "You'd only be able to come as a guest until we decide the consequences."

Scratching his chin, Clint flicked a piece of pepper that had managed to get stuck in his scruff. "For the record, I would have done this as soon as you gave up your limits if you hadn't gone on your little rampage to find yourself a dangerous Dom."

"Fuck." Keady bit into his hand as his tears overwhelmed him. He couldn't make it without his friends. And what if Clint kicked him out forever? It would only take so long for rumors to spread across other communities.

"It shouldn't be a problem, anyway. You told me you're moving out of town. You already put an offer in on that new place you were raving about, and I doubt you'd take the two-hour drive just for some playtime at my place."

Is Clint...pouting? Keady should have been livid, grieved and everything in between. Instead, seeing Clint scowling so obviously on the couch with some kind of ranch sauce smeared all over his lips, made his heart break.

"Could we still be friends?" asked Keady, wiping his eyes with the back of his hands. He didn't mention that the deal on the new place had fallen through when someone had come in with no conditions and had steamrolled Keady's offer.

"Of course," said Clint, finally seeming to brighten up. "Sorry... I fucking hate this part of the job. I hate thinking about turning someone away who has been by my side for so long."

"Then I'll try not to be an asshole about it and hope you'll let me stay."

Clint gave him a long look. "You know it's not just up to me." He paused, narrowing his eyes. "You're taking this all very well. Did he have you in subspace all weekend or what?"

Nodding, Keady ducked his head for a completely different reason. "Pretty much. Cutler's fucking amazing, even if he is a sadistic bastard. I am sorry, Clint, even if it doesn't mean much. I was in a rough space before this weekend. I have been for a long time." That was the understatement of the year, but it still wasn't an excuse.

"On the plus side, I got a wrap out of the deal." Clint polished off the last bite, licking his fingers before wiping them on his shirt. He seemed a touch less tired than he had a few minutes before, his shoulders not quite as stooped. There was still a stiffness about him, though.

"Just out of curiosity, Cutler said you scened with him."

Clint paused before reaching for his drink and taking a swig. "Yeah."

It sounded like he was trying to be nonchalant, but Clint's cheeks had flushed, and he was putting a lot of effort into looking everywhere but at Keady. He looked more like the friend Keady knew and loved with all his heart. A bit of tightness in his chest eased. *Everything will be all right.*

"Can you tell me about it?"

He knew so little about Clint's previous relationship and had only heard rumors of him recently sitting in on some scenes. He'd seen the scars, though, and he knew Clint liked to play with fire and liked to play hard. But he'd also been certain that Clint was mostly a Dom, which wouldn't have worked with Cutler at all.

Cutler was a Dom through and through.

"Yeah—no. Not happening, Keady." Clint snorted. "Where did you get the ink? It looks good. Suits you." Kicking up his feet, Clint lay back on the couch as if it were a bed. It was nearly big enough to be one and just as comfortable.

"Um." Keady looked at it, touching the dark marks on his skin. There was one spot of scarring that hadn't taken the ink up, but Scotland had said that was easily fixed. He had an appointment the following week for a touch-up, and maybe more if he was feeling brave. *Not.* The rest had healed well… amazingly so. "His name was Scotland. Cute guy. Young, but talented. Not that I know ink that well."

"Fuck." Clint shook his head, a smile on his lips. "That guy shows up everywhere, I gotta tell you. I almost regret signing off on his membership. He's like a fucking leech." Rubbing his hand over his face, he looked to Keady. "What are you going to say to Cutler when he comes back?"

Swallowing his curiosity along with the clog in his throat, Keady looked back to his feet, all his bravado dropping away. If Cutler removed him from his life, then Keady would probably never see the inside of Unkinked again. No one would trust a dangerous sub like himself who didn't respect safewords.

"Probably nothing. I'm good at that."

"You're good at watching things go to shit and doing nothing about it, you mean," said Clint, sitting up on one elbow. "But it's your call. Give me your color so I know if I can hit the road. Maddy is probably rearranging the entire place right now. He's always up to something when I step away. Fuck'n kid."

It was strange how he called Maddy 'kid', even though he really wasn't that much younger than Clint. He did have a certain innocence to him, though, especially when Keady was telling him a dirty joke. He just really didn't seem to understand them.

"I'm all green, although I'm sure my ass won't be when Cutler comes back. You can take off. Nothing I can't handle."

Clint pursed his lips. "You know this isn't about 'handling it' right? This is about enjoying yourself and being open and honest with your partner. Give society the middle finger and get your ass whooped at the same time. It's the life—or it was." Clint cleared his throat, cutting himself off. "Anyway, I'll hit the road. Call me if you need something. There won't be a decision today, but sometime soon when I have a chance to call a meeting. *My* door is always open to you, no matter what happens."

"Thanks, Clint."

Keady stood as soon as Clint had left, circling the couch once. His cheeks and thighs were sticky, the lube mostly dried in a tacky film. Scrunching up his nose, he headed to the bathroom, running the sink and slowly wiping himself down while being as gentle as possible. He really was sore.

His reflection caught his eye and he paused, staring at himself for a long moment. Clint was right, the ink did look good. The collar did, too—a streak of darkness against his pale skin. It was too bad he didn't deserve it.

His gut thrummed when he thought of Cutler punishing him, and it wasn't all in dread. But Cutler had told him more than once that he *never* punished his subs. He'd never had to. He'd probably never had a sub be quite so bad, though. It couldn't get much worse than ignoring an established safeword, even if it had been outside their scene with another Dom.

"There's always a first," Keady mumbled to himself, staring in the mirror. Or he could just punish himself, get it over with and save Cutler the trouble.

Leaving was out of the question. He didn't even want to go there. So was putting on clothes, seeing as that was more of a reward than anything. Sexual stuff was out, too, seeing as Cutler had already said he wasn't up for another round.

Then what?

Wandering out of the bathroom, Keady bit his lip as he stared at the door to the basement. He flicked the light on, taking a deep breath as he took the first step. Each one was harder, and he was trembling by the time he stepped into the room that Cutler had first taken him to.

They had visited it since, so Keady could *refresh* himself, but they hadn't touched the ginger again, thank God. He hadn't had to touch the bare mattress or the cage, either.

He stepped toward the small enclosure of metal bars, leaning down as he pulled the door wide. He would have to crouch to get in and there wasn't enough room for him to stretch out once he had. It had probably been built for a mastiff or something similar, but there still wasn't much room within.

Dropping to his knees, he shuffled inside, thankful for the blanket on the bottom that protected his knees from the worst of the bars. They would have made the unbearable even worse. The door closing nearly did him in, the latch settling in the grooved notch.

The blankets were soft as he settled on them, leaning against the freezing metal that now surrounded him. They quickly warmed under his touch, almost comforting once they were above room temperature. His heart calmed, his breaths coming easier since Clint had shown up at the front door.

The squeal of the door opening caught his attention, but Keady didn't look up. He could hear Cutler breathing, slow and soft and hopefully calm. He always seemed calm, though, except when he was seconds from coming.

"I'm sorry," said Keady, not lifting his gaze. He didn't deserve to.

Cutler didn't respond until he crossed the floor, settling with his knees on the concrete. "Are you okay, Keady?"

Keady clutched the blanket, fluffing it under his head as he lay the rest of the way down. "I'm just really sorry. I lost track of things and completely forgot to touch base with Clint. It's no excuse. Safewords are important—the most important."

"That's not what I asked." Cutler reached through the bars, tracing the parts of Keady he could. Keady squirmed under the touch, not sure if he loved or hated it. It chipped away at his misery, warming his limbs.

"I'm green."

"Still not what I asked." There was a hint of exasperation that cut through his calm, his jaw tense.

"I'm not sure." Keady bit his lip. When was he ever sure about anything? "I broke Clint's trust—again— and yours. I know you're fine with me being a brat, but that was very rude of me. And I really can't believe I let

Clint down after everything, either. It just doesn't seem to sink in with me." He shrugged, even if he wanted to scream.

"Did you want to talk about it?" Cutler moved his hand until he was caressing the base of Keady's skull. He slid his fingers under the collar — not tugging, just feeling.

"Are you mad?" That was something he couldn't stand. He couldn't fix anything if Cutler was angry with him.

"No. But you are." Cutler tugged a strand of hair and Keady whimpered, leaning into the touch.

He was right. Keady was furious, but only at himself.

"If I punish you, would it help?"

A shiver racked his body as he thought of pain and reproach. "I don't want to hurt right now."

"I don't have to hurt you to punish you, Keady. Hell, I don't have to be in the same room. In fact…call 'yellow' or 'red' if you need me. I'll be listening."

Something clicked on the cage and Keady shot his head up, staring wide-eyed at the lock that was now looped through the latch on the door, anchoring it in place. Cutler looked on impassively as Keady snuck his fingers through the bars, touching the gold steel in disbelief.

"I'll turn the light off so you can rest. No bathroom breaks unless it's an emergency. Goodnight, Keady."

Gasping, Keady clutched at the bars, gritting his teeth. "It's fucking lunchtime, SB. You really want me to stay in here all day *and* night?"

Cutler turned, leaning against the wall, the first hint of a smile on his lips that he'd had since Clint had dropped the news in the living room like a wrecking ball. "You'll stay in there as long as *you* need. Then we get to talk." He raised one brow. "It will be something to look forward to."

Flicking the light off, Cutler plunged the room into darkness that was only interrupted with a strip of light beyond the door. The room instantly seemed smaller, closing in on every side. The bars were the only things keeping them at bay.

"Remember… I'll be listening."

Chapter Seventeen

Keady

"Oh my God, are you serious?" asked Maddy, his voice hushed in the phone. There must've been people close by that were listening in for him to keep so quiet. "Like in a cage...all day? That's insane. What if you had to pee? Derreck would never get me in a cage."

Keady snorted, tapping his earpiece to increase the volume. The more he talked to Maddy, the more he liked him. He'd originally called Unkinked to talk to Clint, but Maddy had answered, and it had spiraled from there. He'd thought Clint was a gossip, but he'd been so wrong. Maddy had said he gossiped now because he was '*making up for lost time around the water cooler*', whatever that meant.

"I *did* have to pee," said Keady, chuckling at the memory. "But I held it until about five in the morning. Then I woke the sadistic bastard up from a dead sleep by screaming my brains out."

Cutler had run down the stairs so quickly that Keady had heard the loud thumps that got progressively closer and the smack into the door as Cutler hit it at a run. The light had nearly blinded him when Cutler had switched it on, immediately unlocking the cage and pulling the door wide.

Keady had looked at Cutler, trying to keep his eyes from watering and the smirk from his face. "I'm done with my punishment now. Oh, and I thought I felt a spider on my arm. Sorry if I woke you."

The look Cutler had given him was pure exasperation, but he'd let Keady out as promised and he'd squashed the spider that *had* been spinning a web between the bars of the cage.

My hero.

After relieving himself, Keady had spent another hour on the bare mattress in the basement before he'd given in and joined Cutler upstairs. He'd woken his Dom up with the blowjob of a lifetime before he'd snuggled into his arms, still hard and wanting but not ready to do anything about it.

The morning after, they'd finally *talked*. It had been just as terrible as Keady had imagined it would be, and he was already reaping the unwanted side effects.

"I can imagine that." Maddy laughed. "I've seen him flat-out dismiss subs for looking at him the wrong way. The guy is like a holy grail. He's got all the right stuff, but he's impossible to get to."

"Does that make me a crusader?" Keady mused, clicking a document to open it before sliding it to his third screen. He had a stack of four, but sometimes he needed just one extra.

Maddy snorted. "So, sorry to get so off-topic, but why were you calling? I thought I saw your name on a sign-up sheet for the next event, but last time I looked, it was stroked out."

Blinking, Keady stared at his screen, not seeing a single word. "Did Clint not tell you?"

"Tell me what?"

"That he suspended my membership." Every time he said it, it sat harder in his gut. Sometimes he wondered how he was still able to eat, but he knew the reason for that, too. Cutler had had his lunch delivered when he'd found out that Keady's schedule was more insane than his own.

Keady had never taken him for a Daddy Dom before, but all the signs were there, especially the snuggling part, which was apparently something Cutler didn't do with just anyone. *That's a great way to make a guy feel special.*

"Uh, no. Are you fucking kidding me? Clint—"

Keady winced as Maddy yelled into the phone, obviously shouting for Clint himself on the other end.

"Jesus, Maddy. *Don't.*" This was going so much worse than expected. "I just need to talk to Clint— Aw fuck, you aren't even there anymore."

Maddy had obviously covered the mouthpiece with something, as it gave off a warbled loud screech that made his ears ring. Why the hell was Maddy picking up Clint's phone anyway?

"Holy shit," said Maddy, his voice clear and out of breath. "I don't believe it. You finally ran out of your nine lives."

Grimacing, Keady shot a glare toward his phone. *Hopefully I've got one more.* "You aren't helping, Maddy."

"I'm sorry." At least he sounded a touch more somber. Maddy was usually a pretty sensitive guy, but he had come into his own since Derreck had first scened with him in the club. He was like a whole new person, according to Derreck.

"I should know better. That was really insensitive of me, and I apologize, Keady."

But sometimes he sounded just like he used to — Mr. politically correct auditor who could find a flaw or solution for any business in the province.

"It's okay, I just needed to talk to Clint." That, and the conversation needed to be over ASAP.

"He's a little busy at the moment. He's helping Harold with one of his rope bunnies, and they are just getting to an intricate part. You know how that goes."

He sure did. One rope, all those hands, and enough knots that he'd been secure enough to stay still in a hurricane. Unfortunately, it did very little to float his boat.

"Okay." Keady bit his lip. "I just wanted to let him know that Cutler wants me back on the schedule. I had to call as part of my...training."

Training was exactly how Cutler had put it. It made him sound like a pup — and not in a good way. What it really was was a big fat punishment. "*I don't punish my subs — my ass!*

"I could pass along the message," said Maddy. "You sure you're okay, though? I feel really bad. Clint said you could come as a guest until the decision's made, and Cutler seems like an okay guy."

"Compared to Derreck or compared to a serial killer?" They were both equally as scary, but Derreck knew how to hide the damn bodies, too.

"I'll let Derreck know that you mentioned that," said Maddy, the humor suddenly back in his voice. "He's going to be Dungeon Master for the event, and I don't think he'd be averse to joining in for a bit. We've been talking about something just like it."

He was doomed. Absolutely doomed.

* * * *

"How did the assignment go today?" asked Cutler as he took another bite of the sandwich Keady had prepared for him. Keady had half-surprised him at work for his lunch break, showing up after he'd texted to make sure that Cutler wasn't caught up with any cases or emergencies.

It turned out that Keady hadn't needed to pack anything at all since there was a cafeteria on site that had actual restaurants he was familiar with. It smelled *good*, unlike the rest of the hospital.

But Cutler had waved off Keady's awkward suggestion that they buy food instead. His sandwiches weren't exactly stellar, seeing as they were PB&J. Most other kinds were out with his meat problem.

"I've worked in hospitals long enough that I can't stand the food," was all that Cutler had said before he shoved the first bite into his mouth.

Cutler seemed chipper, his eyes bright and his scar nothing more than a touch pink. When he really started to touch it, it went red, and that only seemed to happen when he started getting stressed or uncomfortable. It was crazy how much more Keady noticed everything after their weekend together.

"It went okay," said Keady, picking at the crust on his own lunch. The wooden chair in the booth was rock hard, and his ass was already aching. He needed lumbar support and cushions in his life at all times. "I talked to a lady at the grocery store today. She was nice. And I talked to Clint— Well, Maddy."

He'd gone to bed early the night before so he'd been able to wake up in good time and get everything done before his impromptu lunch.

"Good." Cutler nodded, taking another bite and chewing slowly. Swallowing, he took a swig of his drink—a homemade lemonade that Keady had spent way too much time making. "I'm proud of you for doing those things. Good job."

His stomach tingled, and Keady flushed. The simple praise made the terrible human interactions so much easier. "Maddy is my friend, though, so that one wasn't hard. Maybe it shouldn't count."

"Don't belittle your accomplishments. Take the praise, Keady." Cutler wiped a few crumbs from his mouth before leaning back and tenting his fingers.

Well, if you put it that way. "And there was someone in the elevator that asked me to push a button for them. I did it— I didn't say anything, but I pushed the button."

Chuckling, Cutler reached across the table, squeezing Keady's hand. "That's my boy."

The conversations from the dozen or so others in the cafeteria around them washed over their table, leaving them in a comfortable lull as Keady took his first bite. They were nothing to the crowd at the restaurant, and he didn't even have a plug in his ass. *Easy-peasy.*

Cutler stiffened as Keady took another bite, his lips thinning as a man approached from across the room. His eyes were suddenly pinched and narrowed, and Keady had to blink at the sudden change, wiping his lips with the back of his hand. His mouth was too sticky with peanut butter to ask Cutler if he was okay, his tongue coated in delicious sweetness.

"What the hell do you want, Klein?" asked Cutler, his voice suddenly cold and emotionless. If that tone would have been directed at Keady, he would have hidden under the table. Even when he'd disappointed everyone, he still hadn't gotten *that* tone.

"Just checking in." Klein was tall, dark and handsome by any means, with a roundish face and pleasing looks for a man who seemed to be about the same age as Cutler. He appeared to be going for more of the sitcom type of doctor, who knew exactly how attractive he was, but the smirk on his face was anything but sexy.

Cutler gripped the table, his knuckles bleeding white for a moment as a muscle flexed in his jaw. Keady would have missed it if he hadn't been watching so closely.

"Check in on your own time."

Klein's smirk only got wider before his gaze landed on Keady. "Who's your friend?"

Pure panic engulfed Keady in seconds, every moment of gained confidence burning out. What the hell was he supposed to say? He didn't know if Cutler was level with his colleagues about his lifestyle, or if he was even *out*.

"His cousin—"

"My partner—"

Keady and Cutler chimed in at the same time.

Partner? Keady was sure that he was absolutely glowing, his cheeks flushed as a smile lit his face. Partner was pretty broad, but it was something— something *equal*. It was a position that had to be treated with respect.

Cutler's lips twitched, his eyes glowing as he looked to Keady. Oh, he could get used to that look, especially with the tiny dollop of jam on Cutler's lip that made him look softer.

"Your cousin and your partner. Got it," said Klein, looking between them. "I didn't realize that you had a business on the side. I guess that promotion wasn't enough for you."

Promotion? "Congratulations!" said Keady, ducking his head as Cutler snorted outright. His cheeks flushed as everyone in the room probably looked his way. He was such an idiot sometimes. *Most times.*

"I'm not laughing at you, baby," said Cutler, instantly severing every negative thought. "And thank you. There were a lot of people up for that promotion — even Klein here." Cutler reached across the table, squeezing Keady's hand again. "But administration settled on the best guy for the job."

So humble. Keady struggled to keep his laughter to himself. He was sure that Cutler probably was the best guy for the job, but the man didn't seem to know the meaning of the word 'modest'.

Cutler turned a glower on Klein again. "And if you think I need a business on the side to keep things afloat, then you must be assuming that we have the same proclivities for controlled substances. He's not my business partner, you imbecile. He's my partner."

Klein went pale, the conversation around them seeming to pause as he turned on his heel and marched toward the room's exit without looking back. The tension immediately eased from Cutler's shoulders.

"Wow." Keady sucked in a breath, trying to calm his racing heart. "That was the coolest thing I've ever seen, but can't something like that get you fired?"

Cutler shrugged, running his finger over the scar on his lip. "He's already been reported by at least three nurses here, and I suspect his time is limited. I might as well kick him in the ass on his way out."

Hiding his grin behind his hand, Keady glanced toward the door where a few nurses had just stepped through. Each of them sent Cutler a wave, which he returned with a nod.

"Oh, good. I was starting to think you were a dick to everyone, on top of being a sadistic bastard," mused Keady, pulling his hand back and sneaking another bite of his sandwich.

"Your ass must be feeling better," said Cutler softly, his eyes glowing.

"Yep." Keady grinned. *So much better.* The reddened skin of his ass hadn't bruised, and his hole had gone back to its normal cute self despite having four fingers shoved into it. Keady had been a bit worried.

"Just wait until this weekend," Cutler growled, a noise that didn't belong anywhere near a hospital. Keady shivered, clutching at the table as his body attempted to betray him. He'd heard little snippets of the plan, but not enough to piece everything together.

"Can you just tell me? Everyone else seems to know what's going on." Maddy had seemed in the know, which just wasn't fair, especially if Derreck was going to be involved.

"Don't worry, little one. I'm going to make you a star."

Chapter Eighteen

Cutler

The place was packed, with cars winding all the way out of the private drive and double-parked in the lot. It was the biggest turnout that Cutler had seen so far at the new place, and Keady looked like his heart was in his throat. Cutler was downright chipper as he did a five-point turn, tucking the car into one of the last available nooks along the lane.

"G-good crowd," said Keady, stammering as he stared around with wide eyes. Maybe he was doing the same calculations that Cutler was. It was doubtful that most of the cars had single occupants, which meant two or sometimes three passengers each. Cutler wasn't one for crowds, but he wasn't *afraid.*

Cute. Cutler hadn't filled Keady in on a single piece of information, although they had talked safewords and limits before he'd agreed to permanently put Keady back on the sign-up for the event.

"They know there will be a good show," said Cutler, running a hand through his hair. He liked it a little lengthier, although in longer surgeries it was a bit of a bother. With a full gown and gloves in summer, it didn't matter if the air conditioning was cranked, he was still covered in sweat by the end. Bald would probably be the best, but his hair had brought on a lot of dreamy looks from the nurses.

His ego was never too big to stand a little stroking.

Keady wilted in the seat next to him, wrapping his arms around himself. He'd donned a thick hoodie, despite the weather, probably trying to do his best to hide himself. The guise wouldn't last long in the summer's heat.

Stepping out of the car, Cutler looped around, opening Keady's door and offering his hand. Clammy, sweaty skin met his, and he couldn't help but pause.

He loved to push... It was his thing to take a limit and slowly grind it to pieces until it was a drug. But he'd, unfortunately, developed a soft spot for Keady that was terribly sappy and even romantic. He'd even considered buying him flowers, which was fucking ridiculous.

"We can call it," said Cutler softly. "Or grab a few drinks and head out. I have an appointment with your ass later, and I'm flexible on the 'where'."

The distant sound of music broke through the quiet forest, with the low thrum of the rock that Clint loved so much. It was a reminder that, although it felt like they were in the middle of nowhere, they were about to be the center of attention. Keady looked toward the sound, biting his lip.

"I don't know if I can do this. There are so many people, and I just asked for help in a retail store for the first time." His breaths came in quiet gasps, and he glanced at the car. "Can we just go?"

"Yes," said Cutler, leaning back against the car and dragging Keady with him. The hoodie was hot against him, so he played with the hem, tugging it a few inches up Keady's belly before dipping under to stroke his sweaty skin.

"Oh." Keady blinked at him with something like wonder in his gaze. Cutler loved that look, especially when Keady met every challenge Cutler set for him. "I didn't expect you to say yes."

"Do you think I'm a bad Dom?" asked Cutler teasingly, placing a kiss on his nose. It was still a serious question, even if he kept his tone light. People had different opinions on what made a bad Dom, and it was often directed at him.

"No, because I *know* you're a sadistic bastard. Hell, I could probably upgrade you at this point to the king of all degenerates...but only if I could be your prince."

Keady was also the only one that Cutler wanted to simultaneously destroy and fuck. Under his shy exterior was a brat like no other, and Cutler wanted to get to know every part of him. Keeping Keady from getting distracted was half the battle, and he relished in it.

"I see what you're doing," said Cutler, stroking Keady's bottom lip before leaning in for a kiss. It was soft and sweet and over before he was ready for it to end. "And it's working. Distract me enough and piss me off so I lean you over the roof of my car and fuck you right here. I have no problem at all with that. Fuck, that's why we're here."

Narrowing his eyes, Keady looked up as another car rolled past them. They'd be back in a minute once they realized there was fuck-all for parking. Cutler would have to mention to Clint about setting aside some disability parking for those in need.

"You keep saying stuff like that," said Keady, pulling back enough to cross his arms and let out a huff. "You can fuck me anywhere. Why does it need to be in public?" *Hypocrite.* He knew Keady loved it, just as much as he did.

"And you can pretend to hate *everything*, but why bash something that you really love?" asked Cutler, catching Keady's lower lip between his fingers and tugging it. Keady flushed brighter, the few new freckles standing out on his cheeks. He would bake soon if he kept the sweater on.

"That's right. *I know.* You're a slut for attention, even if you're too shy to ask for it. Don't worry. You'll never have to ask me." Cutler chuckled, releasing Keady's lip and leaning against his car. The trees offered some much-needed shade, but that came at the cost of leaves and bird droppings. Even now, the robin above them was eyeing up his sparkling windshield and letting out a high alarm.

"One drink and two conversations," said Keady, "then we go home and you fuck me how I want it — and I get to wear the collar. Oh, *and* you have to choke me. You can't say no this time."

Fuck. This guy. He struggled not to roll his eyes. "I'm not sure what gave you the impression that you have any say." Inclining his head, he acknowledged the same car as it rolled past them again, searching for a parking spot in the stretch of vehicles. "Are you safewording?"

Keady snapped straight before lowering his eyes to the loose gravel. Cutler caught his chin, forcing their gazes to meet. "No, Sir. Green, Sir."

Such a stubborn boy.

"Good. Then get your ass to the house before I decide to start the scene right here." Reaching for his keys, he locked the car before shoving them deep into his pocket. Hopefully, he didn't lose them in what promised to be absolute chaos.

"And that scene would entail...?" Keady asked with a smirk, raising one brow as he tugged his sleeves up.

"Nice try."

* * * *

Keady

The house was packed tighter than sardines in a can. It looked like every kinky bastard in the province had suddenly descended into the front hall of the house, tendrils of conversations sneaking into the stage area.

Shrinking against Cutler, Keady cursed his hoodie again as he reached for his Dom's hand and held it tight. He was so fucking hot and sweaty that he would probably slip right out of his clothes if they caught on something. His freshly showered skin was probably already going not-so-fresh, and his balls were practically dripping.

Squeezing his hand once, Cutler tugged him to the side, guiding him to the area where they had come down after their first scene together. It hadn't been that long ago, but it felt like so much had changed.

Keady had changed completely, which was something he never thought would happen. A few weeks ago, he would've taken one look at that many cars and turned around, hightailing it all the way back home. But now he was in the middle of it, sweating his ass off with Cutler at his side.

"Open the door," said Cutler, whispering against his ear. Every part of his body was on full alert as he glanced at the crowd, recognizing almost every person there. Still, he'd never seen so many in the same place at the same time, caught in conversations as others tried to push through unsuccessfully.

With his hands shaking, he grabbed for the door, tugging it wide and stepping inside. As the door closed behind them, he let out a sigh of relief, leaning against Cutler and letting his body go slack. *Almost yellow.*

Thankfully, there were only a few people in the room, most of them looking to be in a similar state as him. Maddy and Derreck were on one of the couches, Maddy looking flushed as all hell with Derreck tenser than Keady had ever seen the man.

"Clint still hasn't taken care of them?" asked Maddy, his voice strained. His eyes were wet, and he wiped at his cheeks, snuggling deeper into Derreck's lap.

"No," said Cutler, filling in as Keady tried to get his breath back. "I'd take care of them myself but I don't want to leave you." He looked to Keady, his eyes narrowed. "I apologize, love. I wasn't expecting a crowd that big."

Love, aww. Some of Keady's tension drained. "I can always sit with Maddy and" — he looked to Derreck, steering clear of his intimidating gaze — "the others."

"Derreck?" Cutler asked. "You look like you have your hands full already. What are your thoughts?"

"Get them the fuck out, or I'll take them the fuck out myself," Derreck growled, sending a bolt of fear straight up Keady's spine. Maddy's eyes drooped lower, strain dropping from his shoulders. *Because threatening murder is apparently relaxing.* There was a big reason that Keady had never approached Derreck as a play partner a second time.

"Got it," said Cutler, looking back to the door. "Keady, sit next to Maddy on the couch. I have too many plans today to get caught up treating multiple concussions."

Sliding onto the couch, Keady perched at the far end, leaning away to give Maddy and Derreck extra room. From this close, he could see Maddy's trembling and the way he pulled at the sleeves of his long-sleeve shirt. The material was thinner than Keady's hoodie, but obviously had a similar purpose. Keady couldn't remember the last time he'd seen Maddy so self-conscious.

Maddy's throat bobbed as he closed his eyes and swallowed, letting out a small whimper. "Can't you just? *Please*, Derreck?"

Derreck grunted in response, a low sound that carried across the room. The couple across from them stood, sending them a wave. "We're going to take off. Too much action for us."

It wouldn't have been so bad if people were all around the house like they were supposed to be. What the hell had they all been doing at the entrance?

"What about now?" Maddy whined as the door closed, leaving just the three of them and the tinkling of soft music. "It will help."

Derreck only grunted again, tapping his palm against Maddy's thigh. It was dirty, as if he'd dipped his hands in the mud and had scrubbed them clean, only to miss most of it.

"Did you guys need me to leave or something?" asked Keady. He tended to steer clear of their dynamic, mostly because he was terrified of Derreck. "Or can I help?"

Maddy, he was one hundred percent okay with. He was fairly new to the scene, but he was extreme, and he kept Derreck under wraps, too, which was best for everyone.

"Stay put," said Derreck, sending Keady a glare — or maybe it wasn't a glare. He seemed to have a similar expression as Cutler, but his eyes were softer now that it was just the three of them. "Cutler would take my kidney if I let you wander off. Maddy just wants something I can't give him right now."

Maddy grumbled, crossing his arms. "Something you *won't* give me right now."

Derreck rolled his eyes, and Keady had the impression that it was something that didn't happen often.

"I can help?" asked Keady again, shoving his hands into the front pocket of his hoodie. "I can change the music, or I think I saw some different scents for the diffuser...lavender, peppermint." He stood from the couch, pulling out a small box that he'd noticed by the diffuser. "There's *'breathe'*, whatever that means."

He held up the little bottle, squinting at the tiny label before screwing off the top. Taking a whiff, he broke out into a fit of coughing as his lungs filled with the most potent *something* that he'd ever smelled. "Shit, it's like a skunk fucked a peppermint plant."

Derreck chuckled and Maddy's lips twitched in a smile before he hid his face against Derreck's collar again.

"*Please.* It's not just the people. You know it was starting before I even came to work tonight, and I was just caught off guard." Maddy breathed the words over Derreck's skin, the pure pleading in it calling to Keady's soul.

"You're my friend, Maddy. What do you need?" Keady set the box down, twisting the cap back on the bottle and tossing it in with the rest before heading back to the couch. He doubted peppermint was going to help if Maddy sounded this desperate.

"Not your place," said Derreck, his eyes pinched as he rolled his shoulders. He strained his hands on Maddy's hips, digging into his tight pants.

"Fuck you," Maddy grumbled, going tense as he leaned back to glare at Derreck. "If you would just give me what I want, then we wouldn't be in this situation. Just a touch — a taste."

"Don't fucking push me. I'll drag you to *Nightmare* right now." Derreck grabbed Maddy by the hair with one powerful hand, twisting his wrist until Maddy's neck was arched. One more inch and Maddy would fall from his lap in a very grumpy pile.

"Um, I'm gonna go," said Keady, slipping toward the door. Neither of them looked up as he twisted the knob, letting himself out. But he wasn't going to stay another moment with the tension rising in pure tsunami fashion.

A wave of terrible heat and human humidity struck him, soaking his sweaty face in a film with the first step out of the door. The murmur of voices had thankfully faded, though, the sound of Clint's distant yell tinted with the edge of exasperation.

Clasping his hands together, Keady stepped down the hall that had been packed before. The exit was in clear view, but without Cutler and his keys, escape was impossible.

"You kinky fuckers listening?" Clint's shout came from the direction of the main stage area. It was followed by a few catcalls and some laughs. "Good, because we have a Shibari master in the house today. I know he already roped a few of you right at the door, but we'll get started soon."

Shibari? Keady crinkled his forehead, turning to look at the front door. That explained why the crowd hadn't been dispersing, but it was the last thing he would have expected. Shibari was *not* his thing. And being on stage, without even being tied up by a strange Dom, should probably have been on his limits list. *Is it too late to send Cutler a text?*

His heart picked up as he heard steps coming closer, the rhythmic tap completely unfamiliar. Whether it was Cutler or not, sweaty and flustered, he didn't want to be seen by *anyone* right now. Rushing away from the entrance, he grabbed at the handle of the nearest kink room, glancing at the name before he let himself inside.

Nightmare. Since Derreck had mentioned the room, it probably meant it was empty at the moment.

He was through the door before he had time to register the darkness and the pure silence that enshrouded what he had to assume was one of the new kink rooms. It was one that hadn't been available on opening night and had been locked every time he'd come since.

A red light shone opposite him, only giving him enough of a sign to let him know that he wasn't dead. It was cold, so blessedly cold that his hoodie immediately stuck to his skin as he broke out into goosebumps. If there had been an overhead light, he was sure that he would have seen his breath in the chilled air.

Sensation play was a bitch, and *Nightmare* was a fitting name for this brand of it. One of the other rooms, *Feel,* was the much calmer side of things, offering feathers and vampire gloves instead of the pure torture that *Nightmare* seemed to promise.

Sliding his hand along the wall, he searched for the light switch, flicking the first one he found by touch. Instead of lights, sounds broke into the room, the thick metal tones startling a scream from his throat. The base of heavy music rocked his lungs as he plastered himself against the wall, blinking to try to see anything in the darkness.

He *hated* metal music, but only because it was absolutely terrifying. His heart pounded as the music numbed everything else from his brain, until the cold and the beat were everything he knew.

Whimpering, he blindly found a second switch along the wall next to the first, taking a deep breath before he flicked it. Light finally flooded the room as he touched it, the music continuing to thrum the walls. He blinked as his eyes slowly adjusted, his cock going harder by the moment.

He'd always been wired differently. He could hardly stand to watch a horror movie, because as soon as fear prickled across his skin and his heart rate picked up, he got hard. It wasn't so bad at home, but being caught with a boner in a theater had made him swear them off for the rest of his life. Sometimes commercials were even enough to get him going, which were almost impossible to avoid.

The room did look like the stuff of nightmares, with a few other switches on the wall that probably did horrible, terrible things. Different manacles hung from various heights, a few bolted in the ceiling along with an actual set of stocks that looked like it had rolled out of a museum.

The walls were painted black and red to match the music, with speakers hidden between the implements. He flicked off the music, sighing with relief as the sound ended.

There was even a small bar fridge along the far end of the room that probably had something dead in it. Keady was almost certain of it.

But the biggest threat was the door across from him, the engraved words carving themselves across his skin.

Are you sure you're ready? Safeword now, little subbies.

All Doms were assholes, Clint right along with them. They probably thought it was funny, too. Keady would never admit that it turned him on something fierce to see those words and let the terror rocket through him.

With a surge of confidence, he strode across the room, grabbing the handle and tugging the door open. A narrow set of stairs greeted him that were probably barely to code with how steep they were. They looked like something out of a century-old farmhouse that hadn't been lived in for half that. A sign just to the side of the door read 'wheelchair access to the basement is available. Please ask Clint or the Dungeon Master for details.'

Okay, so Doms were courteous bastards…but still assholes. If Keady had had the balls for it, he would have started his own sub patrol that would put the damn Dungeon Masters to shame. Although most of them lived up to their names—like Derreck…or Nikita.

The stairs were well lit, but the landing beyond appeared quite dusky and the bright red paint dimmed to something dark and leery. Swallowing, Keady took the first step, gripping the handrail tight. At least it wasn't made of a dulled chainsaw blade or something to set the mood.

The stairwell seemed warmer than the room above and he wondered if some poor soul had cranked the air conditioning and forgotten. Clint would see it on his utility bill and probably flip a lid. He grinned. *It's the little things that make the best revenge.*

Keady tugged his hoodie off before he took another step, tossing it back toward the room and finally taking his first refreshing breath.

This was why he loved kink. It was the same thing he had been missing for years as he jumped around and searched. The unexpected and terrifying were as beautiful as they were liberating. But no one could have taken him there except Cutler.

He hadn't known what he'd been holding back until Cutler had demanded it from him, stripping him of his boundaries and control.

He would have to send his Dom flowers or something. He would aim for the pinkest and brightest ones he could find and send them to Cutler's work on a busy afternoon when all the nurses would see. That would get his ass railed good for sure.

A shadow moved at the bottom of the steps and Keady paused, his palms going slick and his cock throbbing. "Somebody there?"

Cutler appeared, crossing his arms and sending Keady a light glare. "Are you trying to ruin my surprise, little one? Derreck should have kept you for a while yet."

Keady gulped, shaking his head. "Derreck and Maddy needed some alone time, and I—uh—came looking for you." It wasn't a complete lie. From Cutler's narrowed eyes, he didn't look like he bought it.

Had he planned it all? Maybe Maddy had Derreck had only been a distraction, and the crowd and footsteps had herded Keady right to the nearest escape.

"If you're so eager, we'll start now," said Cutler. The hint of amusement was wiped off his face in a moment, leaving only a ruthless Dom behind. Keady groaned automatically, pre-cum soaking his boxers in an almost Pavlovian response. "What are your safewords?"

"Red for stop, yellow for slow down, green for if you stop I will hurt you." Keady grinned, quickly tapping the rest of the way down the stairs. He turned when he reached Cutler.

"Ready or not, here we come," said Cutler, reaching for Keady and jerking him back by the hair. His other hand slapped over Keady's eyes, cutting off his view before he could catch much of a glimpse of the basement. "Someone pass me the blindfold, and I'll get this slut trussed up for us."

Chapter Nineteen

Cutler

It had taken him all of two seconds to check on Clint and make sure he had everything in hand before he headed to the basement to make sure final preparations were in place just in case Keady changed his mind and wanted to continue with their scene. He hadn't even needed to enact his plan to corral Keady to him. He'd done that all on his own.

Keady was hard to read, which was a nightmare for any Dom, but for Cutler especially. The way he played, he *had* to be able to predict someone, and if he couldn't, it could turn dangerous.

He should have known that Keady had no intention of backing out. The way his pants had pulled tight as he took the first steps down the stairs was a pretty good indicator of how much he was into it.

Too bad he hadn't been able to go through with his whole plan. He'd left the playroom dark and had fully intended to snatch Keady there and blindfold him before leading him down the stairs.

Walking down the stairs blind was a terrifying journey, if not a touch dangerous. But that was why Cutler was going to be there to guide him...and maybe forget to tell him about the last step.

He was trying not to be miffed that his plan had gone awry, but it was nice to see Keady so on board. And the way he writhed against Cutler as he covered his eyes, then strapped on the blindfold that Trick handed him, had him just as hard.

"Thanks," said Cutler, shaking off the last of his nerves. There were five other Doms in attendance and two subs. He'd vetted them all extensively, pulling their medical records, even though they had been willing to hand them over. One could never be too careful.

None of them were getting close to Keady without a condom, either.

With the blindfold secured, Cutler grabbed Keady's wrists, bringing them behind his back in a move that had to be a touch painful. Cutler knew just how far he could stretch the tendons before it would be too much and reveled in Keady's whimper. "Let's put this bitch where he belongs, boys."

The table was ready, with leather straps for Keady's arms, neck and waist. He wouldn't need any for his feet, because it was situated in such a way that his ass would hang over the edge at the perfect height. Plus, it would be much more fun to watch him try to kick.

Trick approached again with a pair of sterile scissors, cutting Keady's shirt in a few sure strokes. The blonde Dom had the soft kind of features that probably fooled everyone but his sub, Nav. Nav watched on, licking his lips as his Dom went to work.

It looked like Cutler wouldn't have any jealous partners on his hands, and Trick had assured him that he was fulfilling one of Nav's fantasies. Their style was just like Cutler's — barely on the side of allowed.

"You could have just asked me to take my shirt off," said Keady, pulling at his hands as Cutler eased the angle. Cutler placed a kiss on his shoulder, breathing in the scent of sweat and desire.

"Where's the fun in that?" It was nice to see that Keady's confidence had returned with the blindfold. His sub's control of his shy demeanor was tenuous at best, and Cutler wasn't quite ready to cut the strings completely.

Maybe he'd be on a different page an hour from now.

Trick carefully dragged the pointed end of the scissors over Keady's belly, and he let out a whimper, sucking in as he was slowly tortured. Trick's eyes went dark as he cast a look to his own sub. *Oh to be a fly on the wall in their next scene.*

"Not my p-pants. I like these," said Keady, trembling as the blade was dug in enough to scrape a white line over his skin. Trick grinned as he grabbed the waistband, cutting them free with a few snips and the drag of the blade.

"Fuck you, SB. I said I liked those pants."

Cutler chuckled, leaning his chin on Keady's shoulder and squeezing his arms. His blood was pumping fast as a grin tried to break free. Did Keady really think it was just him there? *Not to toot my own horn, but fuck, I'm good.*

"I'm right here, Keady. Both hands." He squeezed again. "I didn't do a thing."

Keady froze, slowly opening and closing his mouth.

When Cutler had approached the stairs after hearing the music blast through the speakers, he'd asked the others to stay in the shadows at the edge of the mirrored basement room. Keady must've been so focused on the decorations that he'd missed the group. And when Cutler had spoken to them the first time, Keady must've thought he was bluffing.

Not that I would ever. He suppressed a snicker, letting the mood flow through him.

"W-who?" Keady asked, pushing back into Cutler's arms in an attempt to get closer. His skin was prickled with goosebumps in the cool basement, sweat dripping down the middle of his back. Cutler peered over his shoulder. Keady was rock hard, the head of his cock red and wet.

"Do you really want to know?" Cutler whispered, placing a kiss on Keady's neck. "The next time you see them in a room, you'll have to meet their eyes and remember everything that happened down here."

Keady let out a shaky breath, swallowing hard. "How many, then?"

"If you can guess, I'll give you a reward."

Keady squirmed, his cock flexing. A few chuckles came their way.

"Three?" Keady asked softly.

Cutler hummed, inhaling the smell of Keady's skin without the scent of another man. Later he would smell him again with the scent of the other's cum and sweat. He wouldn't let Keady shower until he'd gotten his fill.

His sub wasn't the only one who was a filthy fucker.

"Good job." Cutler eased his grip, leading Keady to the table and strapping him in. The strap around his neck was tight enough to hold him, but nowhere near enough to cut off his breathing. His hands and the straps over his waist were the same way.

"Clench your hands into fists." He watched Keady make fists, testing the tightness of the leather. "Any tingling or if you lose feeling, you call 'red' immediately."

"Yes, Sir." Keady tilted his cheek into the table, a smile on his lips. "I'm green, just in case you were wondering."

Cheeky little thing. Cutler covered his own mouth with his hand as he fought another smile. He would laugh when he didn't have an audience.

"Now, to decide who goes first," said Cutler, running his finger down Keady's spine all the way until he paused at his hole. He was slick with sweat, which gave him just enough moisture to ease his way in past the tight sphincter.

"Uh, lube?" Keady moved his hands on the table, only making it an inch before the restraints stopped him. "And seriously, you're just going to tie me to a table and gangbang me? That seems a little soft...pun intended."

Is that a pout? Cutler caught Trick's gaze, a look passing between them. He'd met a few people in his short time in this community that had been in the game as long as him, and Trick was one of them. His sub Nav was a newbie in comparison but seemed completely devoted to the lifestyle, as far as Cutler could tell.

Among the others were Shelvin and Elliot, the two who were actually responsible for the building of the new Unkinked. They weren't a romantic partnership per se, preferring to keep it kinky instead of throwing roses in. Scotland had been a surprise. When Cutler had first expressed an interest in setting the scene up, Scotland had come forward. He'd said he had hoped to catch Clint in on the action.

But Clint would be upstairs, monitoring the Shibari display and the huge turnout for it. The camera in the corner of the room with a live feed of the basement had probably helped the numbers surge.

Derreck was still MIA, and Cutler expected him to be gone for quite some time with the state he'd seen Maddy in. He hadn't meant to use their stress as a distraction, but Clint had been busy.

That left two other Doms without partners, both of which had seemed trustworthy and more than willing to help set the scene. Philip had joined in, which was a surprise. He was a sadist like none other, but Cutler had been certain that he was straight.

And Turin, who was the nicest and only Italian who Cutler had ever met. From what Cutler understood, Turin's last long-term sub had crashed and burned their relationship to the ground before leaving the community. Turin had left the bar behind, and this was one of the first steps for him getting back into the lifestyle. It was an entrance sure to make a bang.

Cutler rubbed his scar, twitching his lips as the numbness fluttered against his nerves. Raising one brow at Trick, he motioned to Nav with a question in the air. They'd set up a loose order of who would go, but nothing too strict that it couldn't be changed.

Nav seemed ready to burst from his skin as he stepped forward, grabbing for the front of his pants and jerking the zipper down. He shook his head as he started to speak. "You have no idea how long I've been waiting for this. It's been nothing but the bottom for *so* long that I think my dick is dryer than the desert."

"Nav?" Keady's voice hit the air, his shock evident in the way he tensed his arms. *Oh, baby, don't tense. It'll only hurt so much worse.*

"Get on with it, slut," said Trick, his voice and eyes dark. He didn't look quite as friendly when he appeared like he was ready to fuck to destroy.

Cutler reached for a small bottle of lube, leaning over and lining the narrow neck up with Keady's hole. Keady let out a gasp as he pushed it past his entrance, squeezing the bottle and emptying the entire thing in Keady's ass. Lube dripped from him as Cutler drew back, running along the back of his balls until Keady tightened up with a groan.

Nav eyed the dripping lube, rolling a condom on one-handed as he licked his lips. When he reached forward with his fingers, probably to prep Keady, Cutler shook his head.

"If Keady wants to lip off, then he can suffer the consequences," said Cutler, slapping Keady's ass once before circling around to the front of the table.

Nav's pupils dilated until his eyes were nearly black, and Trick sidled up behind him, guiding his hips closer. Trick whispered something into Nav's ear, too quiet for Cutler to hear. He didn't really need to hear with the intent rolling off Trick in waves.

Nav was one lucky sub, even if their relationship had had a bit of a rocky start from what Cutler had gathered.

The moment Nav began to nudge inside, Keady scrunched his face up, digging his nails into the surface of the table as he pulled at his restraints. The muscles in his ass jumped, and Keady let out a whimper as he bit his lip.

"Don't make it look so hard," said Cutler, his voice dark. "You're just lying there so we can fuck you, after all. Just do what you're supposed to and take it."

"Fuck." Keady arched his back as Nav bottomed out, his hips flush with Keady's ass. He had nowhere to go—no escape—even as a whimper burst from his throat.

"I'd ask you your color, but you'd probably just get snarky again. I'll try to set you up for a reward next time instead of failure." Cutler kneaded the muscles of Keady's back, feeling them jump under his touch at every little shift of Nav's cock inside. Trick was right against his sub, pulling Nav's pants the rest of the way down until they tangled at the level of his ankles.

Cutler couldn't see what was happening between the two of them, but he could guess as Trick lowered his own pants and Nav's face scrunched up as they suddenly settled that much closer and more intimately.

They were just beginning, and there was already a fucking chain blooming before him. *Fuck*, he loved gangbangs. It was starting to sound like one, too, with more than one person moaning and dual cries hitting the air.

Trick set the pace, grabbing Nav's hips and rocking him back and forth—pulling him back on his cock, then plunging him deeper into Keady. Nav's eyes rolled back, already floating as his Dom took control and fucked him hard. Cutler felt each thrust as he stroked Keady's back, bracing against the table that was bolted to the floor.

He could see them from every angle, the mirrors around them showing off the clenching of Trick's ass, and the way Nav's cock disappeared inside Keady. Even Keady's cock was visible, hanging between his legs and dripping every time Nav presumably hit his prostate.

But Keady was still fighting, flexing on every stroke with his hands clenched into fists. He'd gritted his teeth, biting back the whimpers that were probably desperate to escape.

Cutler leaned in, tucking a stray hair behind Keady's ear. He was soaked with sweat already, his skin flushed and beautiful. If only Cutler could see his eyes, hidden behind the blindfold, but he wasn't ready yet.

"You're taking it so well." He let the praise wash over his sub, wondering if that was all Keady needed. "But there are still cocks that need warming here. If you need to safeword and your mouth is full, knock the table. Do it now so I know you understand."

Keady knocked the table immediately, dropping his mouth open as Trick's pace changed. Nav must've shifted his angle in response, because Keady suddenly arched into the touch, welcoming it completely.

Sending a look to Scotland, he motioned to Keady's mouth. Scotland didn't need to be told twice, exposing himself and rolling a condom onto his cock before guiding himself to Keady's mouth. Scotland's eyes narrowed at the ink on Keady's arm, reaching for it and giving him a tender caress.

"It turned out well." Scotland's voice rolled over Keady, and at his tension, Cutler realized that he probably recognized his voice. "Can't wait for him to come back for that piercing you promised."

"I haven't forgotten," said Cutler, adjusting himself as he started to ache. "I just can't decide between nipple and cock." Keady groaned around Scotland's cock, his mouth stuffed full and gagging as Scotland bumped deeper. "Nipple would be fun, combined with clamps, but I could put a leash on his cock so I could correct him every time he talks back."

He was only partially bluffing. Keady would probably enjoy that style of correction as much as he would, but it would probably happen pretty constantly. Keady's cock would be mighty sore before he finally learned.

"Fuck, that's hot," said Scotland, pulling out for a moment to let Keady breathe. Keady gasped in a few breaths, licking his lips to catch some of the drool that had started to leak from him. His cheeks were flushed, a few tears escaping from beneath the blindfold.

"Getting bored, Keady?" asked Cutler, dragging his nails down Keady's back. White lines bled to red as Trick's pace increased again, jamming Nav deep with quick thrusts. Nav looked like he was barely holding on, his hands digging into Trick's forearms and his mouth opened wide in a near-constant groan.

Keady only grunted before his mouth was filled again. His hands were flat on the table, nowhere near to a safewording by any stretch. And if his cock was anything to go by, Cutler would have to get the cock ring out fairly soon so he didn't come too quick.

Cutler reached for the flogger that he'd set on a table close by. He'd spoken to everyone beforehand—except Keady, obviously—letting them know his plans. Elliot was the only one who had given any hint that he might have a problem with impact. Cutler approached him, keeping a watchful gaze on Keady the entire time.

"Will this be an issue?" He showed Elliot the flog, flaring the many leather strands over his hand. The ends were tied so they would leave an extra sting with each blow, painting Keady's flesh to perfection

"That will be fine," said Elliott. "Just don't bring out a belt."

"I'll keep an eye on him, too," said Shelvin, a Dom who was substantially shorter than his sub. "We're still trying to decide ass or mouth. Both look delicious."

Sending them a nod, Cutler strolled back to the table just in time for Scotland to withdraw to let Keady catch his breath again. Cutler patted Keady's head, sweeping his sweaty hair back from his face.

"How are we doing, Keady? Need a break yet? Or are we still *just* fucking you?" Cutler ran the strands of the flog over Keady's back, letting him know what was coming, even when he couldn't see. "Don't bite Scotland, now. He might mess up that piercing of yours if you do."

Keady drew in a shaky breath, nodding his head slowly. "Green, Sir. So fucking green."

Glad to hear it. Keady was just starting to slur his words, but he was still clear. He was probably barely hanging on, slipping deeper into subspace with every stroke of cock. Cutler gave his cheek one last touch before Scotland slipped back into Keady's mouth, testing the edge of his gag reflex.

Nav's eyes went wide as he spotted the flog, eyeing the strands like they were the best thing he'd ever seen. "I can't. I'm gonna come. Trick!" He dug his nails deeper into Trick's arms, moaning over the slapping of his hips against Keady's ass. They would probably be able to hear him at the top of the stairs, and that was without the microphone built into the camera.

"Make it last, slut. This is the last time you'll get to top until I decide you need a reward," Trick growled, sinking his teeth into Nav's shoulder.

"Fuck. *Fuck!*"

Nav cried out as Cutler brought the flog down on Keady's ass, his sub's muscles jumping as the leather spattered over his skin. Keady must've clamped down because Nav's shout morphed into a moan as his hips jerked against Trick's grip.

Cutler didn't hold back. He brought the flogger down again, painting the top of Keady's ass and his back in bright red. Even as Nav finally withdrew and Trick grabbed him to retreat to the corner of the room to a waiting chair out of view of the camera, Cutler didn't ease his strokes.

Scotland grunted beside him, pulling his cock out just as Turin slicked up his covered cock and slid into Keady's ass. Scotland ripped off the condom, and with a few strokes, came over Keady's back, his cum landing on the reddened streaks.

Fuck. Cutler's pants were way too tight for their own good, his cock throbbing with every stroke of the flogger. Leaning in, he licked the cum from Keady's skin before biting down *hard.*

"Ah, fuck!" Keady squirmed, his voice so fucked out that it was barely recognizable. Elliott and Shelvin were at his head, pushing into him at the same time and stretching Keady's mouth to its max.

"Color?" Cutler dragged his tongue over Keady's cheek, licking at the edge of Elliot's cock as he pulled back. Keady groaned low in his throat and a moment of slick fucking passed before he slowly formed his hand into a thumbs up. "You floating, baby?"

Keady nodded, sucking in breaths whenever he could, his mouth so stuffed he could scarcely breathe.

"I'll take good care of you."

Chapter Twenty

Keady

Cutler was everywhere. He'd somehow gained a dozen hands and enough cocks to keep Keady busy for hours. His voice and moans had taken on a new light, too, sometimes high and other times lower than Keady had ever heard.

Logically, he knew there were many men — so many more than the three he had guessed — but they were all still Cutler. Cutler was directing their every move, every stroke, his powerful presence drowning out the rest until they were barely a flicker.

Another cock pushed into his ass, slick and cold with latex and fresh lube. It only took a few moments for it to warm, then it was edging even deeper and splitting him wide.

The first one had been rough, his ass on fire from no prep. Even if he had deserved it, it had still fucking hurt. But when it had started to feel good, it was better than anything he'd ever known.

This one was wider and thicker, settling just a touch deeper. The two cocks in his mouth became one and he groaned at the loss, sticking out his tongue and reaching for more. He wanted three — no four — in him and on him at every angle until he was bursting.

And the flogger… It seared across his skin, making him flinch and tighten with every stroke. His rim ached from clenching so many times, but the flog never stopped, even when it wrapped around his ribs and tickled his sides in a flame of pain and pure sensation.

He'd lost himself what felt like decades ago, every breath dedicated to Cutler and not himself. It didn't matter how many had gone or how many were left. He felt open, used, sore, beaten and so fucking perfect that he wanted to fly.

"Color?"

Cutler's voice cut through his calm madness, bringing a frown to his lips. Couldn't he see that Keady was in the perfect place? That he could take so much more? The blindfold between them was suddenly too tight, cutting off his air along with his sight.

"I want to see," said Keady, the moment his mouth was finally empty. His jaw ached so fiercely that it hurt to talk. He would be sore for a long time — weeks, hopefully. He reached for his face but his restraints held him tight, refusing to let him go. "You need to see how much I want this — love this."

Bright light assaulted him, Cutler's face shining above like some sort of angelic demon. His eyes were wild, his hair a complete mess and his pupils so blown that his eyes were nearly black.

"Fuck." Keady groaned once before his mouth was filled again with two cocks instead of one. He choked, gagging as one went too deep. His eyes rolled back, and he fought not to come.

"One moment please," said Cutler, his voice quiet and calm among the thriving lust. The cocks withdrew and Keady whimpered, struggling to follow them and failing completely.

"Please. I want it. I want more." He looked to Cutler, frantic in his need. The other faces and people blurred, so wholly unimportant that he didn't care who they were. He just needed to be filled, everywhere and always.

"The slut wants more. Give him hell, boys," said Cutler, grimacing in his smile that only Keady knew.

His chest constricted, his belly fluttering and warm. He could look at Cutler's face for the rest of his life and feel the same contentment as when both cocks slid back into his mouth, the big one going too deep and choking him again.

Someone leaned against his lower back, pinning his hips to the table hard. He was probably bruised to all hell, and he couldn't wait to see every mark. Shutting his eyes almost all the way, he let himself go completely, slipping away as he was used.

He lost count and time for a moment until a finger pressed beside the cock in his ass. He was close to breaking already, his rim twanging from the largest intrusion he'd had so far. The flogger flared over his back, and he bore down, the finger slipping inside him easily.

"Can his ass take as much as his mouth?"

Keady didn't know who said it, but it was still Cutler to him. Something shuffled around him as someone straddled his ass. They weren't heavy so they must've been standing on something as they slid into him from above as another lined up behind him, searching for his hole with a blunt cock.

When they struck true and pushed home, Keady whimpered, the sound caught in his full mouth. Suddenly his mouth was free, and the neck restraint was gone. There were lips against his, searing and molten at the same time. He couldn't taste much between the different flavors of lube and latex he'd swallowed down, but he'd recognize the shape of those lips anywhere.

Cutler devoured his mouth, seeking with his tongue and taking as Keady arched off the bench as he was pounded into by two men. Something hot lanced over his skin, soaking into his welts a moment before a stray tongue lapped him clean.

Oh God. Oh fuck. His cock had remained all but dormant thus far, hard and dripping but never getting close to orgasm. Now he was there, then past it, slamming head-fist into pleasure so complete that he lost himself. There were only sounds and aches so warm that they were more soothing than not.

And Cutler. Cutler was everywhere.

When he roused, with his ass aching but not empty and his lips still occupied, he blinked his eyes open. The table had been replaced with a couch, and somehow he was upright, cradled to a chest that smelled completely like home.

There was a cock inside him, and he knew in an instant that it was Cutler's. Same with the tongue in his mouth and hands on him. There had been so many before, but now there were only two. One behind his head, keeping him upright and guiding his lips, and another beneath his ass, prodding his loose hole that hurt so badly he wanted to cry.

"You back with me, baby?" asked Cutler, pulling away for one moment to allow Keady to breathe. Keady sucked in a few deep breaths, his lungs aching as much as his too-full chest.

"Yeah." Numbly, he searched for Cutler's mouth again, finding it in an instant. He poured everything into the kiss, along with the thank you that he couldn't communicate. Cutler rocked into him from below, his cock as unforgiving as the rest of him.

"Can you take one more?"

Keady nodded before he even had time to think. Of course he could. He was invincible. It didn't stop him from whimpering as he was adjusted along the couch until he was lying on Cutler's chest. Someone leaned over his back, their breath against his ear.

Turning his head to the side, Keady caught the sight of tanned hands on his hips, the redness of his welts scraping against their callused palms.

"Trick?" Keady asked, already knowing the answer as Cutler nodded and brought him in for another kiss.

Trick sank inside in one long thrust and Keady started sobbing almost immediately. It was so much that he wasn't sure he could take it. Cutler cradled him, shushing him and kissing away his tears. "Color, Keady?"

He trembled, his teeth chattering as vulnerability smashed into him from nowhere. But he was still powerful, the drunken energy surging under his skin. He never wanted it to leave. Bearing down, he met Trick's thrust, taking him to the excruciating base.

"Green, SB." A smile flickered over Keady's lips as he said it, laying his head on Cutler's shoulder. He heard kissing above him and craned his neck to see Nav standing next to them, kissing Trick as he thrust inside Keady.

Everything blanked again into a haze of contentment that burned itself into his memory. He would never forget a second of it, even though it felt like he had been outside of his body, watching himself take it.

He felt the chill of Trick's withdrawal, then the splash of warmth as Cutler removed his condom and plunged back inside, coming deep. He was full, dripping, but as Cutler's cock slipped out, so abominably empty. He whimpered at the loss, reaching for himself.

He was so swollen and sensitive, and he slid his fingers in easily. They did nothing to fill his emptiness.

"I've got you, baby." Cutler kissed his temple before dragging Keady's wrist away, forcing the emptiness upon him again. "I've got you."

* * * *

It must've been hours later by the time Keady was ready to pull away from Cutler's arms. He'd already drunk nearly a full bottle of water and had nibbled on a snack without moving more than a few inches.

Blinking, Keady surveyed the room, glancing from the table to the few couches near the darkest side of the basement. Most of the others were gone, slowly filtering out after they'd checked on him and come down. He'd watched them go through the mirrors that gave him every angle without having to move.

There were other things in the basement, too— things that he wondered if Cutler would ever let him experience. There had to be a line somewhere, right?

Scotland had lingered longer than the others, casting a glance at the stairs every so often, as if he were still waiting for someone to appear. He'd changed his hair from purple to blue and it had grown just enough to give his handsome face a shaggy tilt to it.

Keady didn't take Scotland's distraction personally. He had enough rolling around in his body that he had no energy to track someone else's love life at the moment.

The only two who remained were Derreck and Maddy.

Derreck hadn't joined the foray, instead dragging Maddy to the bench and grabbing the flog. Keady had watched through heavy lids as Maddy had come alive in the same way he had, with pain as his catalyst.

Now they were snuggled up next to Cutler and himself, Maddy looking as if he were about to drift off and Derreck practically purring in contentment.

Keady shifted on the couch, flinching as he dragged himself off Cutler's lap. His Dom had fallen asleep about ten minutes before, and he didn't want to wake him quite yet.

Every part of him was filthy, even though Cutler had already cleaned him with a cloth. A cloth couldn't replace a shower. *And hell, do I need a shower.*

Maddy peeked at him, opening one eye. "You good?"

Nodding, Keady looked back to the table. The leather straps were gone, the table polished and sanitized as if he'd never been there. But his wrists were bruised from where he'd pulled against the restraints and his hipbones were blackened from every slam into the surface.

He held his finger to his lips as Maddy opened his mouth to speak again, motioning to Cutler's sleeping face. He looked so peaceful, his perpetual tiredness finally wiped away from his features. Keady could hardly notice the facial paralysis that Cutler was so self-conscious about as he relaxed deeper into sleep.

Maybe he would suggest that Cutler take a chill pill, because no one ever noticed his small scar. He didn't think his ass could take the consequences of that conversation at the moment.

Running his hand over the table, he looked at the multiple types of restraints in the room. Between the wooden cross, manacles and stocks, Cutler had settled on the nicest set for a restrained orgy.

He could still feel the echo of hands and cocks, a smile touching his lips as he closed his eyes and breathed deep. He could still *smell* them, too.

The steps creaked behind him and he whirled to the sound, catching himself on the table as he wobbled. Clint was standing on the bottom step with a tired smile on his lips. "Everyone okay down here? Sorry I couldn't get away sooner. Harold went all out tonight with his Shibari demo."

Running a hand through his hair, Clint looked past Keady. Keady couldn't help but follow his gaze, a silly smile on his own lips.

"Are you sure you weren't avoiding a certain tattoo artist?" asked Keady, clasping his hands behind his back. He was still naked, but his lack of clothing didn't matter for once. He'd already connected the dots as to whom Scotland had been looking for.

"Shush, I don't need it from you, too. Maddy is already playing matchmaker."

"He waited for you," said Keady, giggling as Clint sent him a mild glare. He could take much worse than that right now. "I think he pretended he was fucking you the whole time he was inside me."

Clint rolled his eyes before rubbing a hand over his face. "Don't sell yourself short. I haven't seen a gangbang this popular in years."

A warm tingling moved from his belly all the way to his fingertips as he looked to Cutler, his face still relaxed in sleep and his mouth partially open. "Do you have a room we can stay in tonight, Clint? I'm not up for driving home."

"Yeah." Clint swallowed, looking away. "And one more thing, Keady. The decision was made before tonight could happen. The last thing you need is to be banned from this place, and I know what it's like to get distracted in an intense scene." He let out a wistful sigh, his gaze suddenly distant.

Keady's heart stopped, his jaw dropping as he stared at Clint. "What are you saying?"

"Eh, you'll figure it out. But I don't think Cutler is through with you yet." He patted Keady on the shoulder before turning back to the steps. "Welcome back, kid. Stick around this time and keep that serial killer of yours in line."

"I heard that," said Cutler from the couch, his eyes closed but his voice void of sleep.

"You were meant to," said Clint, leaning against the entrance to the stairway. "A few people mentioned that you have a pet name, Cutler. SB? What is that supposed to stand for?"

Keady flushed, looking to his toes. There was a smudge of cum on his big toe that was crusty and flaked. "Sadistic bastard."

Maddy snorted from the couch as Clint let out a long sigh.

"Well, it fits, I'll give you that," said Clint. Cutler opened one eye and Clint visibly wilted under the intensity of his glare.

Keady could only grin. "Damn right, it fits."

Epilogue

Keady

Keady leaned against the glass, taking in the view of lush greenery and the park that was surrounded by a full city block of buildings. One side was newly built and seemed to stretch toward the skies and sway in the heavy breeze blowing in from the north. The other side was the older part of town where buildings were made of thick brick instead of windows and cheaper siding.

He could even see a bit of downtown from his roost, a few shops for shoes and clothing calling to him. Maybe he'd even go one day…but not today.

"Everything to your liking?" asked Cutler as he came up behind him, wrapping an arm around Keady's waist.

Keady nodded, swallowing back the swarm of tears that threatened. 'Like' didn't even begin to cover it. "It's beautiful."

He hadn't known what he'd been missing in his last place until Cutler had found out about his search for a new apartment and taken it upon himself to help. He'd thrown out Keady's tentative choices in a heartbeat, doubling his price range in an instant.

"I can't afford these places," Keady had said, looking from the pool to the gym that was included with the condo. There was no way in hell he could ever afford a balcony or a barbecue, especially not on his own.

Cutler had silenced him with a glare. "If you won't move in with me, at least let me take care of you."

Keady had spluttered. Cutler hadn't even offered for them to move into together, which was probably a good thing. Keady needed his space as much as Cutler did some days, and he wasn't quite ready to admit how madly he'd fallen in love with Cutler, either.

He'd let it slip during aftercare once, but he didn't think Cutler had heard, thank God. That was not how he wanted that confession to go.

"Maddy used to work around here," said Cutler, pointing to one of the buildings. "He recommended this area because of the park close by and easy access to downtown. We'll have to try out a few of the restaurants."

Keady couldn't express how grateful he was for the crew at Unkinked. They'd welcomed him back with open arms, and Clint had even seemed a touch bashful the last time someone had mentioned Scotland's name.

It was what he'd been missing for years and what he'd been keeping himself from by isolating himself.

That didn't mean he exactly loved Cutler's methods for breaking his shyness.

Cutler trailed his hand down Keady's chest, settling on the dip of his waist. In the window's reflection, Keady could see every exposed inch of himself.

"The windows are tinted, right?" he asked for the third time, turning his head into Cutler's shoulder. He'd tried looking up from the ground floor, but he hadn't been able to see a thing. His neighbors were another story altogether. Just because he couldn't see into their condos didn't mean they couldn't see into his.

"I'm not sure," said Cutler, letting out a soft chuckle as he kneaded Keady's ass. There were a few lingering bruises, and Keady let out a huff as his cock started to stiffen.

"You are not fucking me against this window." He tried to put every ounce of stubbornness into his tone, but Cutler gave him a simple look, and he already felt like he was going to cave. "Dammit, no."

Cutler only grimaced, his reflection not giving anything away.

"Seriously? The window?" Keady let out a huff, doing his best not to cover himself with his hands. That only ever made the situation much worse.

Cutler only nodded, his eyes dark. "Unless you want to try out your new leash." He fingered the ring through the head of Keady's cock.

That was just fucking cruel. Keady squirmed, butting against Cutler's hand. "I'll be good, Sir."

And he meant it with everything he had. He'd never been happier, with more friends than he could ask for and a Dom who was made of dreams.

"Did you have to head back to work?" asked Keady, a touch more serious. In their time together, Cutler had received another promotion, which had probably paid for a portion of Keady's condo. On the other hand, it meant less time together.

"My pocket has been buzzing for the last ten minutes, but I doubt it's more important than making sure you're settled in okay," said Cutler, pulling back even as he said it and sliding his phone from his pocket. He furrowed his forehead, tucking his phone away a moment later. "I was right."

Keady grinned, leaning against the glass and spreading his legs wide. It was rare that he had moments of bravery, but he'd learned to take them as they came and use them to the greatest extent that he could. "Good, because I have another joke for you, and if I make you laugh, you don't get to come but I do."

Cutler's lips twitched as he clasped his hands behind his back. "That's a dangerous game, my love."

His stomach flipped and Keady struggled to keep his emotions at bay. Of all the pet names Cutler had for him, that was his favorite by far.

"Okay, so July first is International Doctor's Day—"

"Oh, for Christ's sakes, come here," said Cutler, grabbing Keady by the hips and tugging him close. "I will do anything if you don't finish that joke. *Anything.*"

So many choices. Turning in Cutler's arms, Keady placed a kiss on his neck before leaning his head on Cutler's shoulder. Even after a shower, he could still catch the faint whiff of the hospital. It lingered, almost soothing in its constant presence.

"Smile. Always. You don't need an excuse or a joke, just always smile for me," said Keady, steadying himself as Cutler jerked back. "You are beautiful."

It was something Cutler had told him a thousand times, but Keady had never said it in return—had never thought to. Their scars no longer mattered — and neither did their pasts.

Cutler stared at him, his gaze dark and searching as he held Keady at arm's length. When he spoke, it was soft and sweet.

"Anything for you, love."

Want to see more from this author? Here's a taster for you to enjoy!

All Hallow's Harem: Candy Magic
M.C. Roth

Excerpt

Crean leaned against his car, peeking at his belongings through the back window to make sure they were still safe. The little Rav 4 was barely hanging on to its last life, with every handle wrapped in duct tape and an engine that had more quirks than an old farmhouse. Hopefully, it would last the rest of the trip.

"Hey! You can't park there like that."

Looking toward the shout, Crean rubbed his eyes with the back of his hand, letting out a long sigh. It had only taken the store owner six hours to notice him.

"I'm just leaving. Sorry." He patted his car as the man got closer, a black apron wrapped around his bright red shirt. From the guy's appearance, they'd had about the same amount of sleep.

"There's a hotel a few minutes from here if you need to rest, but my lot's not a truck stop." The guy put his hands on his hips but seemed to soften as he took in Crean's appearance.

Do I really look that bad? He was about to meet three strangers and his brother, who he hadn't seen in years, and he probably looked like he'd just crawled out of a trash fire.

"Sorry. I didn't know. My phone died last night so I followed the signs to the nearest place. It was either here or across the road, and your place looked way safer." He glanced to the other side of traffic to what looked like a car graveyard. "I'll be on my way."

The man waved him off with a grumble as Crean reached for the handle on his car door. The tape stuck to his fingers, a bit of dirt tucking under his fingernails. Jerking his hand away, he tried to pick it out from under his nails as the man disappeared into his store, but it refused to budge.

Just five more minutes. His legs were aching, and his back was beyond help from the night he'd spent cramped in his driver's seat, trying to catch a few winks. He circled around the back of his car, fiddling with a rust patch on the fender as he shifted from foot to foot to ease the pins and needles racing through his limbs.

He could still remember the day he'd pulled into the driveway back home and his mother had scowled at the car like it were better suited for a scrap yard than their neighborhood. They had a reputation to uphold as one of the most powerful shifter families in the province, and junkyard scrap didn't jive with that.

Still, it was the first thing he'd bought with his own money. It had barely limped along then, and his neglect hadn't done it any favors.

Is it still neglect when I have no idea how to change a tire? He'd had great intentions when he'd bought it, but keeping the interior clean and tidy didn't do much for the engine—that, and the fact that the door was held together with a healthy portion of duct tape, courage and a small touch of magic that he hoped no one would notice.

Magic was also responsible for helping the engine start on even the coldest winter mornings when his breath crystalized on his eyelashes. A little extra edge for the igniter was worth the risk.

But magic was something he wasn't exactly supposed to be able to do. Witches had been pushed to the brink of extinction during the Middle Ages and had died out completely by the sixteenth century. He knew because he'd heard about it dozens of times, sneaking tidbits of conversations when he was younger when he was supposed to be sleeping.

Vampires, were-animals and faeries all thrived in secret droves alongside humans like himself, but there wasn't a drop of pure magic left in the world. If anyone ever found out...his magic would be the least of his problems. People didn't tend to react well when they were faced with something they believed was long dead.

A were-animal was expected to be able to shift at will, but if things started flying around the room, the house was suddenly possessed, and they had to hire an exorcist and move. He'd had one slip-up when he was younger, which his mother had blamed on ghosts. She'd ordered the house burned after she'd dragged the entire family to a new city.

Vampires were a whole different level of weird — and faeries? Well, he didn't want to think about those winged bastards anymore. Every one he came across was a conceited, self-centered, beautiful monster. *Or a murderer.*

Stretching his arms over his head, he cracked his back, blinking away the sleep from his eyes. Three days of endless roads and late summer wind buffeting his hair through his cracked window without a shower or a decent sleep were taking their toll.

The road trip would hopefully be worth it. He hadn't been able to pass up the job opportunity in one of the highest-paying cities in the country, even if it took him away from the protective shroud of his family. Everything he owned was packed away for the drive that had pushed his car to the limit.

Pulling out his cell phone that he'd been charging all night, he brought up his mom's contact info. She'd been texting him twice a day throughout the entire journey, calling him if he didn't answer right away. It had taken years to convince her to let him move out and make a life on his own.

Well, not really on his own.

I'll be at the house in a couple of hours.

His phone buzzed immediately as his mom answered. She'd probably been hovering over the screen for the last hour, counting down until the next time he would text.

Between crying so much that her eyes had been completely bloodshot and accidentally shredding his shirt when she'd partially shifted into her panther form when trying to give him a hug goodbye, their parting hadn't gone too well.

I'll call Rian now to let him know. His roommates should be there to help you unpack so you can rest after your journey. Call me as soon as you get there. Drive safe!

Cracking a yawn, he ducked into the car, starting the engine then pulling onto the road.

It was the only downside to the 'moving out' ordeal. He was thirty-five years old, and by human standards he should have been married with kids, a house and one-point-five cats. But shifter families didn't really work like that for the eldest children, especially panthers. Even though he'd been born without a drop of panther in him, his mother had still tried to arrange his last six girlfriends, who'd had claws instead of fingernails.

He still hadn't mustered up the heart to tell her he was gay. He'd been half hoping she would figure it out on her own.

It was a miracle that he'd been allowed to move out at all, but he'd been given one condition. His mom had insisted that he move in with his brother and his three roommates, refusing to let him get his own place. Even if three-quarters of them weren't panthers, it was better than him flying solo.

It wasn't so bad. The city was pricey, and splitting expenses five ways was sure to help him get ahead.

But three days of driving was as close to hell as he'd ever gotten, and he'd almost turned back after the first night of shivering in the car. Most truck stops didn't mind him camping out for the night, but his seat didn't fully recline, and the weather seemed to get colder every night.

It's worth it, though.

"Wow." He blinked in the bright mid-morning sun, letting out a low whistle as the first wisps of mountains came into view. When he squinted, they almost looked like clouds instead of the perpetually snow-covered peaks. The hills back home had nothing on them.

They disappeared out of view as he took a ramp into the city, diving between rows of fresh buildings. As he pulled onto Ridge Street, he perked up for the first time in days. The houses were exotic and nothing like the cookie-cutter versions of subdivisions he saw all the time back home. Most of them were tall and skinny, unlike the sweeping bungalows that he was used to.

There! He spotted the number plaque stamped into the house. It appeared to be two stories from the outside, with a red metal roof and deep green siding. The windows were clear and new, along with a porch, and he caught a hint of the backyard as he pulled into the driveway.

Grinning, he slid into the lot, parking next to his brother's familiar blue Honda pickup. There were three other cars in the wide and shallow driveway, all of them putting his trusty car to shame.

"It's going to be okay." He shifted the car into park before leaning heavily into his seat. His heart had picked up at the first sign of mountains and hadn't calmed since, his palms sweating against the steering wheel. "Change is good."

He knew a little about his new roommates — enough that his brother vouched for them, at least. One of the roommates was in university classes, apparently, while the other two had day jobs like his brother, but that probably didn't stop them from partying like animals and making out with their girlfriends on the couch.

Yuck.

He'd seen enough straightness to last him for a lifetime.

Swallowing, he killed the engine, popping the trunk as he stepped out. The sound of rushing traffic greeted him, along with the distant laugh of someone down the street. The neighbors were stacked right next door, with nothing but a flimsy fence between the properties.

So no naked sunbathing… His bucket list was going to end up the shortest in history at the rate he was going. A new town meant a new start, leaving his old ways and the majority of his family behind him. That meant the magic, too. *I'm done for good.*

"Maybe I'll sunbathe anyway." He nodded to himself, treading a few paces so he could peer into the backyard. There was a lawn chair and everything, and he'd packed lots of sunscreen. There was bound to be a nice day or two left in the season before the hornets came out in full force.

Grabbing one of the lighter boxes from the trunk, he hefted it up on his shoulder, wrapping his arm around the broad side to hold it tight. The cardboard edge scraped against the inside of his arm where his sleeve had ridden up, a strand of unstuck tape flittering as he moved toward the deck.

The deck itself was large enough to fit five or so chairs and had a second staircase leading into the backyard. Beyond it was a stainless barbecue paired with a smoker, the small silver bucket swinging back and forth in the wind. There was only one tree, but it was massive, its looming branches filled with leaves that were just starting to shift from green to rusted red. With a strong enough gust of wind, the entire backyard would be buried in them.

He stared at the welcome mat in front of the door, a single stray stone tucked between the thick fibers. He'd expected a frat house with beer cans strewn about and broken windows repaired with duct tape and hope.

Do I knock? It wasn't exactly his house — at least, not yet. Maybe he'd fit in in his own way in a few weeks, but for now, he was a long way off. Being with his brother would probably help because Rian had never been shy a day in his life.

Pinning the box against the door, he freed one hand and tapped out a few knocks against the stained wood. A shout sounded immediately from the other side before a loud whoop came that should have been reserved for a hockey game. He winced at the pounding footsteps that rattled the frame, the vibrations even traveling along the deck.

He looked back at his car as he bit his lip. *It's not too late.*

The lock clicked a second before the door was flung open, the glass catching the sun and blinding him for a moment. The heaviness of the box hit him at full force as his door support disappeared and he caught a flash of blond hair and blue eyes before the earth started to tilt.

He scrambled to catch himself, but the box was too heavy, gravity sending him tumbling through the frame and over the box in a mess of limbs. His elbows hit the ground first, then his hands, the tip of his nose stopping just shy of a faceplant. As the corner of the box struck his solar plexus, air whooshed from his lungs, hair prickling on the back of his neck as danger loomed closer.

There's something in this house.

"Holy shit, I think I killed him."

Rolling to the side, Crean peered up as he struggled to catch his breath, blinking at the change in lighting from outside. His chest ached, his gut still spasming from the hit.

The man above him was definitely not his brother — not unless his brother had gained a few inches and a shit-ton of muscle with the smell of wolf clinging to his aura. He'd only met a select few werewolves in his life and never one with the sense of danger stuck to him like glue.

Hot damn. Wolves tended to be on the sleeker side, but this man was built, with crystal blue eyes and a jawline he could cut grass with. But that *feeling* – His skin prickled, his eyes watering as he struggled not to blink.

He shook his head. The full moon must've been looming closer than he'd thought. *If Rian trusts him, he can't be too bad.* The house was big enough that Crean could always avoid him if he needed to.

Despite Rian being determined to move in with people who weren't panthers, their mother had warned him about them…repeatedly. Wolves were *different*.

"Sorry, man. I didn't think you'd be leaning on the door like that. You okay?" The hulk loomed down at him, holding out one hand when Crean didn't answer. His nails didn't look all that sharp, but that could change in an instant with a shift. A panther would win against a regular wolf, but not a shifter — especially one built like this guy. *And I'm just a human.*

"Yeah." His voice came out as a strangled mess as the hairs on the back of his neck stood. The wolf wasn't the only dangerous thing in the house.

Thumping footsteps reached them, and Rian appeared around the corner. His smile dropped as he rushed ahead, pulling Crean to his feet. "What the hell did you do to him, Conner? You okay, Crean?"

The familiar warmth of Rian soaked into him, pushing away the danger of everything else. His little brother had grown since he'd last seen him, but he was still the same person who had chased a ball of string around the house as a kitten and who had gotten stuck in an actual tree one day.

Their mother had been so pissed about the latter. It was hard enough to keep secrets from the majority of the human population when it came to shifters. They couldn't hypnotize anyone like a vampire or faerie could, so they had to rely on stealth alone. Calling the fire department because of a baby panther stuck in a tree was the opposite of stealth.

"Yeah." Crean let out a huff before pulling his hands free to rub at the back of his neck. "Thanks for letting me stay here."

He looked down the hall to the other curious onlookers that had appeared during the ruckus. His mouth went dry, and he cleared his throat. *This is going to be hell.*

All of them had to have been over six feet, leaving him the sole one in the five-foot club. And although he'd spent most of his life hanging out with people much stronger than him, he was way out of his league.

"No problem," said Rian, throwing his arm over Crean's shoulder. "Guys, this is my bro, Crean. Crean, this is Conner." He pointed to the blond wolf. Conner sent him a small wave and a smile, apparently oblivious to Crean's panic. "Then we've got Nate and Tristan."

Nate was the shortest of the three strangers and maybe a bit leaner, his dark hair pulled back into a ponytail that was resting on one shoulder. His hair was silky and straight, and his skin glowed with a fierce unnatural paleness.

Tristan was the opposite, with light brown hair that was buzzed short. There was a speckling of dust on his hair and clothes, some of it sticking to his skin like it had painted itself to him while he'd been sweating.

Crean tried to keep his face passive as his magic touched them inadvertently. Rian was at his back, the same calmness that he remembered, but the other three were something very different. He tried to rein himself in, mustering a breath of control before it snapped.

Fuck. I promised myself it would be different this time. His magic surged beneath his skin like a wild animal, soaking into the house and the people around him against his will.

A metallic tang slid over Crean's tongue as he shook Nate's hand. He had to be a vampire, with life and copper clinging to him like a virus. He shook as he took Tristan's hand next, trembling as the wrongness of the touch creeped in.

Faeries were dangerous, even more so than any other person in the world. They flitted through existence, lying and cheating unsuspecting folks who were just trying to get by. He hadn't believed the rumors until it had happened to his own family. During a disagreement between families, one of his uncles had been murdered.

Then why is Rian living with one?

He took a half-step back, ducking closer to his brother. The familiar presence of family engulfed him in an instant. Crean gave the others a small wave before pointedly focusing on Conner. He was probably the safest bet out of the three. At least wolves were loyal.

"Nice to meet you," said Tristan, brushing a bit of dust from his hair. His hands were thick but paler than any faerie he could recall. Usually, they were tanned and glowing from spending so much time in the sun and immersed with nature. At least he had the decency to keep his wings tucked away.

Maybe Tristan was mostly human, like a shifter who couldn't turn into their animal but growled a little and got excited around a full moon. *Or like me.* It had been a shock to his family when a human had been born among them, but his mother had still cherished him.

"I'm gonna hit the shower, but I'll order pizza before I jump in." Tristan caught his gaze, before ducking his head and turning away. Crean shuddered, smoothing the front of his shirt as he fought the urge to fidget.

Fucking faeries. Always thinking they can have anyone or anything they want.

"Trying to get out of the real work, as usual," said Rian with a snicker as he flipped Tristan off behind his back. "Crean, why don't you look around, and we'll bring your stuff in? We've got you set up on the second floor just past the bathroom."

Rian gave him a pat on the back before nudging him into the house. He was gone before Crean could protest.

"I can help," he said softly to the others, flushing with all eyes on him. His gut clenched, his mind already spinning. The house was thick with their presence, already becoming familiar, which had to be a good sign.

About the Author

M.C. Roth lives in Canada and loves every season, even the dreaded Canadian winter. She graduated with honours from the Associate Diploma Program in Veterinary Technology at the University of Guelph before choosing a different career path.

Between caring for her young son, spending time with her husband, and feeding treats to her menagerie of animals, she still spends every spare second devoted to her passion for writing.

She loves growing peppers that are hot enough to make grown men cry, but she doesn't like spicy food herself. Her favourite thing, other than writing of course, is to find a quiet place in the wilderness and listen to the birds while dreaming about the gorgeous men in her head.

M.C. Roth loves to hear from readers. You can find her contact information, website details and author profile page at https://www.firstforromance.com/

PUBLISHING

Sign up for our newsletter and find out about all our romance book releases, eBook sales and promotions, sneak peeks and FREE romance books!